THE LONGEST SILENCE

A child is missing.
Every mother's nightmare is happening to Susan Rolph on a carefree family holiday in Turkey. Nothing in life has prepared her for the shock of losing one of her six children. Her husband cannot comfort her. Her remaining children are out of their depth. Susan's ex-husband hurries to her side, but her only real hope lies with the enigmatic Yilmaz. He appears at the villa to act as a police interpreter. Only gradually does Susan realize he is a senior detective—and that he may be more interested in smugglers than kidnappers...

Described by critics as 'a natural and fluent storyteller' and 'a mistress of the craft'

THE LONGEST SILENCE

THE LONGEST SILENCE

by
Anne Melville

Magna Large Print Books
Long Preston, North Yorkshire,
England.

British Library Cataloguing in Publication Data.

Melville, Anne
    The longest silence.

    A catalogue record for this book is
    available from the British Library

    ISBN 0-7505-1046-3

First published in Great Britain by Judy Piatkus (Publishers)
Ltd., 1995

Published in Large Print 1997 by arrangement with Piatkus
Books and the copyright holder.

Magna Large Print is an imprint of
Library Magna Books Ltd.
Printed and bound in Great Britain by
T.J. International Ltd., Cornwall, PL28 8RW.

Chapter One

It is the blackbird that breaks the dawn silence with a tentative arpeggio, like an opera singer wishing to test her voice without spoiling it for the performance to come. Within moments the garden is full of sound: an orchestra tuning up. Only after ten minutes or so does a crow somewhere in the distance give four hoarse caws. As though a conductor has tapped his baton to attract attention, the birds fall silent again.

With the instinct which has always summoned her from sleep in the second before a baby whimpers for the morning feed, Susan Rolph awakens as the blackbird is drawing breath for those first notes. Immediately alert, she slides quietly out of bed without disturbing her husband, who continues to snore gently. David is an owl and Susan is a lark: it is one of the many differences which she failed to recognise before her hasty second marriage.

With the exception of David, each member of the household is an early riser. For more than twelve years there has always been a hungry or teething baby in the house, or a toddler revving up friction cars or banging drums while waiting impatiently for breakfast. It is as if a six-o'clock alarm bell rings in each small head, and Susan has never attempted to discourage this. All too soon, no doubt, adolescence will beget laziness, but she hopes that the habit of rising with the sun will persist for as long as possible. It goes—in her opinion—with alertness, creative curiosity and good health, and makes it possible for the family to enjoy a leisurely breakfast, sitting round a table, rather than a grab and scramble.

Despite her pleasure in the time the whole family spends together, these early-morning moments are especially precious to her. Slipping on a satin robe, she makes her way downstairs. It is half past five: already light on a May morning. Stepping out of her bedroom slippers, she lets herself out of the garden door, ducking underneath the spider's web which is every day broken—although not by her—and every night repaired.

She shivers with pleasure as her bare feet tread the chilly dew on the lawn into a track as silver as any snail's. Taking a first deep breath of the cool air she glances up at the clear sky.

The best time of the day!

Every morning she wills herself not to

let this banal thought present itself to her mind as though it were a new idea; and every morning the words force their way through, refusing to be suppressed. That is because they are true, presumably. What else is a cliché but a truth endlessly repeated? It is irritating, though, that the same series of actions at the start of each day should so predictably trigger the same response. She shakes the thought out of her head as she walks towards the meadow, savouring the silence.

Silence is a treasure which can only rarely be enjoyed by the mother of six children, and is all the more to be appreciated because of that. Susan knows and values its every facet. She is a connoisseur of silences.

There is the silence of contrast. When she shouts upstairs in her this-is-the-last-time voice, 'Turn the radio down!' and a sulky finger somewhere on the children's floor flicks the switch off instead, other domestic sounds may in fact be continuing without interruption; but her ears register only their sudden freedom from the beating of drums.

There is the silence of relief, when a sick or inconsolable child at last surrenders to sleep, to the breast or to a bribe and ceases to wail.

There are the listening silences of held

breath and unreasonable fear. Has the baby stopped breathing? Why can't I hear anything? Or the opposite anxiety. What was that sound a moment ago? Is there an intruder moving quietly around downstairs, taking care not to disturb anyone? Why can't I hear anything?

Worse than this, far worse, is the silence of traumatic terror, which has descended on her only once in her life. Summoned by the urgent shrillness of a schoolteacher, she arrived at the gate of Stanton House just in time to see Tam—blood-smeared, unconscious, perhaps dead—being lifted from his crushed and twisted bicycle on to a stretcher. As she rushed towards the ambulance she could tell that people were talking to her, because she saw their lips moving. But she was unable to hear words or even sirens. Sound, for a little while, ceased to exist. She prays that she will never need to experience such a silence again.

There is the happier silence specific to the hours she devotes to her painting. There may be noise all around her but her ears register none of it, because all her concentration is on her eyes and what they see.

There is the silence of snow, deep and dense; frightening to anyone who is lost, but warm and comforting to someone who is sure of herself and secure in her home and family. Susan loves the snow.

There is the silence—familiar to any parent—of shame and confrontation: a silence of patience and steady eyes. The longest silence of all, when an accusation has been made but guilt has not yet been admitted. Susan's sons have been brought up not to lie, but that doesn't mean that they are always quick to confess the truth.

But no, this is not the longest silence of all, for there is one that is far longer: that lasts for ever. Susan tends to forget about it, because her life has been fortunate. No one she loves has yet died. One day, inevitably, she will be forced to confront such a silence, but not yet. Even her mother is still under sixty.

Certainly this is no time to be thinking about death. Indeed, it is the thought of new life that is flushing her body with happiness at this moment. She has a secret.

Susan and her first husband, Hugh Sutherland, welcomed each of their first five babies as they arrived. It was only after Donnie's birth that Hugh made his unwelcome declaration that their family must now be considered complete—and the firmness of his ultimatum was indirectly responsible for the ending of their marriage.

Her second husband, although delighted by the birth of his daughter, has been equally definite in his view that there should be no more babies after Kara. Susan, though, has always made it clear that she is not prepared to use any kind of contraception herself. All that sort of thing is up to David; and, although it is too soon yet to be certain, with every day that passes her suspicion grows that he has been careless. She hugs her delight to herself as she makes her way through the orchard and leans on a gate which opens into the meadow.

The meadow is an Impressionist painting. Buttercups and daisies are encircled first by a wide band of Queen Anne's lace and then by hedges white with mayflower. Breathing deeply, she keeps very still. This is a moment for contentment.

The moment is disturbed. Someone else is in the meadow. Roy—it must be Roy—is running steadily round its boundaries and now nears the gate. His hair is tousled and he wears only a brief pair of shorts and running shoes. His skinny body seems too fragile to maintain the pace he has set himself, and his skin has the pallor of an English winter. Never mind: a few months at The Lookout will deal with that.

He nods, acknowledging his mother's presence, as he passes the gate, but does not check his stride. Susan smiles affectionately as she watches him pound on.

It was one of the earliest differences of attitude to show itself between Susan and Hugh, the father of her five sons. Susan wanted her children to be happy, whereas Hugh wanted them to be ambitious. Because at that time the marriage was a harmonious one, it was not difficult to reach a concordat. Susan accepted her husband's argument that the greatest happiness is to be found in setting a target, a standard of excellence, and achieving it.

They have been divorced now for almost five years, but she still plays fair by Hugh's rules, encouraging each of the boys to develop a special talent. Roy's talent is for running.

He makes three more circuits of the meadow before coming to a halt beside his mother and clicking his stopwatch. Panting from the effort, he bends over and rests his hands on his knees. Susan is tempted to run her fingers up the neat little knobs of his spine, but knows better than to intrude on a private moment. At last he brings his breathing under control and looks down at the watch to see how well he has done this morning.

'Best ever.'

'Well done.'

'What's the use, though?' he said sadly,

straightening himself. 'I'd be sure to win the steeplechase on Sports Day, but we shan't be here. Why do we have to go so early?'

'But you love being at The Lookout!' Susan is taken aback by the complaint. For the past twelve years she has spent the months from May to August in a villa on her ex-father-in-law's estate in Turkey, taking with her the growing family of children. Hugh is a professor: an archaeologist who every summer supervises digs on one or other of the ancient sites which surround the modern town of Antalya.

In the early years of their marriage Susan went to Turkey to be near him. Now the arrangement is a more formal one: part of the divorce settlement. Because his present university post is in the United States, weekend access to his sons throughout the year is not a practical proposition, so she has undertaken instead to bring them within reach of his summer dig for four months of every year. As far as the boys are concerned, however, she does not wish to introduce any element of obligation into what she has always tried to present as a delightful holiday arrangement.

'Yes, well, it's fun,' Roy concedes. 'But two months would be enough. The ordinary school holidays. All the best things at school happen at the end of the year.'

'I thought examinations were what happened.' Susan tries to make a joke of it as together they walk slowly back towards the house. 'You always say you hate examinations.'

'I do, yes, but Calum loves them. They're what he's good at, but he never gets a chance to prove it. The Christmas tests don't count for prizes and things. And the masters get all shirty because they think we're dodging exams. They keep picking on us in class because they hope they'll catch us out on something we've missed.'

'But you don't miss anything. That's why we take a tutor with us, to be sure that you keep up with everybody else.' Susan's protest is made all the more vehement by a flicker of guilt at what Roy has told her. Eight-year-old Calum, her fourth son, is almost pathetically anxious to prove himself the equal of his elder brothers. Naturally he is less strong than they are, and has yet to find a hobby activity at which he can excel, but already he shows signs of being as academically gifted as his father. Is she really depriving him of a chance to shine?

She shrugs the thought away. No doubt there are battles to come, but the boys are still only children and must recognise her authority.

'That's not the only thing.' Roy is making the most of this chance to state a case on behalf of his brothers. 'Tam would have been Head Boy if Mr Fitzgerald had expected him to stay till the end of the year. Murdo's the best trumpeter in the school and he can't ever play in the end-of-term concert. And Donnie likes acting, but he never gets a part because they know he won't be there. It's all right for Kara, because she doesn't go to school, but the rest of us would rather be around till the end of term.'

He speaks with unaccustomed firmness. It is almost certainly Tam who has instructed his younger brother to speak out if ever an opportunity arises. Tam, twelve years old and the eldest of her children, is a natural leader but also an efficient delegator.

Dismayed to realise that the boys are attempting to gang up against what she has always thought of as a treat, Susan produces what she knows to be a feeble argument.

'Well, this will be the last year when we can all go off early.' In September Tam will be starting at Winchester. It is because he had to be in England to take the entrance examination that the family is later than usual in leaving. But the results came through three days ago, and there is

16

no longer any reason to wait.

'Next year, then, can we stay till school finishes?'

'I'll think about it.' What she means is that she will have to discuss the matter with Hugh. Recognising that Winchester will not be as amenable as a small prep school, she has been planning in the future to travel at the same time as usual with most of the family, leaving Tam to fly out later to join them. There is no need to make any decisions yet.

They are back in the cultivated part of the garden now. She reaches into the garden shed for a pair of secateurs and cuts an armful of sweet-scented spring blossom. It is a form of pruning, which will have to be done in any case once the blossom fades. Only that argument helps her to overcome her aversion to mutilating the shrubs. She would prefer to leave everything living to pursue its own cycle without disturbance, like the huge chestnut whose magnificent white candles will before too long fade and fatten into conkers.

Hurrying Roy off to have a shower, she fills the drawing room with the blossom and pushes the fading flowers which have been displayed into stoneware jars on the kitchen windowsill. It is a family tease that she treats the kitchen as though it were an intensive-care unit in which the dying may perhaps recover. It is someone else's duty to observe that heads are drooping and petals dropping, and to throw them away.

Back in the drawing room, made light by four deep windows and decorated in a style of which its Georgian architect would have approved: flat green paint on the walls, brightened by touches of pink and gold on the plaster frieze. The furniture is old where age is appropriate and modern, where comfort is the first requirement. Both this room and the morning room act as galleries for her own watercolours.

Susan is a rich woman. Her American father, who died before she was born, left her a trust fund which has kept her in comfort all her life. She can afford to maintain an English manor house and to employ what staff she requires. She can afford to bring up six children without demanding maintenance payments and she has never had any need to work. Motherhood is her career.

By now there are sounds of activity all over the house. Water is running. Lavatories are flushing. Mrs Ellis, the housekeeper, has arrived in the kitchen to prepare breakfast. Only David, who can sleep through anything, will still be in bed now. It is well understood, even by little Kara, that he must be allowed to lie in on Sundays.

For five days a week David works under pressure. There is always too much to be done in his office, and every detail requires his full concentration. He is an inspector of taxes; it is a joke between them that he married Susan for her money after discovering from her tax return just how much of her income was taxable at the highest rate—and that perhaps only a tax inspector would regard another man's five sons in terms of benefits rather than trouble. He is prepared to behave as a family man on Saturdays and holidays, but Sunday is his day of rest. He will skip breakfast and wander downstairs only when the papers have arrived.

On her way up to dress, Susan pauses to study the notice board on which all of each day's activities are booked in. There is never very much arranged for Sunday's during the school term. The five boys are weekly boarders at nearby Stanton House, where the school day is long and strictly organised. Like David, they need one day a week to relax and enjoy themselves in their own ways. But for once Susan herself has an important appointment. At nine o'clock she is due to interview Mr Peter Quigley for the post of holiday tutor.

Chapter Two

The silence of the night is broken by a crackle and a screech: Radio Three's protest against being expected to offer sweet music at such an hour. Peter Quigley has taken the precaution of putting the radio alarm where it cannot be switched off from the bed. He lurches towards it, groping for the switch with his eyes still tightly closed. The movement takes him out of reach of his spectacles. He has to make his way back to the bedside table before putting out a hand to locate them in their usual place.

'Wassati'?' Mandy's voice emerges, muffled, from beneath the duvet.

'Half past five.' Yawning, he makes for the bathroom.

'Half past five!' Shocked into wakefulness, Mandy sits upright. 'What on earth...?'

'I told you yesterday, I've got an interview for this tutorial job.' He splashes himself vigorously with cold water.

'At nine o'clock, you said. Hours away.'

'Miles away, as well. There's only one train that will get me there in time and

20

I'd better be on it.'

'What an inconsiderate woman she must be! There must be later trains.'

'Wealthy women who offer gainful employment to impecunious postgrads are entitled to be inconsiderate if they choose. I had the freedom to say no.' Peter is in the kitchen corner of the one-room flat now, heating water for the cup of coffee which will serve for breakfast until he reaches the station. 'But it could be that she's being subtle rather than inconsiderate. Making this the first test of the interview. Is Mr Peter Quigley a punctual chap? And is he an early riser? To both of which questions my arrival at Donnington Manor at eight fifty-nine will triumphantly answer yes. I want this job, Mandy. I want it very much indeed. So whatever Mrs Susan Rolph demands, I shall agree.'

'Then I'm jealous of this Mrs Rolph. You wouldn't do that for me.'

He knows what she means. Mandy makes no secret of the fact that she wants to be married. But at the age of twenty-four, studying for a higher degree with no regular income except his grant, Peter feels himself unready for the responsibilities of marriage. It isn't that he is frivolous by nature, or tempted to play around. If anything, he is unnaturally serious and hard-working for his age. But he planned the whole of this stage of his life at the age of sixteen and, until it is completed and he has been appointed to his first university post, he is not prepared to step too far off the narrow path of academic slog.

'I don't exactly think that you need be jealous of a woman who has six children under the age of thirteen,' he suggests. 'She's probably one of these shapeless earth mothers, permanently harassed by screaming kids. It's not surprising she wants someone to keep them out of her hair for a few months. What do you think I ought to wear?'

For the first time since the alarm sounded he is hesitating. This is something that ought to have been decided on the previous evening. His wardrobe is a limited one, but does nevertheless allow him a choice. He can be neat and conventional in his only suit and a collar and tie, as if to indicate a businesslike approach to what will, after all, be a position of authority in the household if he gets the job. Or he can dress more casually, suggesting that he sees his relationship with the children as friendly, and that he is prepared to rough it.

Part of the difficulty lies in the careful phrasing of the advertisement that he answered three weeks earlier. Instead of stating detailed requirements, which anyone could then claim to possess, Mrs Rolph asked applicants to set out the subjects and ages with which they felt most competent to deal. His summons for interview means that he has jumped that first hurdle, but still without receiving any guidance from her as to the kind of person she wishes to welcome into her home.

However, candidates for the job are required to have the ability to swim, a valid passport and a clean driving licence. From that it is reasonable to deduce that the post will involve travel to a remote part of a foreign country. As he reaches for his casual clothes. Peter reminds himself that any assumption he allows himself to express in the course of the interview must draw support from that uninformative advertisement. At no point must Mrs Rolph be given cause to wonder whether this perfectly qualified candidate knows more about her family than she has chosen to reveal.

He kisses Mandy goodbye, picks up a book to read on the journey and arrives at Paddington ten minutes before the train is due to leave. Everything is going to plan.

The first surprise of the day comes when he is shown into the morning room of Donnington Manor.

Mrs Rolph bears not the slightest resemblance to the earth mother of his imagination. She looks far too slim to have given birth to six children and far too young for the eldest of these to be twelve years old. She has the good teeth and long legs which he associates with Americans, but the perfect pale skin of an Englishwoman. Her fair hair is neatly braided down the back of her head and is long enough to fall from the braid halfway down her back. She is casually dressed for a warm Sunday in a sleeveless tunic and brief culottes.

As the expected inquisition begins, her clear blue eyes stare straight into his, probing his secrets. Peter concentrates hard on the task of revealing only what he can be expected to know.

She has already learned from his letter of application that he has a first-class degree in classics and that for the past three years he has augmented his grant by cramming sixth-formers for A levels in Latin and Greek.

'That's a little different, of course, from acting as a tutor in a wide spread of subjects to younger boys,' she points out.

He nods his head, not bothering to argue. There may once have been a time when tutoring, or even just holiday cramming, was a recognised field of employment, with a sufficiency of practitioners to offer a choice. But that time is past, as Mrs Rolph has almost certainly discovered already. He answers with a good show of confidence.

'Presumably their school will provide the textbooks to be studied, and a note of what point in the syllabus they're expected to reach by the end of term. I know how to teach.'

'By slogging your way through the books with them, you mean?'

Peter shakes his head. 'By making the work interesting. Acting it out. Or field work, if conditions make that possible in subjects like science and nature study.' He has reason to know that he is on safe ground here. Sure enough, some of the aggression fades from Mrs Rolph's eyes as she gives an instinctive nod of the head.

'What modern languages can you offer?'

'Good French. Enough German to read it well, though I'm not too fluent in conversation.' Should he or should he not mention that he is in the process of teaching himself Turkish? He decides against it. This is not a qualification which she can possibly expect. He leaves her to continue the interrogation, working her way through his level of competence in a range of school subjects. 'Do any of the boys learn Latin or Greek?' he asks.

'Yes. They go to a very traditional prep school, as weekly boarders. Tam is due to start at Winchester in September. He was coached for a scholarship, although he didn't get one. I think he's pretty well up to GCSE standard in Latin already, and not far away in Greek. Roy has done three years of Latin and Murdo one year: neither of them is going to take Greek. Calum's only eight, but he's longing to start, so he may pester you for a bit of coaching. He seems to have a real flair for languages. He's very good at French and he's even picked up a lot of—'

She checks herself and changes the subject. 'You said in your letter that you were working for a doctorate. Are you able to take so much time off from that? I mean, you do realise that this job would be full time? As well as teaching, I should want you to supervise the boys in their leisure activities. They're good at amusing themselves, but I need to know that someone is responsible for their safety.'

Much as Peter wants the job, he sees no need to present himself as a crawler.

'Even as a full-time employee, I would expect one free day a week and at least two hours to myself each evening, after the boys are in bed. What I do in that time would be my own business.'

'We shan't be in England. It's because we're going abroad that I need a tutor. So there won't be any libraries handy.'

26

'I've done almost all the preliminary research that I need for the doctorate,' he assures her. 'I'm hoping to break new ground in this field by the use of a computer for textual analysis and as a first stage I shall use a laptop to get my notes and thoughts organised. I can do that anywhere.'

His inquisitor says nothing to indicate disapproval of this statement, and it is almost casually that she asks what exactly is his field.

'Pretty specialised, I'm afraid. The use of tomb inscriptions as historical sources.' She looks puzzled, and he doesn't blame her. 'My particular interest is in a very remote part of the world. In classical times it was continually being invaded. Greeks, Macedonians, Romans—you name it, they were there. But because it was so remote there were small pockets that were bypassed and never conquered at all, and one way of finding out which those areas were is by studying the language they put on their tombs.'

'What part of the world are you talking about?'

'Turkey. Just one part of Turkey.'

'Oh.' He has given her something to think about. 'So I suppose you spend as much time there as possible?'

'No, I've never been to Turkey, and

I'm not likely to either: not until after the thesis is finished, anyway. But that doesn't matter. I'm not an archaeologist, who needs to work on a site. Other people have recorded the words—including a lot that no one can understand yet. That's one element in what I'm doing: it's like trying to break a code. It's an intellectual exercise. I don't have to be in any particular place to work at it.'

There is a long silence. Mrs Rolph's next question reveals that she is—with considerable justification—suspicious. 'Who is your supervisor, Mr Quigley?'

Peter allows his expression to indicate surprise that this should be of any relevance to the interview, but answers without hesitation. 'Dr Harry Anderson.' Since Professor Sutherland's departure for the United States three and a half years earlier, this happens to be true. 'I'm sure he'd be happy to act as a referee if you want one. Although of course he only knows me as a scholar, so to speak; not as a teacher.' He checks himself, knowing that he is talking too much and too fast.

Another silence, and then she makes up her mind. 'I'd like you to meet the boys.' Her mouth widens in a smile, once again revealing those strong white teeth: she has accepted him, although no doubt he still has to jump the hurdle of her sons' approval. She stands up, but pauses before leading the way out of the room. 'They call themselves "the gang", and I have to confess that I tend to speak about "the boys", though I shouldn't. But I regard it as very important that they should be treated and taught as individuals.'

'Of course, Mrs Rolph.' Peter also has risen politely to his feet and now follows her out of the room. Although he conceals it well, he is bubbling with triumph. He's made it!

'They'll be in the wood,' Mrs Rolph guesses. They walk together across a terrace, down a wide flight of stone steps and past the high wall of a kitchen garden. A small girl appears round the corner of the walled garden. She is about four years old and is wearing a blue and white striped T-shirt under a blue denim boiler suit. Her hair, which is fair but not as fair as her mother's, is cut at the front into a fringe which almost touches her eyebrows and at the back has been strained upwards and tied with a ribbon into a perky topknot. To Peter's eyes, her head appears disproportionately large for her body, which at this moment expresses a passionate indignation as she runs to her mother to complain.

'They won't let me play!'

'Where are they, Kara?'

'In the tree house. I want to go too. They won't let me.'

'It's dangerous, darling. You might fall out. When you're bigger. I told you to stay with Rosie. You mustn't keep running off on your own like this. Go and help her put the cherries on the trifle. I expect she'll let you taste one.'

Peter turns his head to watch as the little girl runs of happily enough in the direction of the house. 'Would she be one of my pupils?'

'Not officially, no. She hasn't started school yet. She might want to turn up to classes just because she hates being left out of anything, so I could provide you with drawing materials, that sort of thing, and you could let her stay just as long as she amuses herself quietly. But there'll always be someone else to look after her.'

They are in the wood now, and Peter is conscious of an unnatural silence. He stops abruptly and looks up into the centre of an old and very thick beech tree. Five pairs of blue eyes stare down from five freckled faces topped by five mops of sandy hair.

Mrs Rolph, following his gaze, is surprised. 'I thought—' She nods in the direction of a huge oak, in whose branches Peter can see the tree house mentioned by the little girl. It is linked to the beech by a stout rope about fifteen feet above the ground. 'Come down,' she calls, laughing. 'I want you all to meet Mr Quigley.'

'Stand away, then.' Another rope snakes down to the ground and the boys descend, hand over hand, before lining up to be introduced. The way in which they move around before taking up their positions makes it clear that they are standing in order of age.

One thing is immediately obvious to Peter as he shakes each hand. Teaching these five boys may not present too much of a problem, but distinguishing them from each other will be quite another matter. When all five are together, as they are now, it may not be too bad, but any one on his own could easily be confused with the one above or below him in age. They all have the same features, the same skin and hair, the same way of standing. To make identification even more difficult, the youngest of the boys is taller than one of this brothers.

Introductions start at the top.

'This is Tam, Tammas, my eldest. Tam is twelve.'

'Twelve and a half,' says Tam; and then, shaking hands politely, 'How do you do, sir?'

If he gets the job, Peter will ask to be called Peter, since this is a holiday arrangement. But to say so now would be premature. He repeated each name with each handshake. At some point he will have to find some trick of memory to attach it to its owner. The first one is easy enough. T for Tam. T for tallest. T for top dog.

'Roy is eleven.'

'Roy.' R for the red shorts he is wearing, while all the others are in jeans. That clue will last only for the day, but will have to do.

'Murdo is nine. Nine and a half if we're being precise. Murdoch is his full name, but no one ever uses it. My first husband, the boys' father, is a Scot and we rather went to town on Scottish names, I'm afraid.'

'Murdo.' M for the mouth organ which is tucked into his shirt pocket; another one-day-only label. He is a little plumper than any of the others, though; a little fuller in the face. Peter memorises the difference while trying not to stare too hard.

'This is Calum.'

'I'm eight.' Calum speaks for himself.

'Calum, hi.' C for confident—and perhaps C for clever as well: the boy who is longing to learn Greek and Latin.

'And Donnie is the youngest. Just seven.'

Donnie is the one who is tall for his age. He looks older than Calum until he smiles and reveals the gaps in his teeth.

'I'm going to ask Mr Quigley to teach you something.'

There is a roar of protest. Tam speaks for them all. 'Mum! It's Sunday! We don't even have to do prep on Sundays!'

'Only half an hour. He wouldn't want to travel all the way to The Lookout and then perhaps discover that his five pupils are all as thick as planks. We have to let him find out whether he has any chance of getting anything into your noddles.'

Peter grins. 'What your mother means is that she isn't going to offer me the job unless you approve of me. Your big chance to examine a teacher, for a change.'

The four younger boys look at Tam, who—like his mother earlier—gives a hardly perceptible nod. 'Not more than half an hour, then.'

'I'll come back at half past ten and rescue him,' their mother promises. Peter is left alone with his class.

'You could show us how to do spin bowling,' suggests Donnie hopefully.

Peter, whose eyesight has never been good, is not a games player. 'I don't think that's quite what your mother had in mind.'

'Well, what *are* you going to teach us, then?'

For a few seconds Peter's mind is a blank. He can tell them nothing, because he knows nothing. Then the sight of the tree house gives him an idea. 'Do you know the story of King Charles and the oak tree?'

Four sandy heads shake in ignorance. Only Tam is able to summon a memory. 'I know about him hiding. I don't think I know why, though.'

'Right.' Peter organises his thoughts in a businesslike manner. 'Half an hour isn't long enough to rehearse a play. But we could prepare a tableau for your mother, with words. Let's imagine that we're in the middle of the civil war between the Kings' party and the Puritans. Speaking from memory, I think the year is 1651, but we shall have to check the date later. Who wants to be a Roundhead? Over here, then. Cavaliers on the right. Now...'

When Mrs Rolph returns, as she has promised, Peter meets her at the edge of the wood and asks her to close her eyes. With one hand under her elbow, he guides her back towards the tree house.

'Now you can look.' At the same moment he signals with his free hand. Tam, Roy, Calum and Donnie freeze into their positions, with exaggerated expressions on their faces. Only Murdo is invisible, hiding behind a tree as with surprising competence for a nine-year-old he provides sad or marching background music on his mouth organ. M for Murdo and M for musician.

Roy's expression is one of extreme alarm. His mouth is wide open, with one hand raised in front of it—although not close enough to obscure his speech.

'My name is Francis Cotton. I believe that my sovereign lord King Charles the Second has been given by God the right to reign over this kingdom because he is the eldest son of the anointed King, Charles the First. That is why I have allowed him to hide in my house from the reggy, reggy—'

Peter prompts him. 'Regicides.'

'Regicides who are trying to capture him.'

He resumes his frozen posture as each of the others in turn identifies himself. Calum is the Puritan commander. Donnie is the servant who has volunteered to lead the king to safety. Tam, of course, is Charles, staring anxiously down from the oak tree as he describes the events that have brought him to this hiding place.

Mrs Rolph claps her hands enthusiastically as the brief performance ends. 'Well done, all of you! Well, you'll see Mr Quigley at lunch. You can get back to your game now.'

'Aren't you going to ask them whether they'll have me?' asks Peter, as he walks back to the house with the woman who is certainly going to be his employer.

She shakes her head smilingly. 'They like you. I can't read Latin or Greek, but I can read my boys. If you want the job, it's yours. From next week until September the third.'

'You didn't mention in your advertisement whereabouts you'd be living during the period.'

'In a house called The Lookout, owned by my ex-father-in-law. He lives in the main house of the estate, The Eyrie, but there's a villa which he built in the grounds for his son and me after we married. My first husband, the father of all the boys, was Hugh Sutherland. Does the name mean anything to you?'

'Well, of course! The standard work on the eastern Roman empire. And his discoveries at Sillium were what first got me interested in the area. Are you telling me...? I didn't realise, with your name being Rolph. Does that mean...?'

He is pushing it too far. Once again a flicker of suspicion clouds those clear blue eyes. In a moment she will challenge him, asking him whether he knew of the tutorial vacancy before the advertisement appeared. But his confidence that he is exactly the right man for her job helps him to hold an expression of innocent expectation on his face as he awaits her reply. Her eyes clear again as she smiles.

'Yes,' she says. 'We shall be spending the next fifteen weeks in Turkey. A happy coincidence for you, isn't it?'

Chapter Three

'There it is!'

For an hour already the boys have been jostling for the best place on deck, and now, as the ship rounds a headland, five voices shout as one; five hands stretch out to point. 'Look, Peter. There it is!'

Peter himself is almost speechless with anticipation. He has read so much and imagined so much and now, at last, he is approaching Lycia. He tries to laugh himself out of this unexpected emotion. Most people outside Turkey have never even heard of Lycia. It is the failing of all scholars to believe that the subject which supremely interests them is more important than anything else in the world.

His first reaction, as a matter of fact, is one of surprise. When the noise of the engine cuts to half speed, the ship's prow turns to point towards Antalya, and Antalya, as he is already aware, is a tourist resort. The small boats bobbing in the harbour have been brightly painted to attract day trippers, and above the battlemented walls which have protected the port for many centuries rise the palm trees and the coloured umbrellas of open-air café life. Because the walled city was originally built on a cliff, it is not possible from sea level to see its old houses and bazaars, but there is no way of concealing the huge modern hotel which thrusts its balconies towards the sun and its terraces towards the sea.

It is not any of this that comes as a surprise—indeed, Peter hardly notices. He is staring—as the boys on the deck are staring—at the view that must present itself, across the width of the bay, to all those tourists on their balconies.

Lycia, this part of Turkey, has always emerged from the pages of books and diaries and military reports as inaccessible and unfriendly, even sinister: a land of dark mountains and jagged rocks, of shadows and mysteries, of a people who over many centuries have learned the knack of retreating quietly into their own society while invaders or colonisers pause briefly but then pass on. Peter has not expected anything like this scene. It is beautiful.

The mountain peaks which rise higher and higher as they recede from the shore are still capped with snow and the snow is glistening in the sun. The nearest range falls steeply towards the sea and at its foot is a golden sandy beach which stretches, at a guess, for a mile or more; and this too is bathed in sunshine. It is an idyllic holiday scene—made all the more remarkable by the fact that the beach is completely deserted.

It is ridiculous to be so surprised. Mrs Rolph would hardly have brought six children here on holiday to a place completely lacking in holiday ingredients. The absence of swimmers and sunbathers is simple enough to explain. He knows from the maps he has studied that there is no road along most of this stretch of the coast. He moves closer to the boys, who are pointing to the rocky headland whose cliff, falling sheer down to the water, closes one end of the beach. Five voices construct a single sentence.

'That's Grandfather's house, The Eyrie, up there.'

'The grey one, with the trees in front; can you see?'

'And ours is just below it but you can't spot it from the sea because it's a little way back.'

'But you can see a sort of zigzag path cut into the cliff, the path we go down for swimming, and if you follow the line up and then a bit to the right, that's where The Lookout is.'

'And that's our castle.' Donnie's finger is pointing to an outcrop of rock which does indeed look like the ruins of some kind of fortification. But Peter's attention is elsewhere. He points to some dark shapes in the sheer cliff of the headland.

'Those caves over there. They look very square, as though they've been dug out.'

Even before he raises his binoculars to his eyes he knows what the explanation will be.

'They're tombs,' Roy tells him. 'Hundreds of years old.'

'Thousands!' That is Murdo's amendment.

'They're empty now,' says Donnie earnestly. 'No bodies left. But we're not allowed to go in.'

'Why not?' asks Peter.

'There are curses written all over them.' It is Calum who gives the explanation. 'To keep robbers away in the old days. The curses say what will happen to anyone who steals the bodies or the treasures that were buried with them. Or at least, nobody knows *exactly* what they say, because nobody can read the language, but there are other places nearby where there's a different language and someone has worked a bit of it out and Dad says it's probably the same sort of thing here. Curses!'

'That's not why we don't go, though.' Tam wants to make it clear that he would not be frightened by a mere curse. 'Grandfather says that it's not right to use people's graves for playing in, even if the bodies aren't there any more. And Mum is just nervous, in case we might have an accident or get bitten by a snake or something.'

Susan arrives to join the group at that moment, carrying Kara so that she can see over the rail.

'Go and collect all your things together,' she tells the boys. 'And make sure that you're wearing everything that you started the day with.'

She sets Kara down on the deck and the little girl promptly runs after her brothers. 'Murdo! Look after Kara!' Susan calls after them.

'Murdo's the one you trust with her most, I notice,' Peter comments.

'I try to take it in turns. So that none of them will feel he's always being landed with her. It's difficult. She longs to be one of the gang, but it's true that she holds them up. Just by being small: not necessarily because she's a girl.' Susan pauses, perhaps running mentally through her rota of supervision. 'But you're

41

probably right. Murdo does get more than his fair share. He's so patient with her. And she genuinely enjoys listening to him practise. So whenever she has one of her tantrums, it's tempting to cast Murdo in the role of Orpheus.'

For the moment her children are only of secondary consideration to Peter. 'It's beautiful!' he exclaims, gesturing towards the mountains. 'I hadn't expected it to be beautiful.'

'This is why I always try to arrive by sea. This sudden, unexpected, marvellous view. Because it reminds me of when I saw it for the first time.' She leans forward on to the rail, indulging a sentimental memory.

'I was very young and on my honeymoon. We married at the start of the digging season and Hugh carried me straight off here. I was a bit apprehensive, really. Not sure what to expect. I didn't know exactly what Hugh meant by living in "the camp" on site. But I did know it would be miles from anywhere, so I couldn't imagine what I'd do with myself all day or how much I'd be expected to help in running it. On top of that, he'd told me that I'd better stay in Antalya for a few days by myself while he got things organised, and I was afraid that was going to be terribly primitive.'

'And was it?'

'No. Rather nice, really. Terribly hot, of course. But all the streets smelled of spices. They still do, in the old town. And there's an interesting thing about Antalya. It's built on some particular kind of porous rock which acts as a sort of filter for sewage, so everything drains away and emerges in the sea smelling of roses, so to speak. It means that the town doesn't have the nastier kind of smell. But I didn't know any of that in advance. I'd married straight from home and I couldn't speak the language and I suppose I was worried about not being able to cope. And then the ship turned in, just like today, and suddenly I knew it was going to be all right.'

'The camp was at Sillium, I suppose?'

'Yes, and that was all right as well. When they found that I was quite good at drawing, they sat me down in a tent and brought in bits and pieces that they found. I copied the patterns on pottery and inscriptions on stones and even made drawings of the big carvings: friezes and that kind of thing. If you're careful, you can make a drawing much clearer than a photograph, and very accurate. I was quite sorry, in a way, when I had to live at The Lookout instead.'

'When did that happen?' By now the ship has stopped moving and there is a rattling of chains from the deck below; but it will still be a little while before they disembark.

'Hugh's father, Dr Sutherland, already had a house over there.' She points towards the area which the boys have earlier indicated. 'Behind that row of cypresses. He's immensely proud of those trees. There could hardly have been a less promising place for them. Anyway, as soon as he learned that I was pregnant—when we were back in England—he wrote to say that I must have somewhere reasonably civilised to stay with the baby in future summers. So he had a small villa built on his land, lower down, nearer the sea. And later on, when the family began to grow, Hugh and I added on a wing so that the children could have their own quarters.

'Why did Dr Sutherland himself choose to live in such an out-of-the way place?'

'He's a great rock climber. Used to be, at least, and still pretty good, considering he's in his sixties. Apparently the mountains back there—' she gestures towards the highest of the peaks'—they're over ten thousand feet and full of what he calls challenges. He bought the house and the headland when he first came out to Turkey on an engineering contract, years ago. To start with, after the contract ended, he just used to spend all his holidays here. With Hugh, of course, and his wife while she was alive. One day, quite early on, he was asked by some archaeologist if he'd climb up the cliff of the headland and report on the tombs that are cut into the cliff face. I think he became hooked on the idea of climbing for a practical purpose. He's helped out with the studies of several of the really remote mountain cities which had been lost for centuries. Since he's retired, he lives here all the time.'

That interest presumably helps to explain why his son became a classical historian and archaeologist. But Peter has no time to ask any further questions, because by now it is time to disembark.

Among the passengers there is only one foreign family of six children, so it is not surprising that they are greeted with confidence by a young woman who steps forward to shake Susan's hand.

'My name is Esin. I am to look after your little girl while you are here.'

Peter already knows that it is Susan's habit to employ a Turkish student of English—a different one each summer—while she is in the country. The student has the opportunity to improve her English and is expected to act as a domestic interpreter as well as taking charge of

Kara. Esin is a full-figured young woman: probably she will be fat in middle age, but now her generous breasts and hips give her a voluptuous appearance. She has dark hair strained back off an oval face, and her calm expression takes on a motherly look as she smiles down at Kara and takes her hand.

'Over here are two Cherokees,' she tells the party. 'With drivers. One jeep will stay for you at the house for all the time you are here. The other will return to Antalya.' She leads the way, with the boys jostling behind her.

'Dr Sutherland doesn't come to meet you himself, then?' Peter is curious, but Susan laughs to show that she has expected this.

'He and I are not exactly best friends since the divorce. The boys are still his grandsons, of course, so if he wants to keep in touch with them he has to put up with me and encourage us to go on using the villa. But as far as I'm concerned, there's a certain chill in the air. And he completely ignores Kara. It's tough on her, because she doesn't understand why the others get hugs and presents and she doesn't. Now then, Peter, I'll go with Kara and Esin and the luggage. You stay with the boys, and will you sit next to Donnie, please? When we get to the ravine, keep him talking about something different. He hasn't got much of a head for heights, and he finds the bridge rather frightening.'

The first part of the journey is along a coastal road which is in reasonable repair. But it comes to a halt when confronted with the rocky spine of a headland and the two vehicles need all their power and road-holding qualities as they turn away from the sea and begin to climb. The track is rough and narrow, often with a solid wall of rock on one side and a sheer drop on the other. As they zigzag down again towards the bridge that Susan has mentioned, Peter finds himself able to sympathise with the seven-year-old's unease.

The bridge spans a narrow but deep gully and is about two hundred feet above its floor. From photographs he has seen, Peter can recognise it as being a Selcuk bridge: very narrow, and with parapets only a few inches high on each side. More alarming still is the fact that it has been built at right angles to the road: something to cause no problem to anyone on foot or horseback but needing, in Peter's opinion, a more cautious approach than the Turkish drivers are prepared to concede.

'Do you know how to play Boxes?' Peter

asks Donnie, and keeps his own eyes on the paper as well.

With the hazard safely passed, Donnie abandons the game and begins to bounce in his seat with increasing excitement.

'That's the soldier!' he shouts. 'That's the elephant! That's the great big dragon!'

Peter is puzzled at first, but soon begins to understand. With the crossing of the gully they have entered a completely different landscape: one side or other must at some time have been shifted by an earthquake. In the ensuing centuries, outcrops of rocky columns have been eroded into fantastic shapes which could pass for pieces of modern sculpture. At this moment, as the land flattens slightly, they are passing between a group of squat grey chessmen.

After the chessmen comes a sharp turn in the road and, without any noticeable signal, the boys burst into song: 'We'll be coming round the mountain when we come.' This is clearly a traditional part of their approach, and it brings a tall, grey-haired man on to the track to wave in welcome. There is no sign of any building as the drivers draw to a halt, but the cypresses which Peter has seen from the ship are standing in a row immediately above them. They have arrived.

Chapter Four

The first day at The Lookout is tradition-
ally a holiday for the children, while Susan
explains to the new girl and the new tutor
what their charges may, must or must
not do. All five boys keep close to their
mother during this process, to make sure
that none of their rights is diminished or
forgotten. Kara, although her timetable
will be different and her movements
more restricted, insists on staying with
her brothers, and Esin naturally is present
to hold Kara's hand. So the party which
prepares to explore the territory is a large
one. Before they set out, Susan explains
the timetable.

'Breakfast any time between six and
seven, on the side verandah.' The villa
has three wide verandahs, so that there
is always some shade. 'Lessons from half
past seven to half past twelve in the
schoolroom, with a fifteen-minute break
whenever it suits you.'

'Every day?' asks Peter.

'No. Five days a week. As though they
were at school. Their father will tell you
each week when he's free to spend time

with them. If he asks for Friday and Saturday, then Sunday will become an ordinary schoolday.' She glances at him to check his reaction: she ought perhaps to have made sure when first interviewing him that he has no religious objections to working on Sundays. But the whole point of coming to Turkey every year is so that Hugh can spend unhurried time with his sons—and Peter is taking this on board with a nod of the head.

'Lunch at one o'clock,' Susan continues. 'After that, Kara has to rest on her bed for two hours, and of course any of the boys can do the same if they feel like it.'

'Fat chance!' exclaims Roy, and they all laugh.

'Yes, well, the period from two to half past five is free time for the boys. Within limits—and they know what the limits are—they can do what they like. Donnie, tell Peter one of the rules; any one.'

'We have to wear hats and T-shirts all the time until four o'clock. Even in the sea.' He makes a face to show his disgust.

'Calum?'

'We have to tell Peter where we're going and what we're going to do.'

'Right. And there's a message board, Peter, on the front verandah. Anyone who leaves the villa writes up the time and destination. If I go off somewhere to paint, for example, I shall write down where you can find me. That applies to you as well, Esin, if you take Kara for a walk. Murdo?'

'We aren't allowed to go swimming without Peter. And we have to wear our harnesses for getting to the beach.'

'I was going to say that,' protested Roy.

Peter looked puzzled. 'What does that mean?'

'I'll show you when you get there. Tam, what's the most important rule of all?'

'We can't go past the posts to the edge of the cliff.'

'We'll show you what that means as well,' Susan promises Peter. 'Anyway, after their free time, supper will be at six o'clock. Then for an hour after that it's back to the schoolroom. How they spend that time is up to you. If you've set them homework, so to speak, that's when they'd do it. Or you might choose to give one of them an individual lesson while the others get on with their prep.'

'When is bedtime?' asks Peter.

'There's no fixed time. I expect them to be sensible about knowing when they're tired. Kara goes off straight after supper and Donnie's usually ready for bed at eight; but anyone who wants to can read or

51

play a quiet game. Shall we go and explore now? Tam, bring your harness with you, will you?'

She puts on her wide-brimmed hat and leads the way out, with Peter at her side. As soon as they are outside the villa the boys run ahead, shouting excitedly.

'This is where we play football. Dad gave us a goal for our holiday present last year.'

'And that's for cricket, over there. We put stones round for the boundary.'

'Are you any good at cricket, Peter? Can you coach us?'

The tutor makes an apologetic face. 'I'm afraid I've never been brilliant at ball games. I only notice a cricket ball when it's about to hit me. I'll be more use to you with the swimming. I could teach you some interesting dives.'

'Can we take our hats off for diving, Mummy?'

Susan laughs affectionately at her youngest son. 'Of course you can, Donnie. Just be sensible.'

Roy has his special part of the land to show Peter. 'This is my running track. Grandfather gets someone to scythe it flat for me when he's doing the wicket for cricket.'

The land surrounding the villa is not particularly suitable for games. It is covered with a low scrub which is spiky enough to make trainers or sandals essential wear and is quite capable of tripping up a runner. But it would be impractical to create a lawn in a place that receives almost no summer rain and where water is expensive.

Murdo tugs at her hand. 'Can I show him my practice place?' He turns to Peter. 'I bring my trumpet out here. So that it doesn't disturb anyone.'

'Sick cow noises!' teases Calum, but Murdo doesn't react.

By now they have crossed the open and relatively flat space and are climbing a small hill. On the top is a rocky outcrop which the boys unanimously claim to be their castle: it is the landmark that Donnie pointed out from the ship. Murdo leads the way to a smaller ring of rocks at a little distance.

'This is my turret,' he tells Peter. 'There's a sort of ledge inside, look, so that I can prop up my music.'

'My seat, my seat!' Kara until now has been very quiet. Probably she is still making up her mind whether or not to like Esin. But now she breaks free and runs to sit down on a flat rock, with her legs dangling into the turret. Susan turns to Esin to explain.

'Kara enjoys listening to Murdo, and he doesn't mind, do you, Murdo? So it's all right for you to bring her out here if she wants to come. But of course you must stay with her.'

She watches Esin's face to make sure that her instructions are being understood, but there are no real doubts. Dr Sutherland seems, as usual, to have been careful in his search for a suitable student, in spite of his resentment at Kara's very existence.

The others are by now dashing towards their castle. The slopes of the raised area on which it stands are made jagged by small spikes of rock which give the impression of a tank trap: in their soft shoes the boys have to pick their way carefully through this outer defence before beginning the scramble to storm the keep.

The walls of the castle are formed by a ring of natural fingers of rock which rise in places up to twelve feet high. At some point in the distant past the gaps between the rocks have been filled in with rubble. Some of these loose stones have fallen away, allowing the taller boys to look out. Tam explains to Peter that although it might seem simpler to scramble into the castle over the lower sections of wall, there is a danger that the rubble might collapse, so it is one of their rules that anyone wanting to get in must climb one of the solid rocks. From a distance the surfaces of these look sheer, but there are in fact sufficient small ledges to allow even the youngest boys to haul themselves up to the top, as they now proudly demonstrate.

This is not the most obviously suitable place for any lookout post. The tip of the headland, a little further south, would give a wider view of approaching enemies. But from ancient times the headland has been used as a necropolis, to be avoided by the living; and in fact the land on which they are standing at this moment is higher than the top of the headland. Although an enemy creeping round close to the shore might be invisible, there is a good view of the distant sea.

Susan knows that when he was a boy, brought here for his holidays, Hugh liked to think that the rocks had been turned into a fortification by Alexander the Great: but now, as an adult and a scholar, he believes that it is more likely to have been used as a watchtower at the time of the Crusades. In more recent centuries it has certainly been used as a shelter by generations of goatherds. The boys don't care about the details. It is their castle.

'We can look out for invaders,' Roy tells Peter.

'And play sieges.' That's Murdo.

'There's a dungeon.' The wide-eyed awe with which Donnie makes this announcement suggests that he may at some time

have been threatened by his brothers
with incarceration; but already Calum is
correcting his choice of word.

'An oubliette. That means you can put
someone inside and forget about him.'

'I hope you'll never do that,' says Susan,
laughing. 'You haven't told me about
dungeons before.' The boys are inside by
now: she and Peter are content to look in
over one of the rubble walls.

'We only found the hole last year,'
Tam tells her. 'It's underneath that stone,
the one we use for the king to sit on.
When we moved the stone the first time,
we thought it was going to be a well,
but it isn't. It isn't deep enough. Just
a hole.'

'All the same...' The thought of this
unexpected hazard makes Susan uneasy.
'If someone fell in...'

Tam hastens to reassure her. 'No one
ever will. We might use it to keep our siege
rations, but that's all. And we'll always put
the stone back on top. Even if anyone did
fall in, it really isn't deep. If I stand on the
bottom, my head sticks up, and I can haul
myself out.' He jumps in to demonstrate,
waves happily, and wriggles his way up
again.

Susan is still not altogether happy. 'It's
never to be used for people,' she tells Tam
firmly. 'It could be very frightening, even

for only a short time. Will you promise me that?'

'Promise.' Tam is prompt to respond, and the others follow his lead. Their mother is reassured. Tam always keeps promises. The party moves on.

On the further side of the castle the land slopes down to the east, towards the edge of the cliff above the sea, and more gently to the south, towards the headland. Susan glances back to make sure that Esin is holding Kara's hand.

'This is the dangerous part,' she tells both Peter and the girl. 'It would be impossible to fence off the whole of the cliff. So this is an absolute rule. No one is allowed to go within ten feet of the edge, either here or on the headland, except where the path goes down to the beach. If a ball rolls that way or a hat blows off, too bad; it has to go. These white posts are to mark out the limit. Esin, I don't want you to bring Kara anywhere here at all. Do you understand? And Peter, if you ever see one of the boys near the edge, you tell me and he spends the whole of the next two days in the schoolroom. But in fact—' she smiles, because this is after all a holiday—'they're all very sensible about it.'

'Is the edge crumbling?' asks Peter.

'No. But except for a couple of ledges halfway down, it's a sheer drop. So this is the big no-no. OK? Now, where shall we go next, Kara?'

'My swimming pool, my swimming pool!' Kara begins to run, dragging Esin by the hand.

'Right.' Susan has already warned Peter that water must never be wasted. There is a natural freshwater spring above The Eyrie, Dr Sutherland's home: it is the reason for the position of the house. In addition, Dr Sutherland has excavated a huge cistern from the rock a hundred feet above. It is filled every winter by rain and melting snow. But the increasing size of the visiting family puts a strain on the reserves and there has never been any possibility of maintaining a full-size swimming pool.

He is an engineer, however: a practical man. Several years ago, realising that Susan, pregnant for a second time, could not easily carry her first baby down to the beach and up again, He created a small rock pool—with its own miniature cistern—in which a toddler could paddle and splash and sail little boats. It was made for Tam, but each of the boys has enjoyed it for two or three summers. Now Kara has it to herself. Probably this year it is time for her in turn to tackle the steep climb down to the sea; but that can wait until David arrives to help her.

The last stage of the tour is the approach

to the beach. In the centuries before the spring was diverted to domestic use it cut out a gully, and Dr Sutherland has made use of this to construct a path along one side of the headland. To prevent the gradient from being too steep, the path slopes steadily downwards until it almost reaches the sheer cliff at the end of the headland, then turns a sharp corner to go inland for a little way before making a second turn back towards the sea. Although the land falls away abruptly to the floor of the gully, strong iron posts are linked by thick ropes two and three feet above ground, and another thick rope acts as a handrail on the other side of the path. Susan also points out to Peter a long rail, fastened to the rock, which slopes parallel to the path about six feet above it.

'Tam, will you demonstrate?'

Tam buckles on the body harness which he has been carrying and snaps in the metal fastening of one of half a dozen ropes which dangle from the rail. The higher end of the rope is fastened to a metal wheel, which moves with him as he starts to walk down the path. Although Susan knows that there is no danger, she is unable to control a gasp as her eldest son pretends to trip and fall sideways. But the safety rope holds: of course it does. His grandfather inspects and tests the whole system before re-rigging it each summer.

'Tam and Roy are old enough to decide whether or not they need to wear their harnesses,' she tells Peter. 'But it's compulsory for the younger ones, down and up. I'm afraid it's a bit of a slog coming up after a swim, but it can't be helped—and the water's marvellous.'

The sound of a two-tone horn, several times repeated, attracts her attention, and the boys have heard it as well.

'It's Dad!' Tam hurries to disconnect his harness and they all rush towards the house, with Roy leading the field. Susan does not follow at once. Although, after the chilly year following the divorce, she and her first husband are on friendly terms again, she feels an odd kind of shyness about meeting him for the first time each summer. Instead, she turns to Esin.

'I expect Kara would like to have a paddle in her pool straight away,' she suggests. 'Bring her up to the house in time to be tidy for lunch.'

She and Peter walked back side by side. Hugh is lying on the ground, smothered by his sons like a bitch by her puppies. He can be heard pleading for air, and at last throws them all off and sits up, his red hair tousled. At the age of forty he still looks as young as when she first met him. He is an open-air man, not the sort of professor to spend his whole life in libraries. For as long as she has known him he has lived for his summer digs. Now the happiness of being in the place he loves and reunited with the sons he loves flushes his freckled face. At such moments Susan sometimes wishes... But she checks her thoughts. What's gone is gone.

Instead, she awaits the opportunity first of all to greet him herself and then to introduce the boys' new tutor.

'This is Peter Quigley, Hugh.'

'Hello, Peter.' Hugh grins at the young man as he shakes hands. 'You think you can keep this gang of ruffians in check, do you?'

'I shall try,' Peter is smiling as well.

Susan looks from one to the other. There is something odd about the exchange. Just a shade too much ease; too little curiosity. 'Have you two met before?' she asks.

'A long time ago.' Hugh makes no attempt to be secretive. 'About five years, I suppose. When I was still at SOAS.'

That's another odd thing, then. There is no sense of surprise. Neither of the two is commenting that this is a happy coincidence. The meeting is one they have both expected.

Susan throws her mind back to her

interview with Peter. Commenting afterwards to David, she said laughingly, 'He's almost *too* perfect.' At the time it seemed too good to be true that he should claim to possess all the qualifications she required, without knowing in advance what they were. Now she can't help wondering whether he was after all aware what information to volunteer.

She tries to shrug the matter aside. If an impecunious young student has pulled a few strings in order to earn himself a free passage to a part of the world that interests him, there is nothing sinister about that. Is there?

Chapter Five

'Would you like me to drive the boys over?' Peter makes the offer as the second weekend of the sojourn in Turkey approaches. He has felt it only right to keep away during the first of the boys' access visits to their father, but now he would like to join them.

Susan looked surprised. 'It would mean sacrificing your free day. I thought you were anxious to have the time to get on with your own work.'

'That was before I knew that I should be coming to Turkey,' says Peter untruthfully. 'Now that I'm here...I'm never going to be an archaeologist myself, but all the same it's exciting to see the sites and actually touch the inscribed stones. Any one of them might hold the clue to a completely new interpretation of the history of this part of the world. So I'd really like to go to Termessus. And it would save Professor Sutherland from having to make the double journey twice to collect and return the boys.'

'Well, if you're sure; thank you very much.'

Peter can tell that she is still suspicious about his possible links with her ex-husband; but even if he were to confirm her doubts she could have no real reason to object. It's not as though he were being employed by Hugh to kidnap the boys—but he has to remind himself that although he may know that, their mother doesn't. Still, she must realise that there is no need for anything so dramatic as long as she and their father remain on friendly terms.

The day proves to be an exciting one. Before they arrive at Termessus, there is of course the hazard of the bridge over the ravine to be overcome. Peter tells himself firmly that the width of the roadway would be perfectly adequate if it were running over solid flat ground, but there is no doubt that his fingers clench the steering wheel more tightly than usual as he slowly negotiates the first right-angled bend and straightens up before making the crossing.

After that there are no more problems. For part of the uphill way from the coast to Termessus a decent road has been built, wide enough to carry up tourists by the coachload; and the rest of the climb must be made on foot. The boys run ahead, yelling warning of their arrival, while Peter lingers, allowing a few minutes for them to be welcomed. By the time he joins the group, Hugh is ready to greet him.

'Peter! Good of you to act as chauffeur.' When they last saw each other in England, four years earlier, their relationship was that of teacher and pupil, but since Peter embarked on an academic life himself, they have corresponded and become friends. 'Has Susan guessed yet?'

It is all very innocent. All that Hugh has done is to give his protégé—who could never have afforded a visit like this without help—advance notice of his ex-wife's annual search for a tutor and to coach him in the best way to prove his suitability.

'I think she may have, yes. But she hasn't put it into words.'

'That's very Susanish. She's not good at confronting hard facts. Prefers to shut her eyes to whatever's in front of them. Even when it's something as unimportant as this. But never mind that. I've got something to show you all. Boys!'

Without waiting for them to catch up, he begins to stride across the rough ground. They are in a cleft—too high and too steep to be called a valley—below both the ancient Lycian city on the top of the hill, which is the centre of tourist attraction, and the later Roman remains a little lower down. Excavations on these are in only their third season, and the earth remains littered with huge chunks of masonry, most of them still covered with the shrub growth of several centuries. But the group arrives quickly at an area which has been cleared.

'Just look at this, all of you. Found it three days ago. Marvellous stuff.'

Hugh Sutherland is an enthusiast. His excitement infects the little group even before they know what they are looking at. Or rather, they can all see that what has been exposed is a section of a stone wall with words carved on it, but cannot immediately grasp its significance.

'Part of a dice oracle,' he tells them; but only Peter knows what he means.

'What's that?' asks Calum.

Hugh sits down on one of the larger stones and prepares to give a short lecture. His sandy hair is untidy and the clothes in which he supervises the dig are crumpled and none too clean, but he has immediate authority as a teacher.

'I told you last week, that this area, where we're digging, was a Roman settlement. Had a wall round it, naturally. There must have been a gateway here, and someone's carved some rather interesting verses on it. You know about ordinary oracles, don't you? Tam, suppose you just remind the others.'

It is characteristic of Tam that he takes his time about answering: stopping to think in order to get it right.

'There was one at Delphi,' he said at last. 'People would go there and give a present and then ask some terribly important question about what they ought to do, and they thought they were talking directly to a god or goddess but it would just be a priest or priestess who gave the answer. And the answer would be sort of...' He comes to a halt, unable to think of the right word. 'It could mean two different things, so you could believe that you were taking the right advice and then if things went wrong you'd realise that you'd really been told to do something quite different.'

'Jolly good,' says Hugh. "Ambiguous" is

66

the word you were after. Well, it cost a lot to go off in search of one of the important oracles, and journeys were dangerous. So somebody thought of a different system, which anyone could use. If you had a problem, you could come up to a gate like this. And then you'd throw some dice. They wouldn't look like the dice we use nowadays. They'd be made of animal bones and would only have four sides, four numbers.'

'What didn't they have?' asks Murdo, interested.

'No two and no five. Anyway, you'd throw either five dice or seven. And according to the combination you got, there'd be a verse which would give you some advice.'

'Do you mean you'd add up to make a total?' Murdo checks.

'No. The numbers are set out in the order they fall. That gives you a lot more combinations. This verse we've found here, for example, says 44466.'

'And what does the verse say?' asks Donnie.

'Haven't had time to find out yet.'

This can't possibly be true, but Peter grins as he sees how wholeheartedly the boys accept the statement and are ready for Hugh's next suggestion even before he opens his mouth.

'I wondered whether you could all give me a bit of help. If I gave you each paper and pencil, could you draw out for me what you think the letters are? They're so rough and worn that I'd like you each to do it separately, without comparing notes. If you all get the same result, that'll be encouraging. Donnie's version, and Calum's, will be specially useful. Because they don't know any Latin, they won't be tempted to finish off an incomplete letter just because it seems likely to be right. And then we'll get the Latin scholars among you to tell us what the letters mean, if they can. Bearing in mind that some words won't be complete.'

'Peter's the Latin scholar,' suggests Roy.

'Peter can be the judge of your efforts. But I'd like to see how far you can get without him.'

He has the materials ready, and within a few minutes the boys are jostling for the best position and settling down to their task.

'That should give us half an hour,' Hugh suggests to Peter. 'Cup of coffee?'

'Thanks.' They move further up the hill and make themselves comfortable.

'This is something Susan used to do for me,' Hugh confides. 'When we were first married and she didn't have any children to look after. She got bored just sitting around the camp, and she's a really talented artist, you know. So I suggested she might make drawings of some of the things we found. Patterns on pottery, carvings on friezes: that sort of thing. It saved a lot of time in trying to fit them together, shuffling bits of paper instead of heavy lumps of marble.'

'I can imagine.'

'In fact, these tomb inscriptions you're working on—the Lycian ones—it was Susan who transcribed most of those. She'd spend a couple of nights at my father's place and go off on her own for the day, choosing a couple of tombs and copying everything that was carved round them.'

Remembering the printed illustrations over which he has pored for so many hours, Peter finds himself moved by this information. It provides an unexpected link between himself and his employer and brings an added warmth to his feelings towards her.

'Of course, she never had the faintest idea what the letters meant,' Hugh adds casually. 'That worried her to start with. I think it gave her quite a lift when I assured her that no one else could read this particular language either. She has this thing about not being clever.'

'You mean, she thinks she isn't.'

'Yes. Well, it's true in a sense. She's

not an intellectual: but then, how many people are? She's a beautiful woman who can run a household efficiently and bring up children lovingly, and she has a good many other talents as well. When we first met it used to worry her that she wasn't academically minded and not even particularly streetwise; but it was one of the things I loved about her. A sort of innocence. She believes what people tell her. That's not always sensible, but it's endearing.'

Peter feels a slight embarrassment at the course the conversation is taking. He is himself one of the people Susan ought not to have taken at face value. As he struggles to think of some way of changing the subject, Tam runs up to do it for him.

'I can read one of them already, Dad. The one in the middle.'

'And I thought it would take you all morning! What does it say, then?'

Tam reads proudly from his paper. 'Four four four six six. This is the advice of the god. Stay at home. There is danger outside.'

'Jolly good. Are you going to try any more of them for me?'

As his eldest son runs off, Hugh grins at Peter.

'So, having got the job, how are you

enjoying it? Are you getting on all right with the boys?'

The question is a casual one. He is asking merely for a general reassurance, not for a formal report, and Peter gives him the answer he expects. Only much later in the day, after driving back to The Lookout, does he put the same question to himself for serious consideration. Is he doing his job well?

It has taken him very little time to settle into a working routine, because the boys were there before him. Although he congratulates himself—with some surprise —on proving to be a good teacher, the real truth is that the boys are good pupils.

They know how their day is supposed to go, and they are not rebellious. The prep school which they all attend has accustomed them to discipline and their attitude to their mother's rules is refreshingly simple; if they accept the timetable of their working hours, no one will dare to deprive them of the time set aside for play. They have been accustomed to work in silence at school, and even in the more relaxed atmosphere of this schoolroom do not chatter too much.

Naturally the organisation of each lesson is complicated by the different ages of his pupils; but in this matter too the influence of Stanton House is helpful. The boys have

71

never been exposed to group discussions in the modern manner. Instead of learning through play or by a process of exploration, they have been taught from books and are prepared to continue with the same methods. So Peter can have an intensive ten-minute period with one at a time and then send him back to his place with a text to read and an exercise to do while one of his brothers takes his place.

Although this system works well, Peter enjoys the challenge of organising general lessons from time to time. Taking a period which one or other of the boys is studying for history, for example, he tells them all the story of some event or describes some character. Then Donnie is given the task of writing the story in his own words while Calum and Murdo attempt a short version in French and Roy and Tam struggle to put it into Latin. Peter writes up necessary vocabulary on the wide strip of whiteboard which is fastened to one wall and wanders round the room to offer any necessary help.

Even more interaction proves possible with maths. Although he saw no reason to admit the fact during his interview, this is the subject about which Peter feels most nervous. He knows how to do basic calculations, but not necessarily how to explain the methods by which he arrived at his answers. So it is fortunate for him that two of his pupils prove to have a talent for this subject and willingly agree to test themselves by helping their brothers. This is the monitor system, Peter tells them, smiling: a perfectly respectable educational method.

Roy and Murdo are the talented ones in this field. Roy's speciality is mental arithmetic. He likes to do sums in his head as he does his running practice, calculating how much distance he has covered, how much remains, what his speed is, how long his total run will take him and what difference it would make to each figure if one of the others was to be altered.

Murdo's approach is different, in that he needs pen and paper; but although he is only nine years old, his aptitude is greater. Peter watches admiringly as he draws circles and divides them to teach Donnie the advantages of recognising which pairs of figures add up to a nice round ten; then he moves on to solve his own problems as neatly as though the numbers involved were pieces of a jigsaw to be visualised as pictures and fitted into place. M for Murdo. M for musician. M for maths.

The secret of Peter's success is that all the boys are polite and friendly to their tutor, prepared to be interested if presented with something worthy of their interest and to become positively enthusiastic if offered a challenge. More surprising, perhaps, is their lack of quarrelsomeness. Although there are occasional sulks or bickerings, on the whole the boys appear to like each other. Certainly they think of themselves as a group: the gang of five against the rest of the world. This is presumably one effect of growing up as part of a large family and recognising that their mother will always give most of her attention to the youngest, so that the others must to a certain extent look after themselves.

Within the group, naturally, there are alliances. Tam and Roy pair off because they are older and stronger than the rest. Murdo and Calum do the same because it was the expected way to behave before Donnie was born. But this doesn't mean that Donnie is left out of things, because Roy and Murdo and Calum each in their different ways—running or practising or reading—pursue individual interests so strongly that Tam has accepted a special responsibility for making sure that Donnie is happy within the gang. They are all thoroughly nice boys and Peter looks forward to a happy four months in their company.

Other relationships are more compli-cated. As Susan warned him in advance,

Kara hates to be treated differently from the boys and almost every morning asks to join the class. It is Esin's responsibility to keep her amused—but Esin has her own reasons for liking to be in the schoolroom. She is setting her cap at Peter: asking for help with her English, hoping for his company in their free time and generally flaunting herself in front of him.

It is not the easiest thing in the world to ignore her. The memory of Mandy is fading fast—and it is quite likely that Mandy will interpret this long absence as a final confirmation of his unwillingness to tie himself down yet: she may well have moved out by the time he returns. It is tempting to accept the offer of a holiday flirtation which is so seductively dangled in front of him. He would have expected modesty in a Muslim girl, but Esin wears the shortest of skirts, the lowest of necklines. Her bare arms are smooth and round, asking to be stroked; her lips are full and pouting, asking to be kissed. As long as he makes it clear that there can be no future in it, what harm can it do? He has not succumbed yet, but he is weakening.

However, help is at hand. Kara's father is due to arrive soon for a three-week holiday. He will want to spend time with his daughter, keeping her away from the boys, and so there will be no excuse for Esin to hang around. As he goes to bed that night, Peter feels nothing but contentment. Everything is going well.

Chapter Six

David flies out from England to join the rest of the family at the beginning of July. Although Susan has naturally looked forward to his arrival, the visit is not a great success. His office rules prevent him from taking more than half of his six weeks' annual leave entitlement at a time and it is easy to tell that he is glad of the restriction. He would prefer to have more choice and variety in his family holidays and doesn't really enjoy visiting The Lookout. The nearness of Susan's first husband and the regular discussion of arrangements for the boys to visit him make it all too clear that her extended stay in Turkey is for the benefit of the Sutherlands and not of the Rolphs.

Susan attempts to sympathise with his feelings. There is very little for him to do at The Lookout except read or swim. She likes to spend each morning painting, but David doesn't share this hobby. If she goes off on her own with her folding easel and box of watercolours, he is liable to protest petulantly; but if she sacrifices her own inclinations in order to stay with him, she finds herself becoming edgy. Although they make one or two expeditions together—to Ephesus in one direction and to Perge and Side in another—he is not really interested in the monuments of the ancient world.

Nor does he enjoy the heat, in which Susan herself and the children revel; so that even their lovemaking in the darkness is perfunctory and sweaty. Increasingly in the past year or two Susan has come to realise that she and her second husband have almost nothing in common—except Kara, of course—and three weeks spent continuously in his company leave her stressed rather than relaxed. No, it is not a happy visit.

His efforts to be a good father are not very successful either. Like Hugh, he believes that parents should educate their children; but, unlike Hugh, he is not a good teacher. This year he tries to show Kara how to play the recorder. She loves making noises—just as she loves listening to Murdo—but she is unable to move her fingers quickly or strongly enough to play a tune. She is still very young, and Susan is perhaps not tactful enough about pointing this out.

Another failure is in the water, where David endeavours to persuade his daughter to swim without the buoyancy bands on which she relies. Although she is confident in her own pool, the immensity of the sea overwhelms the little girl and the situation is not helped by all the splashing which goes on when the boys are anywhere near. All too often these lessons end in tears and exasperation. There is a feeling in the air of friction only just controlled; it is necessary to work at a holiday spirit which ought to flow naturally. Although Susan is reluctant to admit it to herself, she is glad when her husband's visit comes to an end.

Next year, she promises herself as she waves him goodbye and prepares to settle back into the normal timetable of the day; next year she will do things differently. With Tam at Winchester, Hugh will have to be content with only the school-holiday period: much shorter than the extended visits of the past few years. Perhaps she could leave the boys completely in the care of their father for two or three weeks and go off with David for a bucket-and-spade holiday more suited to little Kara. She will have to think about that.

In the meantime, the irritability which David has only just been able to control has had an important consequence. She hasn't told him that she is pregnant again, although by now she is certain that this is the case: twelve weeks have passed since her last period. Had she confessed it, he would have insisted that she must return at once to be within reach of a British doctor. That, at least, is what she tells herself. The truth is that she is not at all sure whether he will welcome the prospect of another child. But if she waits until her return to England before breaking the news, the pregnancy will be so far advanced that he will have to accept it.

She has never suffered from morning sickness. Pregnancy suits her. For almost fourteen years it has been practically her normal state, so that it is the months in between that feel odd. Instead of sickness, what she feels is an immense lethargy. 'A contented cow' is what Hugh used to call her teasingly, in those early days when he was as pleased as she was to be building up a family. Like a contented cow she retreats to her bedroom to take a siesta after lunch on the day of David's departure. The shutters are closed to keep the room dark and cool. She lies naked on the bed, stroking her still-flat stomach as if to assure the new baby of its welcome.

Outside the villa there is a brief burst of noise as the boys hurtle off for the adventure element of their day. She ought to look out and make sure that they are all wearing their sun hats, but lacks the energy. Although Peter is not required to supervise this period of their play, he has shown himself to be conscientious in more than the schoolroom hours and she can trust him to have checked where they are going and whether they are safely protected against the sun.

After they have left, silence surrounds her. Kara will have been put to bed for her own siesta. Peter will no doubt be working on his thesis and, because he has proved helpful in giving Esin more formal instruction in English than the chatter of children can provide, the girl will probably be doing the exercises he has set her. Susan allows her eyes to close.

It is half past four when she awakes— later than usual, for as a rule she is disturbed by the sound of Kara and Esin going out to play with a ball or to splash in the pool. For a little while longer she drowses on the bed, before making the effort to dress. Then she assembles a selection of games and toys on the shadiest verandah: the house from five to six is her special time to be alone with Kara, while Esin is helping the cook to prepare the supper.

There is an unusual lack of noise and activity about the place. Presumably Kara and Esin have not yet returned. Susan wanders round to the message board on which anyone leaving the villa is expected to write his destination.

The word 'Castle (5)', scrawled in a childish hand, has been crossed out. Underneath is a second message, this time in Peter's small and very neat handwriting. '4 p.m Peter + boys. Gone swimming. Back before 6 p.m.'

Susan nods approvingly. Peter has proved to be a great asset. He controls the morning lessons well. The boys seem to enjoy them and almost every day are anxious for her to look at a workbook or to hear about some chapter of history which they are just about to act out. Rather too obviously Esin is flirting with him, perhaps hoping for the prize of marriage to an Englishman; but as far as Susan can tell he is handling the situation well, remaining friendly while being careful not to encourage her. He is cheerful about accepting responsibility for the boys' safety on the descent to the beach and in the sea. And it is a particular bonus that he is often willing to drive the boys over to Termessus when Hugh wants to see them, even though it means surrendering time which he could have had to himself. Yes, Peter is a good thing.

So now the boys' absence is explained, but where are Kara and Esin? Susan is not wearing a watch, but the position of the sun tells her that it must be five o'clock by now. Presumably they have gone for a walk—though Esin ought to have written the details down. Could they have become lost? No, that isn't possible. Kara isn't capable of walking any distance that would take her off the Sutherland property, and from anywhere within its boundaries the group of trees below the main house acts as a landmark. Wandering round the outside of the house and then inside, looking into every room, Susan becomes puzzled and faintly worried.

Perhaps they have gone up to Dr Sutherland's house. Her ex-father-in-law himself would not welcome a visit from Kara, but Esin has become friendly with his cook. If she took the little girl up there they would doubtless be offered tea and perhaps would not notice the passing of time. That must be the explanation, mustn't it? Susan picks up the receiver of the telephone extension which communicates only with The Eyrie.

It is answered by the cook, who speaks no English. Susan, who understands little Turkish, is just able to make out that Dr Sutherland is not at home.

'Kara? she asks. 'Esin?'

The answer is incomprehensible, but worryingly long; and both the names are repeated several times. Susan interrupts to ask the question she can just about manage.

'Is Kara there?'

She can understand the answer as well. 'No.' Then the jabbering starts again. She puts down the receiver.

By now she is seriously worried. Suppose Esin has had some kind of fall during the walk and is unable to move. Where might she be? Would Kara stay with her, or wander off? Susan exchanges her flip-flops for a pair of shoes stout enough to protect her feet from the prickly scrub and runs towards the cliff.

Unlike the children, who are in no circumstances allowed to pass the row of posts, Susan has no hesitation in going to within a foot of the edge. She has a good head for heights and knows that she is standing on solid rock which is not likely to break away. She looks down at the little group of swimmers.

Peter is giving a diving lesson. One of the boys—he is wearing his sun hat, so from this height she can't be sure whether it is Donnie or Calum—is drying himself on the sand; but three others form a continuous circle as they scramble up on a rock, dive in, swim to the shore and scramble up again. Murdo enters the sea with a splash, and Tam's dive is no more than workmanlike. But Roy is elegant as he parts the water cleanly and reappears—after an alarmingly long time—some distance away. Peter, applauding him, climbs to a higher rock and does a test dive himself before beckoning Roy to try something more ambitious.

There is one boy—either Calum or Donnie—missing, and Kara is nowhere to be seen. Susan counts the heads again before searching the beach with her eyes for any sign of her other two children. She fights her increasing anxiety by developing a variety of possibilities. Perhaps Esin is ill and has asked one of the boys to take charge of Kara for an hour. Perhaps the two children—without any means of telling the time—have gone for a safe, gentle walk somewhere on the estate.

It isn't very likely. The boys have never shown the kind of protectiveness which big brothers might be expected to feel for a little sister. Tam and Roy may not actively blame her for their father's disappearance from the family home, but they certainly realise that there is a connection, and so loyalty to Hugh makes them cool towards Kara. They tolerate her, but there is little warmth in the relationship.

Calum and Donnie are more actively impatient. Calum, who spends every spare moment engrossed in a book, finds her chatter distracting. Donnie, who held the position of youngest member of the family for longer than any of his brothers, was for more than a year resentful of the attention given to the new baby. By now that jealousy is long past, but it has been replaced by a determination to be one of the gang: a big boy, keeping up with the others and not at all prepared to take part in baby games. Only Murdo, the placid and tolerant nine-year-old, is willing to devote time to his sister. He lays down rules: that she must be quiet and keep still while he is playing his trumpet or mouth organ; and Kara, recognising his friendliness, obeys.

But she cannot be listening to Murdo now, because it is easy to recognise that he—plumper than any of his brothers—is the one who is belly-flopping into the water two hundred feet below. Susan begins to shout, but her voice croaks with anxiety. She waves her hat, trying to attract their attention, but they are all absorbed in the diving lesson. Desperately at last she picks up a rock and throws it far enough out to miss the ledges on the cliff beneath her. The boy on the sand—it is Donnie, she can see now—looks up, startled. Seeing her waving, he waves back, but it seems that eventually some of her urgency is conveyed to him. He calls to Peter and his brothers, who at the same moment look up to the top of the cliff.

She waves at them to come up. The gesture is unmistakable and is acknowledged. She waves at them to hurry, but she knows that it is not possible to climb the cliff path quickly. Rather than wait, she sets off to explore the grounds.

Would Kara want to go into the tombs? Just possibly a little girl might choose to 'play house', but it isn't likely that Esin would be willing to take her there and Calum would certainly not forgo a swimming session for such a game. Susan is not at this point worried about Calum. There is no rule that forces the boys always to be in each other's company. The wish to be alone from time to time is a necessary element in growing up into independence. No doubt Peter, when signing all the boys up on the message board for a swimming session, was taking it for granted that they would all want to accompany him. There is nothing sinister about the fact that the numbers don't match. It is only Kara who must be found quickly.

Leaving the tombs unsearched for the moment, Susan makes for the castle instead, picking her way across the rough, rocky ground which surrounds it, and moving round past two of the high pillars of rock until she reaches a section of the rubble wall. She is tall enough to look over this, into the centre of the castle.

She has found Calum, who is lying on his stomach in the slightly raised area which the boys call 'the throne'; at this time of the day it is in the shade. He is reading. His elbows are on the ground, taking the weight of his head as his hands cup round his chin; his feet from time to time kick up into the air. He is alone.

'Calum! Why aren't you swimming with the others?' Because she is frightened, Susan's voice is sharpened by a trace of what sounds like anger.

Without looking up, Calum moves a finger to mark the place on the page which he has reached. 'I wanted to finish my book.'

'Have you seen Kara anywhere this afternoon?'

He shakes his head and then removes the finger to indicate that he is continuing to read. His total absorption in a book is something with which Susan is familiar, but even so he could not have been unaware of Kara's presence if she were anywhere in the castle. From her vantage point above the wall Susan studies the open central area.

There are no concealed corners inside. If it ever was a real castle and not just a natural rock feature, all towers and inner rooms have long ago disappeared. Kara is not here.

The tombs, then. Susan, although not a nervous woman in general, is frightened of snakes and has to screw up her courage as she hurries across to explore.

There are three different styles of ancient tomb in the necropolis which is part of Dr Sutherland's estate. Some of them are cut into the cliff face of the headland: a climber could reach them, but not a small child. A few of the others are in the form of stone pillars, erected on level ground, and it would be equally impossible for a little girl to climb up to the grave chamber at the top. But there are a dozen or more of what Hugh describes as house tombs. Cut into the natural rock of the headland where the land begins to slope down towards the sea, each of them has an elaborately carved entrance: pillars flank a recessed doorway, with a triangular pediment above. The grave chamber itself in each case is dark. How stupid it is to have come here without a torch! But then, if Kara is alive she will respond to her mother's call. Susan rushes from one entrance to another, shouting, but each time is met by silence.

By now the boys are arriving one by one at the top of the gully. They are not as ebullient as usual; no doubt they are resentful of the interruption to their swimming session. Roy seems particularly reluctant to meet his mother's eyes. Perhaps that is because he is not wearing his T-shirt—although this is hardly a great crime. The boys have always been allowed to expose their skins to the sun in the late afternoon, when there is less risk of burning. Susan waits impatiently for them all to reach the level ground. Peter, in the interests of safety, comes last.

'Have you seen Kara anywhere?' she demands.

'Not since lunch, no. Have you lost her?'

'Boys, what about you? Have any of you seen her this afternoon?'

As they shake their heads, Susan begins to tremble with panic. Peter steps forward and grips her hands.

'What's happened?'

'I don't know. She must have had an accident. But Esin would have been with her. They can't both—'

'I expect they're up at The Eyrie and haven't realised the time.'

'No. I phoned. I couldn't understand what the cook said, but they're not there.'

'Let me have another try.' Peter releases her hands and begins to walk rapidly uphill.

Susan runs to catch up and listens to the conversation which takes place. She hasn't previously been aware that Peter speaks any Turkish, but is too grateful for it now to wonder why he should have kept quiet about this accomplishment. He pronounces the words with the careful articulation of a foreigner, so that once or twice she is able to understand what he is saying: first of all as he asks the preliminary questions and later when he begs the cook to speak more slowly. That is one of the few phrases Susan has memorised for herself.

His expression is grave and he is still holding the telephone when he turns to repeat what he has learned.

'Dr Sutherland is away from home. His cook says that Esin came to the house in great distress at about four o'clock, or a little later. Apparently when she went to get Kara up she found her room empty.'

'Why didn't she come and wake me, to tell me?'

'She was afraid you'd be angry. She thought that if she could find Kara quickly, you need never know. So she searched everywhere, but there was no sign of her.'

'But then surely—where is Esin now?'

'It sounds as though she's run away. The chap who comes to do Dr Sutherland's garden one day a week leaves at about that time, so she might have hitched a lift.'

'It doesn't make sense.' Susan is distraught. 'She can't have thought... She must have kidnapped Kara. It's the only explanation.'

'If that were true, she would hardly have gone up to The Eyrie first.'

'She could have arranged for someone to have transport waiting there.'

'Why would she want to do such a thing, though? She's a student, not a frustrated mother.' But Peter's voice is unhappy. Obviously he can think of nothing reassuring to say.

'Get the police,' Susan orders. 'Tell the cook to phone the police. What do they call them here? The *jandarmes*. Will she know how to do that? They must come at once, with enough men to search for a missing child. Torches. They'll need torches to look inside the tombs.' But by now her earlier fears of an accident have been replaced by a different dread.

Someone has stolen Kara.

Chapter Seven

The nightmare is real. It is not simply the product of an overanxious mother's imagination. It suffocates Susan, as though she is enclosed within a shroud. She can thrust against it and stretch it in one direction or another, but is unable to break out to see what has happened. Suddenly she finds herself unable to breathe. On the brink of hysteria, she begins to pant.

It is Peter who comes to her rescue. Sending the boys off for their supper, he grasps her wrists firmly and murmurs reassurances until she begins to calm down. But she is still gasping for breath. He picks up a beach towel that one of the boys has dropped and puts it over her mouth. For a second or two she struggles, thinking that he is trying to suffocate her, so that he has to tighten his grip. In a soothing voice he explains that his purpose is to make her breathe in the air she has just breathed out. It doesn't make sense, but seems to work. Her breathing steadies into a few heavy sighs. She looks at him uncomprehendingly.

'Something I was taught to do for my first-aid badge, with a brown paper bag,' he tells her. 'Curing hyperventilation with carbon dioxide. Now, tell me what you would like me to do? Shall I go up to The Eyrie? I could speak to the police myself and make sure they're on their way.'

'Yes, thank you. Thank you very much.' It is ridiculous that The Lookout should not have a direct telephone line of its own. In the days when she was still married to Hugh, still friendly with Dr Sutherland, it caused no inconvenience, but now the need to make use of her ex-father-in-law's line is an embarrassment to both parties.

While Peter is gone, Susan interrogates the boys in more detail, but they tell her only what she expects to hear. They all went to play in the castle after lunch, taking their swimming things with them. They had previously arranged that Peter should come and collect them at four o'clock to go swimming, and he did. Except for Calum, who wanted to finish his book, they stayed down at the sea until they saw her waving. They know nothing about Kara's movements. Calum, however, who has by now joined his brothers in the house, volunteers the information that even before Peter arrived he had become bored with the noisy game of breaking down the walls of Jericho. He was reading in the shade outside the rampart rocks when Esin ran up to him to ask whether his sister was in the castle.

'What did you say?'

'I said no, but she went to have a look over one of the rubble walls anyway. She scratched her foot on a bit of rock, and then she started crying, although it wasn't a very big scratch. It only bled a little bit.'

Susan has to restrain a moment's anger. Calum should have realised from Esin's behaviour that something was wrong. But still, he's only eight years old, and a bookworm. He was asked a question and he answered it. The story he was reading was no doubt more important to him than the whereabouts of an independent-minded little girl who has quite frequently been known to take off on her own.

'What time did Esin come?'

'I don't know. I haven't got a watch.'

'And where did she go next?'

'Towards the gully or the pool, that sort of way. I didn't really watch.'

He has nothing more to tell her. Leaving the boys to finish their supper by themselves, because she has no appetite, Susan paces round the house as she waits for the police to arrive.

It is a different kind of nightmare now. Time is stretching like a rubber band. She looks continually at her watch, imagining that an hour, two hours, must have passed, but on each occasion finds that the period can be measured only in minutes.

The journey from Antalya cannot be made quickly, but it is not in fact too long before she hears the sound of a jeep pulling up in front of The Eyrie, where the track ends. Peter appears, pointing the way down, before returning to Dr Sutherland's house. Two uniformed men take up a position which makes if clear that they are awaiting instructions. The other two follow Susan inside.

One of these two is an armed officer. His bearing is military and his movements are stiff and formal. The clean-cut sharpness of his profile blends suitably with the well-pressed neatness of his dark-green uniform. He does not precisely click his heels, nor precisely does he bow; but there is something Prussian about the way in which he introduces himself as Captain Zeybel.

Susan wastes no time on politeness. 'My name is Mrs Rolph. One of my children has disappeared. Her name is Kara. She's four years old, and—'

Captain Zeybel puts up a hand to check the flow of words. He asks a question which she is able to translate. Does she speak Turkish?

'I'm sorry, no. Can you understand English?' Those are two of the few phrases she can manage in his language.

It seems that he is as monoglot as herself. He turns and beckons to the man who has followed him into the room but who until this invitation has remained standing unobtrusively beside the door.

This man doesn't look like a policeman. He is informally—even scruffily—dressed in an open-neck red checked shirt and blue jeans. The tight-fitting jeans reveal that his hips are slim, but the shirt strains over a burly chest. His dark curly hair has begun to recede, just enough to give his fleshy face a high forehead. His nose is wide and his lips full; the colour of his skin is a little darker than that of his colleague. His white-toothed smile, as he is introduced, comes near to being a friendly grin.

Efficiency rather than friendliness is what Susan wants at this moment, and she does not find his casual appearance reassuring. But her instinctive doubts are checked by the look in his eyes. They are watching her with a closeness which would make her uneasy if she had anything to hide. They are intelligent eyes. They are also compassionate eyes. They stare steadily at her as Captain Zeybel speaks in the language which she has always found incomprehensible. Then he steps forward and holds out a hand.

'Perhaps I may interpret for you, Mrs Rolph. My name is Yilmaz.'

Almost without noticing, Susan shakes his hand as she starts to repeat what she has already said once.

'Will you tell him, Mr Yilmaz, that—'

'Just Yilmaz, not Mr Yilmaz.'

She shakes her head impatiently, not caring how he likes to be addressed. As she pours out the few details she knows of the disappearance, he puts up a hand from time to time to halt her while he translates. Captain Zeybel is ready to make notes, but she has pitifully few facts to give him. She doesn't know Esin's home address nor even her surname. She doesn't know Dr Sutherland's present whereabouts. She doesn't know anything, except that someone has spirited Kara away.

The questions come to an end and Captain Zeybel leaves the room. Susan leaps to her feet.

'Where's he going? What's he going to do?'

'To see what can be learned from the cook to whom your nursemaid spoke,' Yilmaz tells her. His command of English is grammatical as well as fluent. 'And his men will search. If the little girl is anywhere near, they will find her.'

'But she isn't, is she? I've looked. She's been stolen. I know she's been stolen.'

'Why should anyone steal a child?' He motions her to sit down again, and takes a seat himself without being invited. His tone is conversational, but Susan recognises that this is still part of an inquiry.

'It's happened before. I've read about it in the newspapers. In Greece, and here as well. People snatch young children to sell to families who can't have babies. There are gangs. Or tribes of nomads, passing through. Or she could have been taken by ordinary criminals, hoping that I'll pay a ransom. And what about these terrorists? They're targeting foreigners, aren't they? With bombs and all sorts of things. Trying to stop tourists from coming to Turkey.'

'To start with, Mrs Rolph, I can promise you that no nomads ever pass this way. Even Alexander the Great found it simplest to leave the occupants of these mountains alone.'

'For Christ's sake!' She can hear her own voice rising hysterically high. 'A history lesson is the last thing I want. The terrorists, then. The Kurds, or whoever they are. You're not going to pretend that *they* don't exist. And there are the people who make those terrible films using little girls to...to...' She can't go on. Her imagination is torturing her.

Shuddering with the effort to control herself, she walks across to the window. Darkness is falling with a suddenness quite different from the gradually deepening twilights of England. The men outside will soon have to abandon this area of search.

'I think we shall find,' says Yilmaz quietly, 'that the solution lies closer to home. We must start with the girl Esin. You don't know her family address, you said, and not even her surname? But you must surely have asked for references?'

'I didn't engage her myself. My father-in-law, Dr Sutherland, made all the arrangements. I know that she's studying English at Istanbul University.'

'There are many hundreds of young women studying English.' But it seems that something else is more immediately puzzling him. 'Your husband's father is Dr Sutherland but you are Mrs Rolph?'

'I should have said my ex-father-in-law.' As patiently as she can, Susan explains the position. It seems to her that for a mere translator Yilmaz is taking a good deal on himself, but her need to feel that someone is actively investigating makes her glad to cooperate. And although it is in a sense disconcerting to hear such idiomatic and almost accentless English spoken by someone whose appearance is a cross between a peasant and a pirate, it is also reassuring.

He checks that he has understood. 'So Dr Sutherland is the grandfather of your sons, but not of the little girl. And the father of your sons is Professor Sutherland, who is also here in Turkey. Where, then, is the father of your daughter? He knows, I suppose, that she is missing?'

'No, not yet. He flew back to England today. But it's an awkward journey. He would have had to change planes at

Istanbul. He won't be home yet.' She looks at her watch. 'I have to wait before I can get in touch with him.'

'You're telling me that Mr Rolph was in Turkey earlier today?' His voice expresses surprise. Earlier in the conversation he learned that Kara's father was not on the premises. 'What time did he leave? Have you seen your daughter since that time?'

Now Yilmaz has gone too far. Susan turns angrily towards him.

'Of course I have. I saw her go off to bed at two o'clock. What the hell are you suggesting?'

The big man gives an apologetic shrug of the shoulders.

'Sometimes, when there are two husbands, one father may fear that the other father is going to take over his child. He might have removed her out of love.'

'It's nothing like that. You don't know what you're talking about.'

'No, I don't,' Yilmaz agrees gravely. 'But before this matter is concluded, we must all know what we are talking about. Mrs Rolph, will you do one last thing while we are still here? Please go again to your sons. I'm sure you have asked them once, but ask them again if there is anything they can tell you. When they see that you are unhappy, perhaps they will confess.'

'What do you mean, confess? They don't

know anything. I've asked them already, over and over.'

'I've used the wrong word, perhaps.' His voice is softer as he tries to be conciliatory. 'Sometimes children, in a group together, have secrets. You know this, I'm sure. Suppose little Kara was upset to see her father leave. Suppose she set off down the road, knowing nothing of distance, thinking that she could find him again. She might have told her brothers where she was going, but made them promise not to tell. Then you would need to make them understand that some promises must be broken.'

Susan makes no further protest. The possibility he has outlined is almost too far-fetched to be worth exploring, but there is an unexpected authority in Yilmaz's voice which persuades her to do as she is asked.

By the time she returns to the room, she is in tears again. She has allowed her distress to show itself, but the only effect has been to embarrass the boys, who have probably never seen a grown-up crying before. Shaking her head in failure, she is alarmed to realise that Captain Zeybel, who has rejoined Yilmaz, is about to leave.

'But you can't—'

Captain Zeybel understands the spirit of

her protest if not the words, and Yilmaz translates his explanation.

'It is too dark to search further here. We will try to discover where Dr Sutherland is, and from him where we can find the girl Esin. We will return early in the morning, Mrs Rolph. You will telephone us, naturally, if you have any news.'

'But if she's been kidnapped, there could be a ransom demand.'

There is a short discussion before Yilmaz nods his head and turns back to Susan.

'We will arrange to intercept any call to Dr Sutherland's house tonight. Tomorrow we will bring a telephone so that there may be direct contact here. And one of Captain Zeybel's men will remain on the property overnight, in case there should be any attempt to leave a message, or any prowler.'

Captain Zeybel makes the stiff movement which is almost a bow and leaves the room, but Yilmaz lingers behind: he has one more question to ask on his own account.

'Did your daughter know that you are expecting another baby, Mrs Rolph?'

Susan gasps in astonishment. How can he possibly...? Even David doesn't know yet. Nobody knows except herself.

Recognising her shock, Yilmaz continues to talk. 'I know that often a youngest child becomes jealous and upset by the thought

102

that a new baby will take her place. And so sometimes—am I right?—a mother will tell the little one the news early, to assure her that nothing will change. I'm wondering whether you did this, and whether she was distressed in spite of your assurances? Distressed enough to run away?'

'What makes you think I'm pregnant?'

'Your body tells me,' he says simply. 'The way you stand, the way you walk.'

His percipience makes her uneasy. He is behaving as though he is a detective himself, instead of a mere interpreter. She is not prepared to admit in so many words that he is right, but nor will she lie. Yilmaz waits for a moment before recognising that he is not to be given an answer. Then he shrugs his shoulders and follows his colleague out.

A few minutes later she hears the engine of the jeep growl into life higher up the hill. It roars for a moment and then gradually fades away, leaving Susan more alone than she has ever been in her life before. The five boys are in the house, of course; but her earlier tearful conversation with them has brought their homework period to an end and they seem to have put themselves early to bed: there is no sound to be heard from the children's rooms. And Peter must have stayed up at The Eyrie even after the arrival of Captain Zeybel and his men. Perhaps the need to be prepared for a ransom demand has occurred to him as well.

All the possibilities she has put to Yilmaz are swirling around in her head, and all of them are terrible. Only one of his suggestions, which she dismissed scornfully at the time, offers any hope. Yes, perhaps it might have happened that way; that Kara set off to follow her father. Picking up a torch, Susan scrambles up the hill to the beginning of the track and then walks along it, calling her daughter's name as she goes.

Every few minutes she stops to listen, in case there may be some answering cry, almost too faint to hear; but there is no response. She has never before been conscious of such a deep silence, as though there is nothing alive anywhere between the sea and the mountains. It is not a sinister silence, but it is absolute. A moment comes when she is unable to make her feet move any further. She switches off the torch and stands as though frozen, longing for some sound to tell her that the world has not after all come to an end.

At last she hears it: the displacement of a stone, the sound of footsteps hurrying towards her. 'Kara!' she calls. 'Kara!' But the heavy footsteps are those of a man. She ought to be frightened, but remains rigid.

There is nothing to be frightened of. It is Peter who comes round a corner and reassuringly turns his torch on to his own face to show her that he is a friend.

'Mrs Rolph, you shouldn't be out here by yourself after dark.' He stretches out a hand towards her as carefully as if he is trying to save a potential suicide. Until that moment Susan has hardly registered the fact that the track is a corniche, with the side of the mountain falling away as steeply on one side as it rises on the other. It is wide enough to take a vehicle, so she has never felt in any danger. She allows him to take her hand protectively, but for a moment resists his attempt to lead her back.

'I can't just sit and do nothing.'

'Yes, you must. You must be there. That's the most important thing, that you should be there, waiting, when Kara comes back.'

'If I don't look for her, she may never come back.' But gradually Susan feels her body unstiffening. She takes a step forwards, and makes no objection when Peter, still holding one hand, puts his arm round her waist to guide her. Weak and desolate, she allows him to take her back along the track.

Before going down the hill again, she tries to ring David from The Eyrie, but still there is no answer.

'There's nothing he can do tonight except get upset,' Peter tells her gently. 'If you sit here trying to get in touch once every hour, you'll only become anxious yourself. Leave it till the morning.'

Wearily, Susan nods. And now there is a new anxiety to be considered. She ought not to have left the boys alone in the house if there is a kidnapper on the loose. Forcing herself abruptly back to life, she hurries down the hill.

Four of them are safely where they ought to be. Donnie and Calum and Murdo have already turned out the light in their room. Roy is reading silently in bed. But Tam? Where is Tam?

'He said it was stuffy here,' Roy tells her, looking startled at her appearance. 'He's gone out to breathe. Only a minute ago.'

Anything that is out of the ordinary on a day like this appears sinister and dangerous. Susan hurries outside, calling her eldest son's name. Almost immediately he appears beside her in pyjamas and sandals.

'What's the matter?'

'You frightened me when I couldn't

find you. You shouldn't leave the house, Tam; not tonight. There may be someone skulking around.'

'Well, if anyone does come, there's one of Captain Zeybel's men sitting over by the castle, so all we need do is yell.'

This is not enough to reassure Susan. 'I'm going to fasten the shutters and lock all the doors,' she tells him.

This is not part of her normal routine. Even in such an isolated place she has always in the past felt safe. But this evening she makes the house as secure as possible, so that nobody can get in or out without making enough noise to alert her. She asks Peter to leave his bedroom door open all night, so that he will hear if there is any movement in the children's part of the house.

Only then does she go to say goodnight to her two eldest sons. They hug her more tightly and for longer than usual, but say nothing. Once again, the house is silent.

Alone in bed after three weeks of David's company, Susan tosses and moans in despair. Wherever Kara may be at this moment, she must be terrified, calling for her mother and not understanding why no one comes. Not until the early hours of the morning is the nightmare at last banished by sleep.

Chapter Eight

It is Yilmaz, and not Captain Zeybel, who returns to The Lookout at six o'clock the next morning, waiting patiently until the sound of doors and shutters being unlocked reveals that the household is stirring.

In allowing Mrs Rolph to assume that he is merely an interpreter, he has been less than frank. He was quite happy during that first visit to give the appearance of merely translating questions and answers, because it gave him the perfect opportunity of studying Mrs Rolph when all her attention was on someone else. No doubt she will take it for granted today that he has been sent merely because he alone can communicate easily with her.

It is partly because of his linguistic skills that Yilmaz has been moved south from Istanbul on attachment to the tourist police in Antalya for the summer. But although he is an easy-going man who has no objection to helping out when there is no one else around to provide a translation, he is a detective who does not as a rule concern himself with run-of-the-mill thefts

108

of passports, credit cards or money. His special concern is enforcement of the law that prohibits the removal of antiquities from Turkey: he is an expert in ancient artefacts and can pursue inquiries in any of six languages. This case—if it proves to be a case—has nothing to do with art smuggling, of course; but nevertheless it may prove to need someone of his seniority and command of English to investigate it.

He has already put Mrs Rolph to one small test. 'Do you think she has killed the child herself?' he asked his colleague, in Turkish, during the course of the conversation on the previous evening. His eyes watched her steadily as he spoke, and were satisfied. She has said that she doesn't understand the language, and it is true. And of course he doesn't believe for a moment that she is guilty of anything except perhaps carelessness. He can recognise genuine distress when he sees it.

The question of language is one he pursues now, as soon as he has reported on the inquiries that are in progress. In exploring what must seem to be a side road, he is attempting to slow down the pace of her expectations; and at the same time he is probing for any crack in the picture which has been presented to him of an ideally happy family. Captain Zeybel and his men will be investigating the possibilities of terrorism or criminal kidnap, and he emphasises this fact now so that Mrs Rolph will not think that Yilmaz himself is wasting her time, and his own, with what may seem to be irrelevant questions. But it is his personal opinion that when children disappear, the explanation is almost always to be found somewhere within the family. It is, however, far too soon to suggest this to the mother of the child.

'I find it curious, Mrs Rolph,' he says, accepting a cup of coffee, 'that after so many visits to our country you should speak no Turkish at all.' By 'curious' he means 'hard to believe', but he is talking to a distraught mother, not to a criminal, and this is not the time to behave in a confrontational manner.

The spoon on her saucer rattles with distress as she lifts her own cup to her lips.

'I wouldn't expect you to understand. You're a clever man.'

'Oh, no.' The words come automatically, out of politeness. He is, yes, a clever man.

'How many languages do you speak?'

'Four well enough. Others a little.'

'There you are, then.'

'To speak a language is nothing. It is the thoughts expressed in it that are important.

And for most of the time I am employed to express other people's thoughts.'

Once again he is failing to tell the truth, but it is not only Mrs Rolph herself who needs to be deceived. The children in the family may be more willing to talk to someone in ordinary clothes, someone who looks unimportant, than to a uniformed officer.

Whatever Mrs Rolph may think, whatever Captain Zeybel may think, Yilmaz himself is already convinced that the boys—whether they know it or not—hold the key to the mystery. He doesn't expect them to be actively involved. There are other candidates for that suspicion: the young Turkish student of English, Mrs Rolph's father-in-law, one or other of her two husbands, or perhaps the tutor. But boys are observant. They notice small things that are out of the ordinary. They know more about adult relationships than they normally reveal. It is from the boys that Yilmaz expects to extract some vital clue—although it may well turn out to be something that they themselves don't think to be important.

Mrs Rolph, naturally enough, is not following that particular train of thought.

'Whatever you say, *I* say that you're clever. I expect you've been to university.'

There is no need to go into details, to

tell her of the three years he has spent at Istanbul University and the further three years at Durham University in England, followed by a diploma course, also in England, on art and antiques. 'Yes,' he says simply.

Just as he doesn't propose to browbeat her, he doesn't need to impress her either. It will take, probably, several hours of cautious probing to explore her character and discover what she suspects and how much she may be able to accept.

'You can't have any idea how it feels to be stupid,' she says. She is speaking fluently now, as though by talking for the sake of talking she can keep at bay the silence which reminds her of her little girl's disappearance. 'People who meet a blind woman or a deaf woman sometimes make the effort to understand how it must feel, but no one who has any intelligence himself can comprehend what it's like to have no brains. The reason I can't speak Turkish, or understand it, is perfectly simple. I'm a stupid woman.'

'Oh, really, I'm sure...' His voice trails away into the kind of deprecating murmur which such a statement demands.

Although his reaction is automatic, it is also sincere. He doesn't believe her.

Yilmaz has known in his time a good many girls in whom ignorance and innocence have combined to leave them knowing little of the world around them—or, indeed, of themselves: girls who reckon, often rightly, that youthful prettiness will be found an acceptable substitute for intelligence.

Mrs Rolph, though, is a mature woman. She has had experience of life. She is the mother of six children, and he respects her for that. Motherhood brings wisdom. He looks steadily across at her.

On first arriving in her presence on the previous evening he had the opportunity, standing unobtrusively behind Captain Zeybel, to stare at her without being noticed. What he saw then was a frantic woman whose distress expressed itself in anger. But what he also saw was a beautiful woman.

It was hard to believe, from studying her appearance at that first meeting, that Mrs Rolph had given birth to six children and must be at least in her mid-thirties. She was wearing a shift of fine cotton, transparent enough to reveal the outline of her body. Perhaps she was wearing some close-fitting undergarment beneath it; perhaps not. At the time when she rose from her siesta and prepared to play with her daughter she was not, of course, expecting to receive visitors; and after that her increasing panic would doubtless have put any thought of her own appearance out of her mind.

This morning her dress is less provocative. But tailored shorts reveal even more of her long, smooth legs, and a cotton sun top clings tightly enough to reveal that her breasts are full and unrestrained. Her skin is fair; it stretches smoothly over her collarbone, over her slim shoulders, over her straight, slender arms. His taste has always been for women with full breasts and slim hips; and during his years in England he has acquired not only an idiomatic knowledge of the English language but also an admiration for the pale, delicate English complexion.

Mrs Rolph's perfect skin, nowhere scratched or blemished in any way, packages a perfect body. It tempts him to touch, to stroke, to caress. But of course he cannot allow himself to do any of these things. This is a police inquiry. They are discussing her stupidity.

'I've been married twice,' she tells him. 'And both my husbands are very clever men.'

This is good. The more information she volunteers, the less he will need to upset her by firing a battery of questions. He waits for her to continue.

'My first husband—the father of all the boys—is a classical historian and archaeologist. A kind of detective, in a way. He reads the ground. There are so many details stored in his memory that the most subtle thing—a particular kind of pattern on a sherd of pottery, for example—may tell him that some date which everyone has believed for hundreds of years is actually a century or so out. And yet I can't even remember, though I've been told over and over, who came here first, the Romans or the Greeks.'

'G before R. As in the alphabet. With M for Macedonia in the middle.'

She stares at him in amazement. 'Why didn't Hugh ever say anything as simple as that instead of quoting dates and lecturing me about which art became decadent in the other's era? Well, I suppose it was because I didn't like to confess that I'd forgotten, after the first time.'

For a moment she is able to set her grief aside as she ponders on this: G before R.

'Why did this marriage end, Mrs Rolph?'

This is perhaps the first moment in which she realises that she is being interrogated, but in spite of a momentary indignation she gives a straightforward answer.

'We were still married when Kara was born, but Hugh—Professor Sutherland—is not her father.'

'I see.' What Yilmaz sees is that the professor—who is apparently less than an

115

hour's drive away—might well resent the very existence of the child responsible for the breakdown of his marriage; might even want to take an indirect revenge on the man who has replaced him in his wife's affections. But he keeps his voice neutral as he returns to the original subject of their conversation. 'And Mr Rolph? Is he also clever?'

'My second husband is a man who can do anything with figures. Someone who's trying to cheat on his income tax can tuck the numbers away as cunningly as he likes and David will still be able to ferret them out. I can't even keep my household accounts sensibly, or work out how much I've got left in the bank or whether I've been given the proper change in the market here. It's ridiculous. It's stupid.'

'You are talking now about the father of Kara?'

'Yes, that's right.' Once again her eyes flood with tears at the thought of her missing daughter.

'I believe that everyone has his own talent. Cleverness is only one. I'm sure you're good at other things.'

'I'm good at having babies.' Now the tears are flowing fast. 'I can carry babies and give birth to babies and bring them up to be healthy, happy children. It's my only talent. But what's the use of that if

116

someone's going to steal them away?'

'I don't believe that's happened. The searchers will soon find her. While we're waiting, if I may ask a few questions—'

'You wouldn't need to ask them if you really thought she was just going to be found.'

Setting down the coffee cup, she moves across the room and picks up a bottle of whisky, preparing to pour herself a drink. Yilmaz steps quickly forward to take the bottle from her hand. Her fingers, beneath his touch, are smooth and cool and manicured: this is a hand which has no dirty work to do.

'It's not yet seven o'clock in the morning,' he reminds her. 'When we find little Kara, you will need your head to be clear. Almost certainly she will be hurt. A twisted ankle, I expect. She is waiting for someone to come to her and carry her home, and then she will need your comfort. It's important that you should keep to the usual pattern of your day.'

'But I need to be doing something. I can't just sit—'

Yilmaz interrupts. 'Have you spoken yet to Mr Rolph?'

'Not yet. He wasn't back at home when I phoned.'

'Perhaps this would be an opportunity to try again. It's a time when you should have his support. I'm sure he will wish to return as soon as he hears.'

She nods her head miserably. 'What will you be doing?'

'With your permission,' Yilmaz tells her, 'I would like to talk to your sons.'

Chapter Nine

Yilmaz does not in fact go straight to the schoolroom, but diverts to inspect the room in which the missing girl was put to rest on the previous afternoon. He doesn't need long to satisfy himself that there is no way in which a small child could climb up to the high window. The room contains very little furniture and it is all built in. The only direction in which Kara could have left the house is by passing through Esin's room.

So, yes, the student must certainly be found. But surely it would not be regarded as part of her duties to remain on guard in her own room for the whole of the afternoon? It is difficult to see why she should feel sufficiently guilty about her charge's disappearance to run away herself. And if she has been involved in any form of kidnap, it makes little sense that she should

118

have wasted time in pretending to search for her charge. Either she would make her escape quickly or else she would remain quietly on the premises to postpone the discovery and then pretend her innocence by expressing surprise and consternation.

He searches her room. This too contains only the minimum of furniture; but there is a desk, and in the desk drawer are some letters. From her mother, he sees as he reads them, but she has not troubled to put on an address. She expresses pleasure that Esin feels her English to be improving and is happy in her work. Then she gives news of other members of the family, but not in sufficient detail to be of help in tracking her or her daughter down.

Clicking his fingers in frustration, Yilmaz makes his way to the schoolroom. One of the five boys is sitting next to the tutor, Peter, and reading aloud to him. The other four are grouped round a large table, heads bowed as they scribble in workbooks. Something about the apparent intensity of their concentration tells him that until they heard his footsteps approaching they were whispering together. But that is natural enough. Kara is their sister. There is a mystery, a possible tragedy, to be discussed.

'Please excuse the interruption. Mr Quigley, isn't it? My name is Yilmaz

I am involved in the search for Kara. There are questions I would like to ask your pupils.'

As he speaks, his eyes move round the table. Distinguishing one boy from another is not going to be an easy task for the family resemblances are striking. The one whose sandy hair is a little darker than the others' is probably the eldest. He is now, by an almost imperceptible nod of the head, giving an instruction to one of his brothers.

This boy, who seems considerably younger, stands up politely. 'I'm Calum Sutherland. I can answer questions.'

Yilmaz considers the offer for a few seconds without accepting. 'Which of you is the eldest?' he asks.

Automatically each head turns towards the one who had nodded. Yilmaz addresses himself to him.

'What's your name?'

'Tam.'

'And how old are you?'

'Nearly thirteen.'

'I would have expected you to be the spokesman for your brothers. The leader.'

'We didn't think you or any of the police would speak English so well, sir. Calum's the best of us at understanding Turkish, so we fixed for him to answer for all of us.'

'So you have all been discussing together

what you will say to me? Deciding on a story?'

'No.' Tam, looking a little flustered, reacts with indignation to the suggestion. 'But we knew you'd want to ask a lot of questions and we thought we might not be able to understand them.'

Accepting the explanation, Yilmaz turns back towards the younger boy and and addresses him in Turkish. 'Is your brother right? Could you hold a conversation with me?'

'If you use ordinary words,' Calum replies in the same language.

Yilmaz nods approvingly, but reverts to English.

'I would like to hear from each of you separately about the last sight you had of your sister. Starting with the youngest.'

'But, sir—' Tam is hesitating, clearly unsure whether he has good grounds for a protest.

'What is it?'

'In England, the police aren't allowed to interview children unless they have a grown-up with them. Donnie's only seven.'

'If a boy is suspected of a crime, that may be a good rule, yes. But I'm only asking you to help me picture where on your land Kara might have wandered to. And if I take each point of view separately, perhaps I shall find every eye converging on one point.' He stretches all his fingers wide and points them forwards until the fingertips touch. 'Which of you is Donnie?'

The boy who stands up is not the one Yilmaz would have pinpointed as the youngest. Calum, the linguist of the family, still has the smooth plumpness of a young boy; but Donnie, apparently his junior, has shot out of infancy on long, thin legs: his very brief shorts reveal almost the whole length of thighs which seem unnaturally stretched. It is easy to see that he is uncertain what he is expected to do.

Yilmaz smiles reassuringly. 'We'll leave the others to get on with their work. You come outside with me, Donnie. All right, Mr Quigley?'

He takes the boy outside, far enough from the house to be out of earshot. Donnie's expression is anxious, and he lags a little behind until Yilmaz takes his hand in what he hopes is a reassuring manner. 'Now start at lunchtime yesterday. What did you do straight after you'd eaten?'

'Tam had told us all to keep a bit of lettuce from our salad so that we could have a tortoise race. There are these little tortoises all over the ground, you know.'

Yilmaz nods. Yes, he knows.

'We each had to find our own tortoise

first. But we knew where to look.'

'Show me.'

Donnie looks less worried as he realises that the questions are within his power to answer. He leads Yilmaz over to an area rough with stones and scrub, some way from the house. Leaning down, he scrabbles with his hands for a few minutes among the hummocks of thyme before bringing up for inspection a small tortoise which shows signs of being accustomed to disturbance. Instead of retreating into its shell, it stretches its long neck and turns to stare at Yilmaz.

'We put different colour chalks on their shells, to show which is which. And after the race, we always put them back here. The chalk doesn't hurt them.'

'No, of course not.' But he pauses before asking his next question. It is easy to tell that Donnie has a confession to make.

'We don't tell Mummy about the tortoise races,' he says guiltily at last. 'She'd say that we oughtn't to pick them up. But it *really* doesn't hurt. And they like having the lettuce.'

'Yes, I'm sure. Where did the race take place?'

'Just over here.' There is a patch of level ground not far away, with a football goal at one end of it.

'Was Kara with you then?'

'No. She has to have a sleep after lunch.'

'But all you five boys were together here?'

'Yes.'

'And where was your teacher?'

'Peter was having a cup of coffee with Esin. He gives her English lessons after lunch every day.'

'Could they—Peter and Esin—see you while you were racing?'

Donnie turns to look back towards the house and points to one of the open doors. 'They were inside there. We could see them, so I suppose they could see us if they looked.'

'And all your brothers were here, racing?'

'Yes.' Donnie doesn't seem to notice that he has been asked the question before. 'Murdo won. He nearly always wins. He whistles at his tortoise.'

'Just one race?'

'Yes. It took quite a long time. They don't go in straight lines. Then we put them back.'

'What happened next?'

'We played Joshua and Jericho. Murdo had made up a new tune for his trumpet and he wanted to try it.'

'Where did you play that?'

'In the castle.'

Yilmaz, who is not aware of any castle in the area, looks round. 'Will you show me?'

Donnie shows signs of unwillingness. 'I'm not supposed to go there by myself. The others can, but I'm supposed to wait till I'm eight. Because it's just a bit dangerous getting inside and out again.'

'You'll be with me.' Yilmaz takes the little boy's hand again and gives it a comforting squeeze. Donnie is still reluctant, and leads the way only slowly. There is some distance to cover. Yilmaz looks back as they walk, and notes that the room in which Esin and Peter were sitting no longer has a view of this territory.

The castle proves to be a more or less circular rock formation. It is not dangerous in the sense that the edge of the cliff would be dangerous. Even the tallest pillar of rock is not more than about four metres high.

A quick walk round reveals that there is nothing that can be regarded as a natural gateway, although there are three or four places where the gaps between the tall fingers have not been filled in right up to the top; and in one of these sections some of the loosely packed rubble has been displaced. It is easy for Yilmaz to look over what remains and study the central area. One of Captain Zeybell's men, left to guard the household, is fast asleep there.

Perhaps he is the one who has created an entrance for himself by pulling down a few stones.

It is not Yilmaz's business to discipline him. Turning away, he finds that Donnie has not moved.

'Can you climb in, or is it too hard for you?'

'I can do it this year. Last year I couldn't unless someone helped from the top.'

'Let's sit down for a moment.' Most of the small rocks immediately around the castle are too spiky to make comfortable seats. Yilmaz moves a little way away and lowers himself on to a ridge of land covered with thyme. Holding out a hand, he waits for the little boy to join him. 'Now then, Donnie, can you remember where everybody was while you were playing?'

'Not really. We were moving about.'

'Just try.'

'Well, the castle was Jericho and Murdo and Calum and me were Israelites trying to get in and Tam and Roy were trying to keep us out. I was Joshua. We take it in turns to have first choice of who we want to be, and it was my turn and I chose Joshua. First of all Murdo and Calum and me had to walk round once ever so quietly and then we had to go round six times with Murdo blowing his trumpet but not too loudly. And then we

126

waited for a bit while Murdo got his breath back and then we walked round six more times with Murdo blowing his trumpet and on the seventh walk round he blew it as loudly as he could and Calum and me were shouting ever so loudly as well.'

'Did you get in in the end?'

'Of course. That's how the story goes. The walls fell down. Not really, of course. We had to climb over.'

'So by the end of the game you were all inside there?'

'I'm not sure. I was. But Murdo was still playing his trumpet and he was making such a row that Tam told him to stay out till he'd finished. He's got a special place where he plays, so that we don't have to hear it so much. I think he went off there without ever coming inside, but I'm not sure.'

'This is the important question, Donnie. While you were playing, did you look back towards the house? Did you see Kara at all?'

'I didn't look that way. I was trying to get in.'

'And you didn't see Esin or Peter either?'

'I didn't look. Peter came later on to take us swimming. I saw him then.'

'Thank you, Donnie. Let's go back, then.' But Yilmaz has not come to the end of his questions. He waits until they are strolling across the flatter ground before asking. 'Do you like Kara, Donnie?'

'She's all right. Except when Mummy makes us look after her, because she can't keep up.'

'And were you expected to look after her yesterday?'

Donnie shakes his head. 'No. In the morning she was with Esin and then she was asleep.'

'Does your mother spoil her? Because she's the youngest?'

'Dunno.'

'I expect you had a few years of being spoilt, when *you* were the youngest. Were you sorry when Kara came along to be the youngest instead?'

A moment earlier Donnie had seemed not to understand what Yilmaz was asking, but now he is suddenly articulate.

'I don't like being fussed over,' he says with vigorous sincerity. 'When Mummy fusses over Kara instead, I can play with the others.'

'Right. Thank you very much. I'll let you go back to your lessons.'

He calls out Calum, the next one up in age. Asking the same questions, he is given most of the same answers. The tortoise race is described, and the capture of Jericho.

'Was Kara part of the game?' asks Yilmaz.

Calum shakes his head. 'If she'd been there, I suppose she could have been Rehab the harlot, but she wasn't. She was asleep.'

Yilmaz opens his mouth to ask who Rehab the harlot was, but closes it again. The only thing that matters is that Kara wasn't there.

'So after you pretended that the walls had fallen down, you were all inside the castle, were you? Did you think of another game to play together?'

Calum shakes his head. 'Murdo was still playing his trumpet. And I had a book to read. Tam told me to go outside the walls so that when Peter came out of the house to take us swimming I could see him and we could all cut across to save him having to come here.'

'What was Tam doing while you were reading?'

'I don't actually know but I expect he was giving Roy a climbing lesson.' Sensing Yilmaz's surprise, Calum explains. 'Grandfather's teaching Tam to be a proper climber, like he is himself. He won't teach any of the rest of us, yet because he says it's only safe to have one learner at a time. Tam can do quite difficult things, like climbing up from the beach to the top of the headland. But he's only allowed there when he's with Grandfather and has proper ropes and everything. Mummy doesn't mind if he climbs just ordinary rocks that stick up out of the ground like the castle walls, though, because they're not really very high. I think he was going to show Roy how to go up when there's a crack between rocks. A chimney.'

'And Donnie?'

'I suppose he was watching. Or climbing some of the easier bits. We're all allowed to climb here if we want to.'

'Now for the important question, Calum. While you were reading, who else did you see moving around? Think carefully, please.'

'I can't see people when I'm reading. But like I told Mummy, Esin came out, looking for Kara. And just after she went, I saw Peter ready to go swimming, so I told the others and they went over to meet him on the headland but I wanted to finish my book so I stayed. Do you think it was an eagle that snatched Kara, sir?'

'An eagle?' Yilmaz is startled, but doesn't wish to laugh at the eight-year-old's imagination. 'No, I don't think that's very likely. What makes you think of that idea?'

'It was in a book Dad gave me for Christmas. Stories of Greece and Rome.

An eagle carried a baby away.'

'But not a four-year-old who would struggle and be too heavy, I think. Now, show me which way you walked.'

The way lies parallel with the edge of the cliff. As they go, Yilmaz steps past the white posts, preparing to look down. He puts out a hand, indicating that Calum can safely join him there, but the boy shakes his head.

'I'm not allowed to go past the posts. None of us are.'

'Not even Tam, when he is learning to climb?'

'He doesn't learn here. Only on the headland. Grandfather says this part of the cliff is too difficult for him still, because there are ledges and the ones at the top stick out more than the ones at the bottom and that makes it dangerous trying to climb up.'

Leaving Calum standing in his permitted place, Yilmaz steps forwards to the edge of the cliff and looks down. Unlike the headland, where the strata are roughly horizontal, the land on this side of the gully appears to have been tilted in some past century by one of the earthquakes to which the country is prone. The ledges which Calum has described, short and jagged, run diagonally downwards. Yilmaz can see stretches of the lower ledges through the gaps in the upper ones, but it is impossible to see the bottom of the cliff. He knows, though, that the beach has already been searched.

He stares for some time, moving along the edge to give himself better views. But there is no sign of a child, any more than there was on the previous evening: no small shoe or shred of clothing, no newly broken edges. They will have to send a man down to be certain; but if Kara had fallen she would surely be visible, lying on one of the upper ledges. He returns to Calum's side and together they walk on towards the gully.

'It's one of your rules, is it, that you can't go past the posts?'

Calum nods solemnly.

'And do you always obey the rules, all of you?' Boys, in Yilmaz's experience, are not famous for being law-abiding. But Calum's answer is definite enough to be convincing.

'Yes. Tam explained it. He says that as long as Mummy can be sure that we'll always keep her rules, she'll let us play whatever we want. But if she thinks we're going to cheat, she'll keep us in the house or get Peter or someone to look after us all the time.'

This is a sophisticated philosophy of freedom for a twelve-year-old to expound and to enforce on his younger brothers, and Yilmaz is intrigued by it. He has already formed the suspicion that Mrs Rolph is to some extent allowing her elder children to bring themselves up; it would seem that in her eldest son she has a useful lieutenant.

And here at this moment comes Tam himself, running from the house, followed by a tall man with a rope wound round his shoulder.

'Sir, there's someone come from Antalya for you.'

This is something Yilmaz arranged before leaving for The Lookout that morning. He despatches Calum back to the schoolroom and explains to Tam what is going to happen.

'Since your grandfather is away and can't help us, I've arranged for another expert climber to come and check out the cliff face and the tombs on the headland that we weren't able to get at last night.'

Tam nods his head in understanding. 'Are you going to start with the cliff?'

'No, the headland.' If it were a simple accident they are investigating, he would have expected to see the little girl's body from above. But in case something more sinister has happened, then those of the ancient tombs that could not be reached in the previous evening's search must be first on the list for inspection.

Keeping up with Yilmaz's vigorous stride, Tam produces a helpful piece of information.

'There's a stanchion at the end of the headland which he could use,' he announces.

'Excuse me?' Yilmaz prides himself on the extent of his English vocabulary and is rarely caught out, but this word is new to him.

'I'll show you. Look.'

By now they have reached the head of the gully, passing the path down to the beach. Tam leads the way to the very tip of the headland. Here too there is a row of posts to mark the boundary of safety. The twelve-year-old stops beside them.

'Just there.' He points forward to an iron post which has been hammered into the rock. 'Grandfather taught me to abseil here. And when I climb up with him from the bottom, I have to wear a safety rope that's fastened round the stanchion. There's a sort of ledge halfway down, and you can get to two of the tombs from it. I've been inside. One of them's enormous. It's got three sort of rooms. Dad says it must have belonged to a ruler.'

'That's very helpful, Tam.' Yilmaz passes the information on to the new arrival, who nods once, hitches his own rope securely round the post and disappears over the edge. Although intending to return almost at once to check if there are any discoveries, Yilmaz walks back towards the house with Tam. This is breaking the order in which he has intended to interview the boys, but it seems a pity to waste the opportunity for a conversation.

'Do you miss your father?' he asks casually.

'Well, we see him every week while we're here.'

'But the rest of the year?'

'He works in America. We wouldn't see him anyway.'

'If he and your mother were still married, you'd live in America too, wouldn't you?'

'I suppose so.'

'Are you sorry about the divorce?'

'Yes, of course I am.' But Tam's freckled face shows no great unhappiness. 'It's actually quite good, though, seeing him so much when we're on holiday. It means we can have fun together all the time. And Mum and Dad don't quarrel or anything.'

'Why do you think they split up, then?'

'It's the baby business, isn't it? Mum's got pots of money, so she doesn't see why she shouldn't have another baby every year. But Dad thinks he can't give proper attention if there are too many children.'

135

'So the divorce was because of Kara, in a way?'

'Well, only sort of. I mean, it wasn't her fault, was it?'

'Do you like Kara?'

'I don't like it when we have to look after her. She doesn't know how to play games properly and she doesn't do what she's told. And if we tell her she can't do something, she runs off and complains to Mum. But we don't have to have her very often. Almost all the time she's with Mum or Rosie in England or Esin out here.'

'Why didn't your mother bring her English nanny to Turkey?'

'Well, she needs to have someone who can tell the cook what she wants, and that sort of thing. You know, an interpreter, like you. And I think she doesn't want Kara to get too fond of anyone else, so that's why she keeps having someone new.'

'You seem to be a very sensible boy.' Yilmaz means the compliment sincerely. 'Tell me, what do *you* think has happened to Kara?'

'I don't know. She could have fallen over the cliff, I suppose. She's always running off where she's not supposed to. That's why she has to have someone to look after her.'

'But if she'd come out towards the cliff,

surely one of you would have noticed her?'

'If we're inside the castle we can't see out, except in a few places. And when we were playing Jericho, there was an awful lot of noise. Or she might have fallen from the headland, not this bit of the cliff. While David was here, till yesterday, she was allowed to swim in the sea, like us. Perhaps she was sorry about having to go back to her pool, and tried to go down by herself, although she's not allowed to. The path isn't very safe and where it turns round in a kind of zigzag—you know, at the tip of the headland—anyone who slipped would fall straight into the sea.'

Yilmaz is interested in this theory, if only because its fluent exposition shows that Tam has been giving serious thought to the mystery of his half-sister's disappearance. But by now the boy is growing impatient.

'I really don't know what happened,' he says. 'Sorry. I ought to get back to the schoolroom now, if that's all right. Oh, and there was someone else who came in the same jeep as the climbing man. He's trying to explain a new sort of telephone to Mum, but I don't think she understands.'

For a moment Yilmaz hesitates. He is anxious to supervise the exploration of the headland. But Tam is right to suggest that his mother will be in need of an interpreter. Sighing, he goes in search of Mrs Rolph.

Chapter Ten

Once Yilmaz has arrived to explain the procedure needed to make an international call, it does not take Susan long, even in her present anxious state, to master the use of the mobile telephone with which the police have just provided her. She is accustomed to carry something very similar, although less bulky, in the car with her when in England, and reproaches herself for stupidity in allowing herself to remain dependent on Dr Sutherland for so long. Perhaps it's because she tends to think of Turkey as being a backward country—in spite of Hugh's frequent declarations that the Turks are the best engineers in the world. Or perhaps she has taken it for granted that the mountainous terrain would make reception impossible in this isolated spot. That may have been true until recently, but with satellites now working their magic overhead it seems that on both counts she has been wrong. She nods her thanks to Yilmaz as she waits for an answer from David's office number.

She has already been up to The Eyrie once that morning to use her ex-father-in-law's telephone. There was no answer from her home number, and by the office she was told that David was expected to return to work that day but had not yet turned up. On this occasion she has more success, for he has just that moment arrived; but the conversation doesn't go as she has expected.

David, she discovers, already knows that Kara is missing. He ought to be desperately anxious. He ought to be booking an immediate flight back. He ought to be consoling her in her distress. Instead of that he dismays her by exploding in anger.

'Half an hour in a bloody police station, that's why I've only just got here. Questions, bloody questions! When did I leave Turkey, when did I arrive, why did it take so long? They must be the only people in England who didn't know there was an air controllers' work to rule yesterday. They seemed to think that I'd got Kara hidden away somewhere. Or even that I'd killed her, for God's sake! You'd think they might show a bit of sympathy instead of—' He breaks off, reacting at last to his wife's silence. 'Oh, Susan, darling, I'm sorry. This is terrible. Specially terrible for you, having to deal with it. Is there any news?'

Susan finds herself unable to speak; but how can he be expected to hear a shake of the head? 'No,' she manages to croak.

'What's actually happened? The police asked all those questions without even telling me why at first. And then at the end they sort of threw it at me, but made out that they didn't know any details themselves. All I know is that you can't find her.'

Susan tells him what she can, which is pitifully little.

'Oh, darling! Shall I come out again?'

It has taken Susan so long to make contact with her husband that she has had time to prepare an answer to that question. Although she longs to have him at her side, the answer is no. Not for the moment, at least.

'If there's any sort of ransom demand and we have to make quick decisions, I don't want you to be in transit,' she tells him. 'And we may need to transfer money out here. It would be easier for you to arrange that in England.'

'Well, how can we keep in touch?'

'I'll ring again before five o'clock. I've just been given a mobile phone to use, but I don't know what its number is, so I can't tell you how to contact me.'

At this moment Yilmaz—who perhaps has not moved out of earshot during the conversation—appears in the doorway. 'Hold on a moment.'

'I have my husband on the line,' she tells him. 'What number should he call to reach me?'

'The father of Kara? May I please speak to him?'

She listens while Yilmaz expresses his sympathy and assures David that everything possible is being done. Her telephone calls, she learns, are being monitored and any call to Dr Sutherland's number will be automatically put through to her, so they agree that it will be best if David is the one to initiate the evening contact. After Susan has had a chance to say goodbye, Yilmaz asks permission to make a call of his own.

She listens to the sound of his voice without comprehending the meaning of what he says. It is an interesting voice; more authoritative than she would have expected and a little deeper in pitch than when he is speaking English. This is like listening to opera, she thinks to herself. You lose something when you struggle to understand the words. Once you give up the attempt to make them out, you can appreciate just the sound of a voice, and the sound becomes the person.

141

But now he is speaking again to her, in the English which is almost too perfect, with its pure vowels and clear articulation.

'My colleagues have discovered from a friend of Dr Sutherland's that he is climbing in the Taurus Mountains, near Pozanti. It may be difficult to make contact with him for a day or two.'

'According to Peter, his cook said that he left The Eyrie in the morning, while Kara was still here with Esin. So he can't have anything to do with her disappearance, can he?'

Yilmaz makes no comment on this conclusion, but even while she is still speaking Susan recognises that there is a lack of logic in her remark. Dr Sutherland might not necessarily have moved far away when he ostensibly took his departure. There would be nothing to stop him returning quietly in the afternoon. But why should he do such a thing?

Yilmaz is presumably exploring the same avenue in his thoughts.

'What was Dr Sutherland's attitude to Kara?' he asks. 'Did he blame her for the ending of your first marriage?'

'How could he? A child!'

'He might have been hurt on his son's behalf, perhaps. Did he hope for a reconciliation, so that he could be a grandfather to his grandsons again?'

142

'He *is* their grandfather. Nothing can change that. He can see just as much of them now as when I was married to Hugh. I mean to say, that's why I'm here.' Her voice rises in indignation that the interpreter should interpret the situation in such a way. 'He doesn't take any notice of Kara. That's his way of punishing her for existing, I suppose. And he punishes me in much the same way nowadays. It's understandable and it's not important. Look, I don't actually *like* him. He's a very rigid sort of man. Not warm at all. Only really happy, I think, when he's on his own in the mountains. But you can't persuade me that he'd ever do anything like...like...' Her voice fades away. She doesn't know, any more than Yilmaz knows, exactly what charge she is defending him against.

He prepares to leave, apparently satisfied that at least she is not accusing her father-in-law of anything.

'Please stay with your telephone today,' he asks. 'And perhaps you will choose to spend time with your sons when their lessons are finished. They may think that boys should not show distress. But their sister's disappearance has upset them. I can tell.'

Susan nods. She is moving into a new stage of anxiety. A numbness which is

143

both physical and mental has replaced yesterday's panic and distress. She can do nothing but wait for something to happen.

There is not long to wait. As she steps out on to the verandah and watches Yilmaz hurry away, a different movement catches her eye. On the tip of the headland a tall man who has been stooping down to pick something up straightens himself and starts to walk towards the house. He is carrying an object in his arms, holding it in front of him as he walks with a careful slowness. At this distance, Susan can tell only that it is white.

She snatches at the binoculars which are kept handy for birdwatching and fiddles clumsily with the focus. Now she can see. His burden is featureless, totally wrapped in a white cloth. He is making no attempt to hold it up to his cheek and murmur words of comfort. It is rigid. It is the size of a four-year-old-girl.

'No! No!' She feels as though she is shrieking the words loudly enough to be heard in Antalya, but in fact no sound emerges. In the sudden certainly that Kara has been found, and is dead, her pent-up emotions are haemorrhaging; like an abscess bursting; like a slashed vein erupting. She lets the binoculars fall to the ground as she flings her arms upwards, crossing them in front of her eyes; as though if she refuses to look there will be nothing to be seen.

The movement is an abrupt one and provokes an abrupt reaction. She is conscious of a sharp and intense pain, as if someone has kicked her in the stomach. For a long moment she stops breathing, trying to hold her body together. But it is no use. As she slowly lowers her arms she is conscious of a different kind of haemorrhage. Blood is trickling down her legs.

Never before in her thirteen years of childbearing has anything like this ever happened to Susan, but she realises at once what is occurring. Pressing her thighs tightly together, she makes her way with tiny steps to her bedroom and lies flat on the bed with a pillow beneath her feet. Surely if she keeps absolutely still, she can prevent her baby from miscarrying.

That is easier to prescribe than to perform. Every few minutes she is winded by another pain, almost as strong as the early contractions of labour. The important thing is that she mustn't push—but her body has a timetable of its own. Her muscles disobey orders. The moment comes when she feels a rush of blood soaking her shorts. There is no hope for the tiny foetus.

For a moment Kara is forgotten as Susan groans with despair at the loss of this newest baby. She pulls off her shorts and makes her way into the shower room which leads off her bedroom. There is no longer any point in being careful. Bolting the door behind her, she sits down on the lavatory.

It is not very long before she feels the foetus passing, but she is still bleeding, and too weary to move. With surprising swiftness she can put this new tragedy out of her mind, because once again she is mourning Kara. She rocks forward and back, forward and back, as she weeps.

'Mum! Mum! Mum, where are you?'

It is Tam's voice, but there is something very wrong about it. Presumably he has been told by Yilmaz that Kara's body has been found, and has come to break the news. But he ought to sound upset, caring, prepared to console her. Instead he is shouting as though something exciting has happened.

'Mum!' He is in her bedroom now, and she hears him give a gasp of horror. No doubt he has seen the blood. He rattles at the bathroom door, but the bolt holds. 'Are you in there? Are you hurt?'

'I'm here. It's all right.'

'What's happened? Has somebody attacked you? Mum, let me in!'

'Go away, darling. I'm all right. It's just—oh, God, I don't want Kara to be dead! I can't bear Kara to be dead.'

She is not so much talking to him as shouting out her despairing refusal to accept the news which someone is just about to break to her; but nevertheless she pauses. This is her only hope now, that Tam will tell her not to be silly; to come out because Kara has been found alive and well. But he says nothing of the sort, and instead continues to rattle at the door.

The sound brings her to her senses. Under no circumstances should a twelve-year-old boy be allowed to see his mother, half naked, having a miscarriage. Steadying herself against the wall, she steps across to the shower cubicle.

'I'm having a shower, Tam,' she tells him through the door, turning on the water to make it true.

'But your shorts. All that blood. Is there someone in there, holding you hostage?'

'Of course not, Tam.' It is tempting to tell him that the idea is ridiculous; but only a day earlier the idea that his sister might be kidnapped would have seemed ridiculous as well.

By now she has taken off her sun top and is shuddering as the cold water attacks her skin. It swirls pinkly around her feet, for the bleeding has not yet stopped. Once she has turned off the water again she rolls up a face flannel and presses it tightly into place between her legs.

'I'm going to fetch Peter,' says Tam. She can hear him hurrying out of the bedroom. Moving faster herself, because she must not be caught in this state, she twists a bath towel around her body like a sarong. There is just time to toss her shorts and the bloodstained sheets on to the floor of the shower cubicle, but no time to dress herself before Peter comes running, with Tam, looking alarmed, behind him.

They find her leaning against the doorframe, faint and reluctant to move lest she should dislodge the pad from between her legs. Peter catches her as she is about to fall and then lowers her into the chair which Tam pulls up behind her. The movement dislodges the towel, which she has tied too loosely. She can feel Peter's hands against her skin as he first of all refastens it and then presses her head and shoulders gently downwards towards her knees. Is this something else he was taught to do as a boy for his first-aid badge?

A few moments pass in silence while his hand continues to press on the top of her spine. Then his other hand moves to grip her arm. Making no attempt to disguise his suspicions, he raises the wrist and inspects its unbroken skin.

'I have five sons,' she reminds him. 'You don't really think... It's just...' In the bathroom she has shouted it: now she mutters the words so that the man and the boy have to strain to hear.

'I can't bear the thought of Kara being dead.'

'You've no reason to think that she is,' Peter tells her firmly. 'And every reason to hope. If she'd had an accident, she would have been found by now. But if someone had stolen her, then whatever the reason may be, it will be in his interests to look after her and keep her safe.'

'But I thought her body had been found. I saw someone carrying something.'

'That wasn't Kara,' Tam tells her. The note of excitement has returned to his voice. 'It's what I came to tell you about, what they've found. It isn't Kara.'

Chapter Eleven

Yilmaz is unaware of what is happening inside The Lookout as he hurries to discover what Ahmet is carrying. The climber is a man of few words.

'Stone,' he announces.

'Set it down.'

Unclipping a knife from his belt, Yilmaz inserts the blade into the row of stitches which have sewn together a white fabric covering. He rips them open to reveal a layer of soft padding. Whatever this may prove to be, someone has prepared it carefully for a journey.

It is a marble statue, its small size suggesting that it was originally carved for domestic rather than temple use: a miniature Aphrodite. Yilmaz runs his fingers over her smooth, cold shoulders and traces the delicate line of drapery while the filing system in his memory goes to work. Given the task of tracing a lost child, he is no more efficient than any other detective, but now he is on home ground.

'This was stolen from the museum at Aphrodisias three months ago. Is there more?'

'More, yes.'

'Do you need help?'

'It will save time.'

Doing his best not to show his excitement, Yilmaz follows Ahmet. He is surprised to find that instead of going to the top of the headland he is being led down a narrow path cut out of the side of the gully.

'Easier for heavy things,' Ahmet tells him. Halfway down, where the path reaches the point of the headland before turning back in a sharp elbow to continue its descent, they come to a halt. Ahmet steps on to the face of the cliff and begins to move sideways. The ledge of rock beneath his feet is only a few centimetres wide; there is hardly room even for his toes. Yilmaz, more sturdily built, is reluctant to follow.

'Easier further on,' Ahmet tells him. 'Wait here, if you will.'

He moves out of sight round the pillar of rock which has resisted the erosion of wind and water. There is a long wait, followed at last by the sound of hammering. When Ahmet comes into view again his feet are pressed against the cliff but his body is leaning out from it. With one hand he holds a rope which is attached to a piton and fastened round his waist. With the other he is holding another article packaged in white. This one is much smaller than the statue. Yilmaz, holding tightly to one of the posts with which Dr Sutherland has made the path safe for his grandsons, is able to reach out and take the booty.

Five more small oval packages follow without pause. Then there is a sound of grunting. Still held by his rope, Ahmet begins to push along the narrow ledge a large flat panel.

'Very heavy,' he warns.

Yilmaz is forced to let go of the post and use both hands to keep this last treasure from falling off the edge. By the time he is able to lay it safely on the path he is sweating as much with anxiety as with effort. Ahmet helps him to carry it up to the level ground before returning to bring up the smaller objects.

This slab, unlike the other items, is unwrapped. Yilmaz stares down at a relief carving of a Hittite warrior. He is seen in profile, wearing a conical helmet, a short kilt and shoes turned up at the toes. There are many such warriors carved on the sides of mountains in Anatolia—but that doesn't mean that anyone has the right to take a power saw and cut one away.

'Bastards!' mutters Yilmaz to himself. Naturally he does not say the word in English—which is just as well, because he looks up to discover that one of the Sutherland boys has appeared silently beside him.

'Peter says, would you like to join us for lunch?'

Although Yilmaz is sick with anger, none of it is directed against an eleven-year-old. He manages to smile.

'That's very kind, but I never eat in the

middle of the day. Something to drink, perhaps, when I come up to the house. Will you tell me your name?'

'Roy.'

'Thank you for your message, Roy. Tell me, why does the invitation come from Peter and not from your mother?' He always likes to know exactly who has asked a question—or volunteered an answer—and why.

'Mum's not feeling well. She's lying down. When she saw the other man carrying the statute, she thought it was Kara.'

'Ah, I'm sorry she has had this new distress. Does she know now?'

'Yes, Peter and Tam told her it was just a statue. Where did it come from, sir?'

'That is something we shall have to find out. All these are stolen goods. We have found them hidden in one of the tombs on the face of the headland. Have you or your brothers ever been into these tombs?'

'We don't know anything about stolen things!' Roy is indignant and alarmed.

'No, no, no. Of course not. But if I can discover when anyone last saw the tomb empty, it will help me to learn when it was used as a hiding place.'

'Oh, I see. Well, Tam's been there. When he's having his climbing lessons. There's a wide sort of platform outside one of them, he said. He used it to have a rest.'

'I'd like to speak to him. Would you ask him to come?'

Roy nods and leaves at a run. When Tam appears, it is at a slower pace. He looks upset and seems unwilling to talk. Yilmaz puts his own concerns aside for a moment.

'What's the matter, Tam?'

'Nothing with me. But Mum... She thinks Kara must be dead and she keeps saying that she can't bear it. Over and over again, in a funny voice, as though someone's hurting her. She's never liked to think of things being dead. Not even flowers. When our cat at home kills a mouse, we always have to bury it quickly, because she gets upset.'

'Well, you can give her a message which may help, Tam. Perhaps she'll find it easier to believe if you say it, rather than me. If Kara was dead, we should have found her by now.'

'Not if she'd drowned. She could be anywhere in the sea.'

'Not anywhere. In fact, not very far away. This is Captain Zeybel's part of the inquiry, not mine, but he can find out how the wind and the water moved yesterday. The bay is very sheltered. Experience tells us that the body of anyone who drowns by accident can be found quickly. If not today, then certainly by tomorrow.'

'I didn't know that.'

'Why should you? I'm glad that you have had no need to acquire such knowledge. Anyway, with every moment that passes with no sign of your sister's body, it becomes more likely that she is still alive. Your mother thought from the very beginning that someone had stolen her. Perhaps that is truly the case. And whatever the reason for taking a child away, she will be well cared for.'

'That's what Peter told her, but I don't think Mum believed him.'

'Well, you tell her the same thing. But before you go, you can help me in another matter. Roy says you've been inside these tombs.' He waves a hand towards the headland.

'Yes. With Grandfather.'

'Right inside? Into every room? Right to the back? With a torch?'

Tam nods.

'And was there anything inside?'

'No, nothing. They were all empty. Grandfather said that grave robbers probably came there hundreds of years ago. They were empty the first time he ever went in.'

'Good. Now tell me. When was this that you went inside? The most recent time.'

'Not very long ago. It was while David was here. About ten days ago.'

'Thank you. That is very useful to me. When you are back in the house, perhaps you will take a pencil and work out what you have done each day, to find the exact date. But ten days is a good help. Thank you very much. Had you any plans to go to the tombs again?'

'I'm not allowed to climb without Grandfather, and he's off on a trip.'

'Ah, yes, of course.' Tam is the boy who believes in keeping rules. The thief, whoever he may be, could rely on that. Dr Sutherland's absence is the best possible way of making sure that there can be no request for another climbing lesson, and there need be no fear of an unauthorised visit. Yilmaz has not needed very long to concentrate his interest on the owner of the land. He has to warn himself that he must not take too much for granted. The most obvious suspect does not always turn out to be the villain. Not always—but very often.

Another of the Sutherland boys appears, running from the house to tell his brother that lunch is ready. Tam introduces him. 'This is Murdo.'

'Ah, yes. The trumpeter, who made the walls of Jericho fall down?'

The nine-year-old gives a shy smile as

he acknowledges the identification. Then he looks down at the objects lying on the ground.

'Are these stolen things?'

'Yes.' Yilmaz has decided to tell the boys what is likely to happen. It will be necessary to bring more men to the territory overnight and their presence, dark-faced and hiding in the shadows, could cause alarm if not explained in advance.

'We have very strict laws in Turkey to prevent antiquities from being taken out of the country illegally. And of course it is a crime to steal something from a museum or to cut it away from a mountain, as this slab has been cut. Whoever stole these things would not be able to take them out of any port or airport. So I think someone will come in a boat and climb up to the tomb to collect them. Very soon. Tonight, perhaps. I have sent for more men, to catch them when they come.'

'You ought to put the things back in the tomb, so that you can catch the people red-handed,' Murdo suggested. 'Otherwise they'll just have a look and go away again when there's nothing there.'

'Yes, we shall do that. Well, only one of these.' By now Ahmet has unwrapped the five smaller objects. These prove to be marble heads, which Yilmaz does not immediately recognise. They are not yet on the list of antiquities known to have disappeared. 'For the rest, we shall wrap up ordinary stones.'

Tam nods. 'Would you like me to take them down for you?' he asks. 'I know how to, and as long as you were here at the top...'

'Thank you for the offer, but there is an easier way. From your path which leads to the beach it's possible to reach a ledge. Ahmet has fastened another rope there. He can manage by himself.'

Tam is ready for his lunch and turns away to return to the house. But Murdo lingers for a moment.

'Have you stopped looking for Kara, now that you're looking for thieves instead?'

'No, no, of course not,' Yilmaz assures him. 'A little girl is more important than any statues.'

The assurance is only half sincere. In the excitement of this new discovery he has indeed pushed Kara's disappearance to the back of his mind, and even as he speaks he is reckoning that Captain Zeybel can take over the whole of that investigation, leaving Yilmaz himself to concentrate on the sphere in which he is particularly qualified. But another thought has occurred to him. When two suspicious events take place within the same small area and the same limited period of time, it would be foolish not to consider the possibility that they may be connected.

Might Kara have seen some activity which perhaps would not seem unusual to her at the time but which she would be able to describe later? Might she even have recognised one of the people involved, so becoming a threat to what could be a regular and lucrative trade? Might Esin be in some way connected with the smuggling? Might she have been instructed to hide the little girl away in order to preserve secrets? Or—a far more sinister possibility—might she have realised that someone else had disposed of Kara—permanently—for that same reason? That would certainly explain why she became distraught and fled.

All this is fantasy until the child is found. Already, while Murdo rejoins his brothers and Ahmet prepares to restock the tomb, Yilmaz is mentally listing what must be done. While Captain Zeybel is calculating where the currents around the coast might deposit a small body, Yilmaz himself must arrange to set observers in position both on the headland and at sea. The source of the marble heads must be identified. Dr Sutherland must be located and for a time prevented from learning what has been discovered. Most important of all, Esin must be found.

The last two points are connected. Since

it was Dr Sutherland who arranged for Esin to be employed at The Lookout, it will be reasonable to grill him about her qualifications and whereabouts. All the other lines of inquiry Yilmaz sets in motion at once. Then it is time for him to go in search of Peter.

Chapter Twelve

Peter has just finished lunch when he sees Yilmaz appear on the verandah to indicate that he wants a private conversation.

It is not altogether clear to the tutor what Yilmaz's precise status is. Mrs Rolph seems to think that he is just an interpreter, and certainly the language problem may be enough to explain why he asks so many questions seemingly off his own bat. But in spite of his casual appearance there is an air of authority about him, and the conversational tone of voice in which he pursues his gentle inquiries does not quite obscure the fact that they are interrogations. He must be some kind of detective, more senior than he is allowing Mrs Rolph to suppose. Peter gestures to indicate that he is just coming.

'You ought to stay close to the house

this afternoon,' he tells the boys. 'Find something to read, or a game you can play on the verandah. Something quiet, so that you don't disturb your mother.'

All morning they have naturally been subdued, and although Tam looks for a moment as though he is about to protest against this departure from their usual routine, he changes his mind and nods in acquiescence. Peter joins Yilmaz, who by now is walking up and down the football area.

'We have to find the girl, Esin,' Yilmaz says without preamble. 'Mrs Rolph has told me that you gave her lessons in English. You must have had conversations, if only for practice. What has she told you about herself? Even little things may be important.'

'I'm afraid there's not much. She told me that her university course was too much concerned with reading books. Not enough idiomatic English or practice in talking. So she'd got hold of a sort of course book published in England. For every chapter she had to pretend to be somebody different, take on a different role and carry on a conversation in that role. It was to give her new vocabulary all the time. So in our conversations she might ask me to be a shopkeeper when she was complaining about some goods;

or an employer when she was applying for a job. It was all pretending.'

'But you must have talked in an ordinary way as well. Two young people, getting to know each other.'

Peter is uncomfortable with this line of questioning. 'I tried not to...not to get to know her too well. She did sort of push it a bit.'

'You mean that she saw a handsome young man and pursued him?'

'I'm not handsome. I'm short-sighted and unathletic and pretty dull, really. But I'm English.'

'You're saying that she would like to be married to an Englishman?'

Peter hesitates. He has been slow to recognise that she may have had something of the kind in mind, and even now is not anxious to admit it.

'I think it was more that she hoped I'd invite her to stay with me in England. But that was never something I could offer. My home in London is a one-room flat. Which actually I share with someone else already.'

Even as he makes that statement Peter has his doubts about its truth. Mandy has written only twice since he left England and he suspects that her next communication may prove to be a change of address card. But none of this is anyone else's business except his own. Returning to the point of the conversation, he tries to remember what he has learned about Esin's background.

'She was born in Üsküdar. Scutari. We talked about Florence Nightingale once. But her father died a few years ago and they moved to the European side of Istanbul to live with her mother's family.'

'The family name?'

'I don't know. Sorry. She has three younger sisters. I commented once how good she was with Kara. She told me that then.'

'And this was true, that she took good care of Kara?'

'Oh, yes. All the time, whenever Kara was awake, she stayed with her, watching her or playing with her; finding ways to amuse her when she was bored or wanted to be with the boys.'

'Did this happen often, that Kara wished to be with the boys?'

'She did come into the classroom quite often in the mornings. I was never quite sure whether it was entirely Kara's wish or whether it was Esin who chose to be there. I didn't mind, as long as they kept quiet. Kara never wanted to stay very long. I think she was just trying to make the point that she had the right to turn up if she chose.'

'I see. But when Kara was asleep, then

163

Esin did not watch her?'

'No. There was never any suggestion that she ought to.'

'So, yesterday. Tell me what happened, minute by minute. You had your meal all together, and then...?'

'Esin put Kara to bed for her rest.'

'Wearing what?'

'Just her knickers, probably. I didn't see, but that was the usual system. While that was going on, the cook brought coffee out to the verandah. Then Esin joined me. We both had coffee and did one of the role-play exercises from her book together.'

'The subject?'

Peter has to think. It hardly seems important.

'She was a traveller. Buying a train ticket, getting a return, asking about times, that sort of thing. I was the ticket clerk.'

'And what were the boys doing at this time?'

'Having one of their tortoise races.'

'All the time?'

'I didn't particularly notice. I'm not expected to supervise them after lunch. I did just look once to make sure that they all seemed to be happy, and then I didn't bother again until it was time for their swim. So at four o'clock—'

'Wait a minute.' Yilmaz's interruption

is not aggressive. He is merely keeping his eye on yesterday's clock. 'You were having this English lesson for two hours?'

'No.' Peter swallows the lump in his throat, hoping it will not be noticed. He would prefer not to lie, but is not keen to tell the whole truth either. It can't be of any relevance to this investigation. 'I went back to my room. I have my own work to do while I'm here, you see. Research. Mrs Rolph knows all about that. It's my free time in the day. The boys like to have free time as well.'

'Yes yes. And Esin, what did she do while you were at your research?'

'I don't know,' Peter mumbles. 'At four o'clock I was getting ready to take the boys swimming when she burst into my room and—'

'Your bedroom!'

'My room. It's a bedsitter more than a bedroom. Anyway, she was in a bit of a state. She'd just been to pick Kara up and found she wasn't there.'

'What did you say?'

'I didn't really think it was any big deal. Kara's a bit of a wanderer, but she didn't usually go far. I just said I hadn't seen her, and Esin dashed off again. Then I took the boys swimming.'

'Kara was lost and you didn't offer to look for her?' Until now the two men have been walking up and down the football area, but now Yilmaz comes to a halt near the goal, forcing Peter to stop as well.

'I know it sounds awful now, in view of what we've learned since. But at the time... It's happened before, you see, and she always turned up within a few minutes.'

'And on those earlier occasions, was Esin equally in a bit of a state, as you described it?'

Peter doesn't answer. It is becoming clear that he will have to confess. And perhaps, after all, it will be better to talk to Yilmaz than to Mrs Rolph. For the moment, though, the detective is not pausing for long enough even to be given an answer to his question.

'I must ask again: where can Esin have been after the English lesson was finished? If she had returned to her own room, Kara would have had to walk past her to leave the house. If she stayed on the verandah, she would have seen the little girl from there also.'

'She could have fallen asleep. It was a very hot afternoon.'

'Children as small as Kara do not tiptoe, hoping not to be heard. They ask for attention. They like to wake people up.'

There is a long pause. Peter tells himself that there is no way in which Yilmaz can know what happened, and yet there is something about his silence which suggests that he is not expecting to be surprised.

'Oh, all right,' confesses Peter uncomfortably. 'For about an hour, between three and four, Esin was in my room.'

'In your bed?'

'Yes.'

'Thank you,' says Yilmaz. His tone of voice expresses no moral judgements. It is as though he has simply been waiting for confirmation of something he has guessed already. 'Now we can make progress. So there was an hour in which Kara could have awakened and looked for her nurse and wandered off to find her?'

'Yes.'

'Would you not have heard her?'

'We'd closed the door of my room, of course. And the boys were making a frightful racket. Even though what they call their castle is some way away, we could hear them. Shouting at the tops of their voices, and Murdo going full blast on his trumpet.'

'Yes, they told me. The fall of Jericho. Did that noise continue all the time?'

'The shouting stopped after a bit. But Murdo was still trumpeting away. And of course, Esin and I—' Peter flushes and does not need to continue.

'So at four o'clock Esin goes back to her room, discovers that her charge has disappeared and needs to find her before Mrs Rolph discovers that she is missing, because otherwise there will be difficult questions to answer. Meanwhile, you are perhaps already regretting what has happened. You wish to keep your distance from the situation, so you hurry to find the boys and take them to the beach.'

'Yes. I didn't seduce her, you know. I didn't really want it, although it's difficult...'

'You're saying that she seduced you? A respectable Muslim girl?'

Peter is silent. To blame the woman is not the act of a gentleman. But all the same...

'This may explain why Esin has run away,' says Yilmaz thoughtfully. 'Not because she has committed a crime, as I have been thinking. But because she is feeling great shame at her behaviour.'

'Unless...' What Peter is about to suggest is even more ungentlemanly, as well as casting a humiliating gloss on his lack of attraction as a lover.

'Yes? Unless?'

'Well, suppose she was in league with some kind of kidnapper. She might have been instructed to keep me out of the way at a time when the boys were at a distance.'

'Like Mrs Rolph, you think the child has been kidnapped?'

'I don't know. How can I possibly know? But if it's a choice between thinking her dead and thinking her stolen, of course I must hope that it's a kidnapping. And Mrs Rolph is a very rich woman, you know.'

Yilmaz gives no indication of his own thoughts on this matter. 'Do you know where the father of the boys is working?' he asks instead.

'Yes. At Termessus. I drive them over on his free days.'

'Then I would like you to drive me there now, if you please.'

'I'm afraid I can't do that. The boys—'

'Their mother can look after them.'

'No. She's not fit.'

'It will do her no good to lie and cry. Much better that she should take responsibility for her sons. Better for her, and for them as well.'

'You don't understand. She's unwell. She's had a miscarriage.'

'Oh.' Now Yilmaz does pause. 'Nevertheless. The boys can look after themselves and her. The eldest one is clearly a most responsible boy. Ahmet will still be here, if there should be any trouble, and before it is dark there will be more men on the headland and on the beach. This is your free time, you told me. You can do what you choose.'

'I'm sorry,' Peter tells him firmly. 'What I choose is to stay with the family. If it's a question of transport, I'm sure it would be all right for you to borrow the Cherokee for a few hours. But I'm not prepared to act as your driver.' He meets Yilmaz's gaze straight on, determined not to be the first to blink.

The long battle of eyes ends in stalemate. Yilmaz nods his head as though another of his ideas has been confirmed. He is the one who first turns away, but he is not acknowledging defeat.

'I shall go and have a word with your employer,' he says.

Chapter Thirteen

In a room dimmed by half-closed shutters, Susan is lying flat on her bed. Flat in every sense. Although her pregnancy was not sufficiently far advanced to reveal itself in the shape of her body, she feels, now that it has ended, as though she is empty. When she pulls in her stomach there is no resistance. No womb, no guts. A thin layer of flesh, that's all. Flat.

170

Her spirits are as flat as her body, for she is overcome by a feeling of helplessness. She has failed to preserve her new baby and can think of no contribution to make in the search for Kara. As a rule Susan is confident in the management of her life and family. She makes all necessary arrangements. Although she can afford to employ help and is an efficient delegator, she is always the one in charge. But today her confidence has ebbed away with her blood. Why doesn't somebody else make decisions on her behalf? She would like to be in hospital, with doctors and nurses examining her and taking charge of her body for a day or two.

No doubt her mental picture is based on the memory of the hospital nearest to her home in England: a place of flowers and sunshine. A Turkish hospital, staffed by strangers speaking the language she has never been able to understand, would not be quite like that. In any case, although feeling weak, she is not ill. In a moment or two, an hour or two, she will have to pull herself together.

Lacking the energy to dress, she has covered her nakedness only by a thin sheet drawn up to her armpits. Her bare arms press down the sheet on either side, outlining the shape of her body like a shroud; and as though she is indeed a corpse her toes turn up, her legs are straight and stretched. She is doing her best to control her mind, to think of nothing at all, to forget the miscarriage and to give herself a moment's rest from the nightmare questions about Kara.

The effect of this effort is to induce a craving for a cup of tea. But the cook is out of earshot and Esin has disappeared. Making a second mental effort, Susan wills herself to get up from the bed. But the attempt is quickly abandoned lest any movement should start the bleeding again; and besides, her head is still swimming with faintness. She is afraid of falling.

There is a knock on the door, which opens at the same moment.

'May I please come in?' It is Yilmaz, who is in already. Has he hoped to catch her in a state of undress? She lacks the energy to look as indignant as she feels, but manages to move her arms very slightly, loosening the sheet so that it no longer outlines so tightly the shape of her breasts and hips. He can see what she is doing, and his look makes it all too clear that for a few seconds he is envisaging her naked body beneath the sheet, before making the apology which politeness demands.

'I'm sorry to disturb you, Mrs Rolph. And sorry to hear that you are unwell.

Your tutor told me what has happened.'

'He shouldn't have done that. There's no need for anyone to know. I was upset. I thought you'd found Kara. Kara's body.'

'And are you upset now because we have *not* found her?'

'Of course not. There's hope again. I must have hope.' But his question disturbs her, defeating her attempts at calmness as she relives the moment when she saw a small, stiff burden being carried towards her. In an effort to control her emotions she tries to breathe deeply, but the breaths come faster and faster. She turns her head away from Yilmaz so that he shall not see that she is crying. Yet why pretend? To weep is a natural reaction.

'I think you should ask your husband to join you,' he suggests gently. 'You need Mr Rolph's support at this time.'

'In a day or two, yes. But not until I'm back on my feet again.' She has not allowed David to know that she was expecting another baby, and now there is no reason why he should ever find out. Peter must be told that what he discoverd should remain a secret. She turns her head sharply back to face Yilmaz, daring him to sneak on her. It is easy enough to tell from his expression that he is a man who believes that wives ought not to have secrets from their husbands, but he makes

173

no comment. Instead, he has a request to put to her.

'I have asked Mr Quigley if he will drive me to Termessus, to talk with your first husband, but he feels he ought not to leave you. It would be a help to me if you would instruct him to cooperate.'

She can think of no reason not to agree. 'You could take the boys with you,' she suggests. 'An extra visit to their father.'

'No!' The sharpness of his exclamation suggests that this is not at all what Yilmaz has in mind. 'It's very important that you should have time alone with your sons, Mrs Rolph. Not just for you to comfort them, but so that they may comfort you and nurse you if that's needed. Bring you tea. Talk to you.'

'Important? Why?' She is still lying listlessly flat on the bed. Without being given permission Yilmaz sits on a chair beside her.

'In any large family there are jealousies. Of the only boy, the only girl, the eldest, the youngest. Your sons know that you love babies and small children. They have each in turn had this special time of love from you and took their place in a larger group when it came to an end. But you mustn't make them feel now that you love *only* the youngest of your family.'

He is being impertinent, and she is

tempted to tell him so. But his manner is sympathetic. He is speaking to her as though he is a friend instead of someone who was a stranger until a few hours ago. She accepts his comment in that spirit because she has no strength for a fight. All the same, she wonders just how qualified he is to teach her her business. She pulls herself to sit up in the bed, the sheet still gripped firmly under her arms.

'Have you got children?' she asks.

'No. I'm unmarried. I have no children of my own. But I am the eldest of fourteen. Since my father died, I have had responsibilities.'

'Fourteen!'

'My parents used always to say that their children were their pension. There is no welfare system here, as there is in England, to care for old people. It is for the family to provide. Unfortunately for me, my father died too young, so I have been the one to provide. Now, about the visit to Termessus.'

'Why do you need to take Peter with you? I'm sure he'd rather work at his books.'

She listens as Yilmaz tells her more about the stolen antiquities than either Peter or Tam has been able to do, and explains his belief that before long there will be an attempt to retrieve and make off with them. 'I shall need to know where everyone is, all the time. Your sons with you. Their teacher—for this afternoon, at least—with me.'

'But you surely don't think...?'

'Until I discover the truth, I must be prepared to think anything of anyone. Your father-in-law. Your tutor. Your husband. Your first husband.'

'Hugh? You can't possibly think that Hugh could ever be involved in anything like this.'

Yilmaz gives an apologetic shrug of the shoulders. 'You must remember, Mrs Rolph, that these people are strangers to me. I have no opinions. I am awaiting to discover facts.'

'You're talking now about these statues. You're more interested in finding the thieves, aren't you, than in finding Kara? Have you given up on her?'

'Of course not.' He reaches out to take her hand in reassurance. 'Of course not. I'm sorry you should think so. One of your sons asked me that same question.'

Only one of them? That will be Murdo. Murdo has always had a protective soft spot for his half-sister. Even when she was a baby in the cot and he was only five, he liked to play his mouth organ to her and to report to his mother with delight that she was smiling at the sound. A little plumper than his brothers, and always less enthusiastic about dashing around in games or races, he is perhaps the least gang-loving of the gang, and so the least inclined to close ranks against someone who is—was—no, *is* not only a girl but too small to take part in their complicated games. 'You're talking about Murdo, I expect?' she checks.

'Yes. He is fond of her, I think.'

'You're right, yes. But you're not answering my question.'

'The first answer is that the disappearance of your daughter is Captain Zeybel's affair, and he is pursuing it. He will find Dr Sutherland in the mountains, and then he will find Esin in Istanbul. His men are making other inquiries also, to discover if there were strangers in the neighbourhood. If you see less bustle around your house, it is because we believe Kara is not here. The second answer is that the two crimes may be in some way connected; who knows? I shall ask Professor Sutherland questions about both matters, and again, until I hear his answers I shall hold no opinion. There is only one person in the world I can feel sure would never have brought any harm to your daughter, and that is yourself.'

His hand, which is still holding hers, tightens its grip. She looks down at it, as though becoming aware that he is behaving disrespectfully, he lets go and stands up.

'But while Captain Zeybel makes his investigations elsewhere, the matter of the stolen antiques must assuredly be settled on this estate. So, if you please, stay in your house, all of you, from sunset tonight, until dawn; and do not use any lights after—shall we say?—ten o'clock. There will be a guard outside the house, so you needn't be anxious. Nothing is likely to happen until there is complete darkness. But for the moment may I have Mr Quigley?'

'Yes, if he's willing. This is his free time, I can't force him to do anything. Will you ask the boys to choose one of their board games? I'll be out in a little while to play with them. And before that, I'd very much like them to bring me a cup of tea here. Donnie and Calum. Will you ask Calum to speak to the cook and Donnie to carry the tea here?'

'Yes, of course.' If Yilmaz is feeling cocky about the speed with which she is accepting his advice, he is too well mannered to show it. And although he had no right to speak to her in such a way, he has in fact filled the need she recognised earlier. She wanted someone to take charge and tell her what to do, and he has done exactly that.

Rather late in the day, she recognises

178

that she has been misjudging his status.

'I thought you were only an interpreter,' she says slowly. 'But—'

'*Only* an interpreter?' Yilmaz's eyebrows rise in a mixture of amusement and protest. 'What can be more important than to help one person understand the words—or the actions—of another? But I know what you mean. In the matter of your daughter, I am here to assist Captain Zeybel, at his request. But where the smuggling of antiquities is concerned, I have my own authority.' He produces from his wallet an identity card. Above the neat collar and tie in the photograph the face is unmistakably Yilmaz's, although his curly hair has been brushed into tidiness. Susan is of course unable to read the words beside the photograph.

'Are you a kind of detective, then?'

'A kind of detective, yes. And now I will leave you to rest.'

Susan waits until he has closed the door before getting out of bed. For a moment she is dizzy, needing to steady herself against a wall before moving slowly to collect clean clothes.

Dressed in a loose-fitting shift, with a sanitary towel securely in place, she sits on the bed again, so that she can put her feet up. Outside on the verandah, a noisy discussion is in progress about which game to choose. The board games kept at The Lookout are all old ones which once belonged to Hugh. The boys will choose Monopoly in the end: they always do.

She is fighting to keep her mind on the boys. She has five sons: five beloved and loving sons. Perhaps she has been neglecting them in a way since Kara was born, and she must do so no longer. So she tries to concentrate on the positive side of her life; but the task is impossible. A single thought dominates her mind.

Please God, may Kara not be dead!

Chapter Fourteen

Peter is at first none too pleased to be told that his employer has instructed him to act as Yilmaz's chauffeur. But his nature is an easy-going one, and in the course of working on his thesis he is continually finding questions which his one-time teacher can help him to answer. He slips a notebook into his pocket so that he can take advantage of this unscheduled visit.

'What exactly is your status in this inquiry?' he asks as they rattle down the first rough stretch of the track. 'I mean to say, Professor Sutherland speaks Turkish. Captain Zeybel could have done this interview himself.'

'Mrs Rolph has just asked me the same question,' Yilmaz tells him with a smile. 'Is it always important to the British that they should know the precise rank of a questioner before they will answer a question? Well, I will show you my authority, as I showed it to her.' He holds out a plastic-covered card, but Peter cannot take his eyes off the narrow corniche track for long enough to study it more than superficially.

'In any case, it's best if all inquiries within one family are made by one person,' Yilmaz continues. 'It will be easier for me to tell whether there are discrepancies, or clues to unusual behaviour.'

'You can't really think that Professor Sutherland—' Peter tries to protest, but Yilmaz does not allow himself to be interrupted.

'Besides,' he says, 'I was anxious for Mrs Rolph to have time alone with her sons. They will talk to her, perhaps, in a way I can't expect them to talk to me.'

'Talk about what?'

Yilmaz gives a shrug of his shoulders. 'Who knows? That's what we must find out. But they are troubled, naturally, and I don't think their mother has understood that she must give them the opportunity to express their guilty feelings to her.'

'Why on earth should you think that they *have* any guilty feelings?'

'It would be unnatural if they did not. Look at this whole situation from their point of view. They have been robbed of the father they love. It doesn't make any difference that maybe his work would have taken him away from home in any case. They could have accepted that as long as their parents remained married. But instead of that, there is someone living in their father's place. Even then, children daydream. In their minds they could push Mr Rolph away and imagine their father returning to them. It is Kara's existence that makes all the difference. Because of Kara, Mr Rolph will stay. Because of Kara, their father will never return. It would be a miracle if they had never said to themselves, silently, in their minds, "I wish she had never been born." Or even "I wish she were dead." And now what they hoped for may perhaps have come true. So they will blame themselves, wondering whether the wish is the cause of the fact.'

'I think you're being a bit fanciful.'

'Possibly.' Once again Peter's burly passenger shrugs his shoulders. 'I have to remind myself that the minds of children don't always walk straight along the paths of adult logic. They consider some action or situation and from it they expect consequences that we, as adults, know will never happen. Tell me how did you come to be offered this post as a tutor?'

'Because I happen to be very well qualified for it.'

'Yes, yes. I mean something different. Why did you choose to apply? Had you a special reason for wishing to work in this part of Turkey?'

'The original advertisement that I answered didn't mention Turkey.' Peter chooses his words carefully.

'You mean that you didn't know in advance that you would be coming here?'

By now Peter, who had not expected to be questioned on this subject, has had time to think. Once before, in exploring his relationship with Esin, Yilmaz has pursued a line of questioning and only at the end of it made it clear that he already suspected what he has forced Peter to confess. If he is now, none too subtly, probing to discover any link between a temporary tutor and the smuggling of antiquities, it would perhaps be best to volunteer the truth from the start.

'Well, as a matter of fact, I did know. I'm preparing a doctoral thesis on Lycian culture; language in particular. I could never have afforded to come and live out here on my own. That was why I applied for this particular job.'

'Although the advertisement gave you no clue of your destination?'

'I knew Professor Sutherland; he taught me for a time, before he moved to the States. He told me that the job was about to be advertised.'

'Ah. And was Mrs Rolph aware of this connection?'

Peter doesn't answer immediately, because they have reached the ravine. Although by this time he has crossed it a good many times, the sharp angle and narrowness of the roadway still makes him nervous. 'No,' he admits when they are safely across.

'But Professor Sutherland wished you to be here at the same time as himself.'

'No, it wasn't like that. Obviously he knew how much it would mean to me to come out here, to actually see the places. It was all for my benefit, not his.'

'I understand.' Yilmaz makes no further comment until they are approaching the point where they will have to leave the vehicle and climb the mountain on foot.

'Two things,' he tells Peter. 'If you are coming up with me, you are to say nothing to Professor Sutherland about what has happened at The Lookout. It's for me to decide when he should know. This is very important. You understand?'

'I suppose so.' Although Peter resents Yilmaz's air of authority, he is prepared to put up with it for Kara's sake. 'And the second thing?'

'The second thing is for later. When you are back at The Lookout. I would like you to listen to the conversations of your pupils whenever you can, and tell me anything they say about Kara.'

'You're asking me to spy on them?'

'I'm asking you to act as a detective. You have the opportunity to be close to them in a way that is impossible for myself or Captain Zeybel.'

'You can ask them questions. You *have* been asking them questions.'

'But am I receiving truthful answers? Who knows? When I interrogate adults, I flatter myself that I can recognise a liar in any of six languages. But the lies of children are different. A boy who has made up his mind to deceive and has had time to think about it is often able to convince even himself that he is telling the truth, and so his words convince others as well. I'm not ashamed to admit that I can be—' for a second he hesitates before remembering the right word '—hoodwinked by children without knowing it.'

'But why should these boys lie? You

185

can't really think that any of them are involved.'

'Involved? What do we mean by involved? Let us use our imagination. Kara is unable to sleep, or wakes too early, and her nursemaid is not at hand to prevent her from going outside. Every day for the past three weeks, I've been told, her father has carried her down the path to the sea, to teach her to swim. But on this day her father has returned to England. She asks one of the boys to take her down instead. He refuses—quite properly—and tells her to wait for Esin. But Kara is impatient. She makes her way alone to the path. But she is not tall enough for the rope to protect her. She falls, on to the rocks or into the sea. And perhaps the boy who refused to accompany her is aware of this. What has happened is not exactly his fault, but his conscience will certainly trouble him.'

'You've made all that up!'

'Yes, of course. I told you, I am using my imagination. Although in fact it was Tam who suggested a part of this possibility to me. There are many others. Perhaps one boy saw her go too close to the edge of the cliff, and shouted, but didn't run fast enough to hold her back. Or he did run, and she went further because she thought it was a kind of race—or because she didn't want to be caught. I could give you ten more such suggestions, and each of them would leave at least one boy who sooner or later will need to share his feelings with his brothers.'

They have arrived at the foot of the mountain on whose slopes Hugh Sutherland is working. Peter pulls up the handbrake and switches off the engine, but does not immediately move.

'You think Kara's dead, don't you?'

'Well, we have found nothing to suggest that she's alive.'

'There are these gangs who've been attacking tourists, aren't there? Taking hostages from buses. Throwing bombs at beach hotels. To destablise the government indirectly, I suppose. They might have snatched her.'

'Mrs Rolph would like to think so. In a way, at least. As being better than to learn of her death. But in that case, we ought to have heard something by now. The aim of such outrages is always publicity. Besides, why should anyone take the risk of being seen in such an isolated spot when a child could be picked from a beach with less trouble? And who could have known that Esin would be out of the way for that particular hour?'

It is so easy to think of an answer to this last question that Peter swallows the lump in his throat without responding. Esin could have been acting under someone's instructions. Perhaps she never had any true interest in him as a lover. Perhaps it is not shame that has caused her to run away, but merely the requirements of a plot.

Yilmaz, however, as he jumps down to the ground, makes no accusation of that kind. Instead, he looks earnestly at Peter.

'I must tell you my own belief. When something bad happens, I look first for the easy answer. Later, if there is no success, perhaps it is necessary to be more subtle and to consider more complicated possibilities. But to begin with, we should never be afraid to pursue the obvious. If stolen articles are found on Dr Sutherland's land, it is Dr Sutherland before anyone else who must answer questions. If I speak to his son today, it is only because the father cannot be found and there is no time to waste. In the same way, when a crime is committed in a family, I look for the criminal first within the household. Nine times out of ten I find him there.'

This strikes Peter as a lazy attitude, but he refrains from saying so. 'There may not be a crime at all,' he suggests instead.

'Exactly. Some unfortunate accident. That is why I ask for your help in listening to the boys. Which way do we go?'

'Up the hill.'

Tourists have worn down a visible track by scrambling up the steep and rocky slope, but they are always bound for the Lycian fortress at the top of the mountain. It is a fortress famous for defying Alexander the Great and there is enough left of its theatres and monuments to give modern visitors an arresting impression of a once proud city. Peter, leading the way, turns off the path two thirds of the way up. Now they are going downhill again towards the later Roman town, threading their way between pine trees and climbing over some of the huge blocks of fallen masonry.

They find Hugh working on his notes under a canvas canopy: a tent with no front wall. Peter expects to perform the introduction, but Yilmaz gestures him to remain behind. He shows his identity card to the professor, but the only phrase Peter can catch is 'Department of Antiquities.'

A promise not to break the news of Kara's disappearance prematurely doesn't mean that he needs to stay out of earshot. After sacrificing his afternoon to Yilmaz, he deserves to know what is going on. Without making any attempt to conceal what he is doing, Peter makes his way to the back of the tent and sits down on a length of fallen pillar.

Chapter Fifteen

Professor Hugh Sutherland is sitting in the shade of a small tent. This, by his own decree, is the rest period of the day, and he is using it to make a drawing. With the help of one of his students he has tried to work out the angles at which an earthquake many centuries ago tilted and split the side of the mountain, and now he is applying geometry as well as imagination to calculate whereabouts in the original Roman fortress each piece of fallen masonry may have stood.

At the end of every day he plots the position and angle of each block on his laptop computer. Once he returns to Texas and has more powerful machines at his service, he will be able to walk his eyes through the virtual reality of the fortress. But Hugh is an impatient man: he can't wait. In the interests of scholarship he is careful to express no certainties until they have been thoroughly tested, but to feed his own enthusiasm he likes to chart his guesses on paper.

This is one of the many occasions on which he misses Susan. Although she was never able to remember anything about any of the ancient civilisations by which Turkey in different centuries was colonised, she had the knack of looking at his stiff, grid-lined drawings and transforming them into imaginative watercolours of what appeared to be real, living places—and these in turn often inspired some intuitive leap of interpretation on his own part. But all that is water under the bridge. He mustn't allow himself to dwell on it.

For most of each day the site is a bustling one. Labourers dig or clear away undergrowth, while the four students he has brought from the University of Texas are busy with chequered markers to indicate the sizes of small objects or the levels reached in the site. They clean stones with trowels and brushes; they photograph what they find. But Hugh insists that they should all take a siesta in the heat of the afternoon, so for the past forty minutes there has been silence. He looks up in surprise at the sound of footsteps approaching over the rough ground.

Although it is an interruption, he smiles to see that the foremost of his visitors is Peter Quigley. But Peter seems unsure of his welcome and fails to return the smile with his usual enthusiasm. Instead, he steps out of his companion's way and then disappears round the back of the tent, leaving Hugh alone with the unexpected visitor.

This is a burly man: not tall, but thick in the chest, although appearing to be fit and even athletic. From his dark-olive complexion and the fleshiness of his face Hugh guesses him to hail from the extreme east of the country. As he introduces himself by name, he is searching through his wallet in a way which suggests that he has the choice of a number of identity cards. The one which he eventually shows announces him to be representing the Department of Antiquities.

Hugh stands up and steps out of the tiny tent, first reaching for the wide-brimmed hat which he wears all the time in the open; he has the fair, freckled skin of a Highlander and burns quickly in the sun. As he settles it on his curly head, he gives an inward sigh, but outwardly shows nothing but respect and politeness. His work here is at the mercy of men like this. He knows the importance of keeping in with officialdom.

'Good afternoon,' he says pleasantly. 'If you've come to check my official permit, I'm afraid it's back in Antalya.'

'I don't need to see that.' The big man is equally pleasant. 'It has the usual conditions, I presume?'

'The usual conditions, yes.' Hugh is

puzzled by the question—if it is a question. If Yilmaz is from the department, he must surely know all the details. But he seems to be waiting for an answer, and so is given one.

'We report everything we find. Your inspectors inspect. All fragments of buildings remain on site. Artefacts are collected and your lot specify everything that isn't to leave the country, but allow us a few museum export licences in accordance with our contract. Not that there's going to be anything transportable on this site. A few incised stones, and I expect you'll want to hang on to those. If that's what you've come to inspect, feel free.'

Hugh is speaking the truth. He has found nothing here that anyone could hide.

'I believe you've also worked on another site in Turkey?'

'Sillium, yes, until three years ago. The permit there was for a British university, not an American one, but the conditions were much the same. I can promise you, I work strictly by the rules.'

The phrase brings a smile to Yilmaz's face. 'Ah, yes. You are the father of Tam, who also is observant of rules.'

'How have you come to meet my son?'

Yilmaz doesn't answer the question. Instead, he produces half a dozen Polaroid photographs from a pouch strapped round his waist.

'Would you be kind enough to look at these, professor, and tell me if you recognise anything in them?'

The unexpectedness of the demand makes Hugh a little uneasy. He studies each picture in turn before speaking.

'One of them looks familiar,' he says when he has reached the end. 'This one. There's something very much like it in the museum at Aphrodisias.'

'When did you last visit that museum?'

'Three or four years ago, I suppose. What's all this about?'

'Bear with me, please. What about these others?'

'Well, these heads could have come from almost any theatre of the Greek period. And the Hittite slab is equally difficult to relate to any particular place. I've seen something of the sort myself at Yazilikaya, but there are chaps like this all over Turkey, on the sides of mountains. Are these objects that have been stolen?'

'Yes. I wonder if you would mind telling me, Professor Sutherland, where you spent the whole of yesterday?'

'Are you accusing me—?'

'No, no. No, certainly not. I think the phrase you use in England is that we need

194

to eliminate you from our inquiries. Is that right?'

'But for Christ's sake—! Oh, all right, since it's easy. I've taken a house in Antalya with two of my students. We all came up here together; arrived just before eight. Worked till five. Went back to clean up and then treated ourselves to the buffet supper at the Antalya Hilton. In bed by half past ten: it's tiring work, this, in the heat.'

'So tiring that you surely didn't work nonstop from eight till five.'

'Not physically, no. An hour and half's break in the middle of the day. The students took a siesta. I spent most of that time discussing with the chap in charge of the labourers how best to turn over a great mass of Roman wall. We actually did it, all hands to the plough, at three o'clock. Does that let me off all your hooks?'

'Just one more question, if you please. When did you last visit The Lookout? Or The Eyrie?'

'About five or six weeks ago. To welcome the family when they arrived. Since then, Peter's brought the boys over to me instead of me going there. Where *is* Peter? He was with you a few moments ago.'

'I expect he's sitting quietly, listening to our conversation. On the way here, professor, he was telling me how he came to be in Turkey as the tutor of your sons. Would you be kind enough to describe the circumstances yourself, just as a check?'

Hugh doesn't understand what Peter's appointment can possibly have to do with any Department of Antiquities investigation. It is tempting to refuse angrily; but since he feels confident that his former pupil will have given a true version of events, he describes his own part in the matter, as he has been asked. Only then, annoyed by the interruption to his work, does he demand to be told the purpose of the interrogation before he will answer any more questions.

'The objects in the photographs, the stolen ones, have been found hidden on land belonging to your father.'

'And you think someone put them there yesterday? They could have been there for months.'

'Not months, no. Your eldest son was able to tell me a date on which the hiding place was empty.' Yilmaz's voice changes to a conversational mode, as though his official inquiry is now completed. 'How long, Professor Sutherland, has your family owned property in Turkey?'

'Oh, more than thirty years. My father first came out to Turkey for a year to work on a big oil-pipeline project. He's an engineer, you know, not a medical doctor.

He got hooked on the climbing here. He's a solitary sort of man. Likes having a mountain to himself, and that's not too easily found in Europe. He built The Eyrie while he was working in the area, and afterwards he used it as a holiday home until he came to live here full time about ten years ago. Oil companies offer early retirement to people who've spent their working lives in uncomfortable places.'

'So he has a good pension? A sufficient income?'

Hugh realises that what he has taken to be a chatty question was in fact still part of an interrogation, but he is not prepared to waste any more time on such an unfocused discussion. As a son, he would like to explode in indignation; but as an archaeologist he continues to recognise the need to keep in with officialdom. He is puzzled, though, about his visitor's status, and wishes he had scrutinised the identity card more carefully.

'I don't think that's any of your business,' he says firmly, although still keeping his voice pleasant. 'If you're suggesting that he could have anything to do with thefts, you can think again. And now, if you'll excuse me, I've got work to do.'

'I will ask no more questions, but I'm afraid, Professor Sutherland, that I have a piece of information to give you. A sad piece of information.'

Hugh, who has begun to turn away, swings back to face Yilmaz again.

'Not one of the boys!'

'Not the boys, no. But their sister has disappeared.'

'Kara? What do you mean, disappeared?'

'Just that. She cannot be found. I suppose, though, that this news is not something to cause you any great concern.'

'Of course it concerns me. What do you take me for, a monster? A child, lost! And my wife—I mean my ex-wife! How is she coping with it?'

'She is naturally very upset.'

'Is her husband with her?'

'No. He left yesterday for England.'

'Then I ought to go up there. She shouldn't be alone.'

'You are still fond of your ex-wife, I think, Professor Sutherland.'

Hugh shakes his head incredulously at the impertinence of the remark, and makes no attempt to answer.

Of course he is fond of Susan. He loves her. It was never his idea that the marriage should end. Until the day when his wife told him that she was pregnant again—with Kara, as it turned out—he was blissfully happy in what he considered to be a perfect relationship.

There was never any possibility that the

baby could be his own. He liked children. He had wanted a family. But enough was enough. With more than five it would be impossible to give sufficient parental care and stimulation to each individually. The children of large families tend to bring themselves up, and no doubt are often content to do so; but Hugh always wanted to be an actively supportive parent, and he knew when he had reached his limit.

What had made the situation particularly difficult was his wife's wealth. Susan could afford to have as many children as she liked; and he had always recognised that she had the right to refuse to use any form of contraception herself. She could see no problem in dividing her love and attention between eight, nine, ten children; so that Hugh had needed to be more adamant than was perhaps tactful about his wish to give each of his sons individual encouragement. It was ironic that their clash of opinions should have stemmed from his sincere wish to be involved in his children's lives: to supervise their education and contribute to their happiness. If he had been the kind of father who thought that the upbringing of children was primarily a woman's business, there might never have been any problem.

It wasn't as if he had slipped off to have a vasectomy without saying anything to his wife. For more than six months, while she was pregnant with Donnie, he discussed the subject with Susan, trying to persuade her to his point of view. She gave in on a day when she was exhausted after a sleepless night when Calum was teething. Murdo had earache and Donnie was still waking to be breast-fed at two and six in the morning. Twenty-four hours later she tried to take back her consent, but it was too late. Hugh had seen that coming and wasted no time in arranging to have the operation. In a way he was ashamed of his haste, recognising that he had not really persuaded her. But the conflict between two points of view, each sincerely held, allowed of no compromise. Susan had lost the battle—and Kara, three years later, was her revenge.

She made no pretence that Hugh could be the father. Had she done so, he would have insisted on DNA tests; but she was open about her actions. She had hung on to Donnie as long as she could, but the moment came when she wanted another baby at her breast and on her lap. Since her husband wouldn't give it to her, she looked elsewhere.

David was tall, dark and reasonably handsome. He and Susan were both on the committee of a local charity. Susan gave fund-raising lunches; David kept the accounts. It has never seemed to Hugh, either before or since, that the two of them have anything else in common at all. But Susan is an exceptionally beautiful woman. Even at the time Hugh could understand why David should have succumbed to temptation.

She couldn't really have believed that her husband would accept another man's child as his own, could she? Well, perhaps she did. But if so, she misjudged him. He refused, naturally. If he hadn't, he might have found himself with a new little bastard every year. He was prepared to overlook the act of adultery and accept that she had no particular interest in the baby's father, but he had no intention of bringing up David Rolph's child in his own family. Since Susan had embarked on this stage of the confrontation with her eyes open, she equally naturally refused either to have the pregnancy terminated or to arrange for the baby to be adopted after the birth. It was the end of the marriage. But he had never intended it to be.

They were both equally to blame for what happened, and perhaps it is the realisation of this that has enabled them to remain on affectionate terms. Since the divorce, Susan has behaved well. She has gone out of her way to accommodate him in the matter of access, and he can tell that she never rubbishes him to the boys. They are good friends.

None of this is any of Yilmaz's business. Hugh doesn't put it into words, even in his own mind: it is past history. Except that perhaps one day in the future, when she realises what a bore she has married... Hugh is abruptly conscious that a flush of emotion is reddening his freckled face. He suspects that the Turk is reading his thoughts, and anger shows through his protest.

'When did Kara go missing? Yesterday, I suppose. That's why you wanted to know about my movements, isn't it? Nothing to do with stolen artefacts at all! You thought I had something to do with her disappearance.'

Yilmaz shrugs his shoulders in a weak pretence of apology. 'I had no opinion of any kind, Professor Sutherland. There were questions that had to be asked, that's all. I'm most grateful for the cooperative way in which you've answered them.'

Hugh snorts in disgust and shouts so that Peter will hear, 'You can come out now!' Then he summons his students and the foreman of the labourers and gives them instructions for the rest of the day.

'Are you planning to go to The Lookout?' asks Yilmaz.

'Yes.'

'I also shall be spending the night on the property. I must ask you either to leave the house before darkness or to remain inside overnight. I did not invent the story of the thefts, as you seem to think. The house and the headland will be under observation until further notice.'

'I'll take my own transport.' Hugh's voice is abrupt. Since it now appears that Yilmaz has not after all been sent to keep an eye on the archaeological site, there is no need to continue the pretence of politeness. The three men make their way down the steep gully in silence.

Chapter Sixteen

Susan finds it surprising and distressing that the boys should be able to settle down to a game at such a time of family crisis; but as a matter of fact their concentration is not particularly good today. Donnie, who is playing as her partner, has never yet grasped how a game of Monopoly may best be won. He likes to buy the cheapest properties and fill them with a cluster of houses rather than a hotel. Murdo, too, lacks the killer instinct which makes Roy chuckle with glee whenever he is able to demand rent. Even Tam, who usually wins this particular game, seems not to be trying. Much more quickly than usual, everyone is bankrupt except for Roy and Calum. Susan and Donnie continue to watch and act as banker as the struggle continues, but Tam is restless.

'Can Murdo and me go out to the headland and see what's going on?' he asks his mother.

'Yilmaz said—'

'Yilmaz said nothing would happen till after dark. All the people out there are police, putting pretend things into the tomb.'

Susan can't think of any good reason to stop them.

'Be sensible. And back for supper.'

The two boys run off. But it is well before the meal that Murdo returns, alone.

'There's a man in our castle,' he reports. 'He's got a special telescope so that he can see things in the dark. He let us look through it. And a special camera as well. I should think he's going to stay there all night. He's got his food with him. And a gun.'

'Where's Tam?' Susan has never in the past been nervous about the boys, but today she is alarmed that one of them should be on his own.

'Over by the gully.'

'Go and get him back, please. Tell him that we've finished Monopoly and we're ready to play another game.'

Tam proves to be as interested as Murdo in what he has seen.

'I thought they'd have to lower everything down to the tomb on the rope I use for abseiling,' he tells his mother. 'And then I thought that whoever was coming to collect the things would have to climb up from sea level. But there's a way of getting on to the ledge from our path down to the sea. I didn't know about it. You have to squeeze round a sticking-out bit and you can't see what's on the other side, but once you're round it seems to be quite safe. They must have fixed something into the rock, because they were swinging a huge slab round on a rope.'

'Tam, you're not to try getting on to the ledge that way yourself.' Susan is immediately anxious, but before she has time to emphasise the prohibition there is an unexpected interruption.

'Susie, love!' It is Hugh who has appeared on the verandah. His hair is tousled, his shorts are dirty and his shirt is damp with sweat, but his arrival fills Susan with such relief and pleasure that she takes no notice of this as she jumps to her feet and runs towards him.

'I've only just heard. I'm so sorry—I

205

don't know what to say.'

He doesn't need to say anything. Susan is in his arms, pressing her head against his chest. The smell of him, the feel of him, is familiar and comforting. There is a moment in which she is able to forget all her fears. She is being looked after once more.

The moment is a brief one. She draws away and manages an ordinary smile of welcome. The embrace has had an audience. Peter and Yilmaz have appeared and are observing them with interest, and the boys are watching as well. Their faces express a mixture of pleasure at seeing their father again and a certain shyness at watching their parents embrace. Hugh holds out a hand and they all come running to cluster round him, but it is still Susan to whom he addresses himself.

'How are you? I wish there was something I could do. Something positive, I mean. But if David isn't here, I'm going to stay the night. You oughtn't to be on your own.'

'Thank you.' It is Susan's own fault that David is still in England. She doesn't want him to learn that she has had a miscarriage when he didn't even know that she was pregnant. She doesn't want Hugh to know about the miscarriage either, but Hugh will not expect to share her bed. She accepts with gratitude the offer of his company, and in the pleasure of seeing him again fails to notice that David has not made his expected telephone call.

Esin's room is available for Hugh, but in fact they are still deep in conversation as midnight approaches. The boys have long been asleep and, in accordance with Yilmaz's earlier request, the house is in darkness. There is nothing particularly intimate about the words of their conversation; at this point in the evening they are discussing the individual talents of their sons and the schooling most likely to suit each of them. But darkness brings an intimacy of its own. Since her second marriage Susan has found it difficult to be completely at ease with her first husband, even though their relationship is a friendly one. But tonight his sympathy has brought them close together again.

Their quiet murmurings are interrupted by the sound of footsteps outside the house, followed by a rattling as someone tries to open the main door but finds it securely bolted. While Susan freezes in alarm, Hugh rises quietly to his feet. He bends over her so that he can speak directly into her ear.

'Have you got a gun?'

'No.' Her whisper is equally faint. 'But I can blow a whistle. The place is swarming with police.' As silently as possible she feels her way across the dark room.

Before she can reach the whistle, there is a shout outside. It seems that the guard is doing his duty and challenging the would-be intruder. The shouting is followed by a loud knocking at the main door.

'Stay here,' Hugh tells her, but by now Susan has found a torch as well as the whistle. They stand together inside the locked and bolted door.

'Who is it?' Susan tried to make her voice sound vigorous, but it emerges in a nervous croak.

'David.'

'David!' She hurries to draw the bolts. As she opens the door, Hugh, behind her, shines the torch directly forward. Yes, it is indeed David, with the uniformed guard standing at his side.

'What's going on?' David demands, shielding his eyes. 'Will you tell this chap who I am before his gun goes off by mistake?'

Susan's language is not up to the task. 'OK, OK,' is all she can manage, trying by gestures and smiles to make her meaning clear. It is Hugh, still pointing the torch, who says enough, in Turkish, to make the guard nod his head and withdraw.

'Who's this?' asks David, suspicious at the sound of a male voice. He raises a hand to switch on the light, but Susan, as she secures the door again, is quick to stop him.

'No, don't do that. We've been asked to keep the house dark. Come in and I'll explain everything. It's Hugh.'

'Hugh! What's he doing here?'

'He came to see whether he could do anything to help, and the police wouldn't let him leave again.'

It is easy to tell that Hugh doesn't like being discussed as though he is not present. He switches off the torch, leaving David stranded in the darkness. David's mood is equally prickly. There is about to be a quarrel—but it is dramatically averted. A short burst of machine-gun fire is followed by the more considered crack of a rifle. Then the machine gun lets rip again. Through the louvres of the wooden shutters it is possible to see a very bright light somewhere outside.

'What's going on here?' David asks; but Susan has heard the voice of an unhappy child. 'Mummy, Mummy!' She grabs the torch from Hugh's hand and runs to the rooms in which the boys sleep.

It is Donnie who is startled and upset, sitting up in bed and rocking backwards and forwards while Murdo and Calum, who share his room, look down at him anxiously.

'He was having a bad dream already, and then all that noise frightened him,' Calum tells her as she sits down on the bed and takes her youngest son into her arms, murmuring assurances that everything is all right now. He is her baby again, surrendering to her love instead of pushing her away in his determination to be one of the big boys.

'I think you could open the shutters,' she tells Murdo after a few minutes. Probably it would be all right to switch lights on again, for there can be no further need for secrecy. Whether a success or a failure, the ambush has taken place. But although the bright light on the headland is not directed at the house, it provides just sufficient illumination for her to see the boys. She can tell that Donnie has been crying, and is not surprised. He is only seven, and she has found the evening alarming enough herself.

Tam and Roy, excited, burst into the room.

'Did you hear?' Tam exclaims. 'Can I go out, Mum, and see what's going on?'

'With people letting off machine guns? Don't be an idiot Tam.'

She recognises, though, that they cannot be expected to settle quickly back to sleep, and offers to read a midnight bedtime story. This is good motherly behaviour—but she is well aware that she is using it to keep her out of David's way, and is ashamed of herself. He will be as upset as she is about Kara. She ought to be in his arms, comforting and receiving comfort. But it was all too easy to recognise, as he came into the house, that his predominant emotion was one of anger at Hugh's presence. She is keeping her distance from that situation because she doesn't know how to deal with it. Soon, she hopes, Yilmaz will appear to tell her that the exercise is at an end and the family need no longer stay inside in the darkness.

He arrives on the verandah just as she finishes the story. He is pleased with himself as he answers the boys' excited questions.

'No, nobody was killed. They came in a small boat, as we had expected, and the machine-gun fire was to show them what would happen if they tried to sail away. But we needed to catch them alive, so that they can tell us about other people who may be involved.'

'Will you torture them?' asks Murdo, wide-eyed.

'Not torture, no. But they cannot expect to be treated very well until they are ready to talk to us.'

'Weren't they hurt at all?' Calum sounds

211

almost disappointed.

'It was necessary to shoot at one of them when he tried to run away along the beach. But not to kill. He is hurt in the leg.'

'Did they take the things that you'd hidden in the tomb?' Tam's question is less bloodthirsty than the others'.

'Yes. We waited until they had taken every item down to the beach and were starting to load the boat. They'd done this before, I could tell. They knew how to use your path from the beach, instead of having to climb up.'

'So the tomb's empty now, is it?' This is Tam again.

'Quite empty, yes. And I'm sure it will not be used for such a purpose any more. Your castle is also at your disposal again. Now I'm sure your mother wants you to go back to bed. There will be no more excitement here. In half an hour we shall all be gone.'

Susan supposes that this is a relief. 'So it's all right for my—for Professor Sutherland to leave?'

'Perfectly all right. Although of course the road is dangerous in the darkness. And you may feel safer—'

'My husband has just arrived from England,' she tells him.

'Ah!' There is a wealth of understanding in the sound, but he shrugs his shoulders.

This is her problem, not his. He surprises her by holding out his hand.

'I don't expect I shall return to The Lookout, Mrs Rolph, so I will say goodbye to you.'

'But Kara—?'

'The search for your daughter will naturally continue. You can rely on Captain Zeybel to explore every possibility. But she is nowhere to be found on this property, and there are no more questions for you to answer. So...'

Automatically Susan has taken the hand he stretches out to her in farewell. She clings on to it, as though if she lets him go her last hope will go with him. When at last he frees himself, he hands her a card.

'You may telephone me at any time, Mrs Rolph.'

'But I can't—'

'Your son's tutor speaks a little Turkish. Enough to help you make the connection.'

This is not precisely news to Susan, because Peter mentioned it when he first offered to ask Dr Sutherland's cook whether Kara was at The Eyrie. But at the time she was too distraught to register the fact as surprising. Now, although it is still almost an irrelevance, she is disturbed to be reminded of it.

Why did Peter not mention at his

interview that he was learning the language? What prompted him to apply for a job that turned out—though he could not have known in advance—to be in exactly the part of the world he most wanted to visit? Well, of course he must have known. Hugh must have told him. She has seen the two of them together. Even at the time, when they were all in happy holiday mood, she suspected that they were not strangers to each other. It has been stupid of her to take Peter at face value. Hugh would never harm a child. But Peter: What does she really know about Peter?

She checks her thoughts, which are leading her down too dark a passage. Yilmaz, she knows, believes that the key to most disappearances is to be found within the family or immediate neighbourhood, but Susan dares not even consider agreeing with him. Kara is old enough to speak, to give descriptions. If she has been abducted by someone she knows, they will have had to silence her. The only hope for her safety is that she has been kidnapped by strangers.

That isn't something Yilmaz thinks likely, so perhaps it will be better after all that Captain Zeybel is in charge. All the same, Yilmaz has proved himself to be both sympathetic and intelligent, and as he takes his departure she feels as though she is losing her chief support.

'Don't cry, Mum.' Tam is trying to comfort her, just as a little while ago she was trying to comfort Donnie.

'I have to go on hoping,' she tells him, grateful for his clumsy hug. 'I can't bear to think... I must be able to hope.'

'Yes, of course.'

Taking a deep breath to bring herself under control, Susan manages to smile down at her eldest son. She sends all the boys back to bed, telling them that they may lie in next morning if they wish, since they have all had such a disturbed night. She looks for Hugh in order to thank him for his support, but he has already left. Then she prepares herself for a difficult conversation.

She has behaved badly to David. With only a few hours between his arrival in England and almost immediate return, he must be tired out. He has made the journey in order to support his wife, and he must be just as upset about Kara as Susan is herself. And how has she treated him? She has allowed him to discover that after telling him not to join her she has accepted Hugh's company instead, and she has disappeared almost without speaking to him in order to be with the sons who are not his sons. He will be angry, and with good reason.

Bracing herself to accept his reproaches without quarrelling, she says goodnight to the boys and goes to look for her husband.

Chapter Seventeen

Breakfast next morning is a scratchy affair. Susan feels drained and silent. More than anything else she would like to be alone, but knows this to be impossible. The five boys, who usually start every new day in a bouncily cheerful mood, are all showing the effects of a disturbed night. Donnie in particular is pale and quiet, while Tam has difficulty in restraining his yawns. Peter is also more reserved than usual, but apparently not prepared to explain what is worrying him.

As for David, Susan can tell that he is poised on the threshold of irritability. Naturally he is tired after so much travelling. Naturally he is put out by having to abandon all the work which had piled up on his desk during the three weeks of his holiday. Naturally he was furious to find another man with his wife when he arrived. Naturally—it was the last straw—he has been frustrated to be told that Susan is having her period and doesn't want to be comforted in the way which would come first to mind. Naturally he is worried sick about his daughter.

Susan has tried to slip out of bed without waking him, knowing that he is not an early riser at the best of times; but he is determined to start the day at the same time as everyone else, because there is a lot to be done. First of all he checks to see what inquiries she has already set in motion. Has she enlisted the help of the Foreign Office? Has she notified the press? He makes no criticism of her negative answers, but Susan's barely controlled panic is increased by the realisation that she can hardly expect members of the public to look out for an unhappy child, probably in incongruous surroundings, if they haven't been alerted to the need.

As the interrogation continues she becomes ashamed of herself for thinking that it would be sufficient to contact the Turkish police and simply leave them to it. Why did she not insist that they should bring with them dogs trained to sniff out survivors of earthquake disasters? Or order a helicopter equipped with a heat-seeking device which would be even more efficient at picking out a human being on a rocky mountainside? The answer is that until hearing David's suggestions none of these

217

possibilities occurred to her. She is angry with herself at her failure to call on every possible resource, and illogically angry with David for taking so much conspicuous care not to blame her. Neither of them seems able to behave naturally. They ought to be united in anxiety but instead it seems to be separating them. They come to the brink of a quarrel as Susan, feeling guilty at her inadequacies, has to restrain her resentment of the criticisms which David is not in fact putting into words.

A small domestic complication arises to distract her. It has been part of Esin's duty to act as her interpreter to the cook, who is now about to be driven down to the market by one of Dr Sutherland's servants and wants to know what she should buy. Susan calls on Peter to help, but Peter's vocabulary does not run to the names of common vegetables.

Susan gives up. 'Tell her to go on in the same way as before.' She hands over cash, not caring whether or not she will be cheated. There is no shortage of money.

David, meanwhile, settles down with the telephone as soon as he thinks anyone is likely to have arrived at the other end of the line. When he has finished several conversations he comes in search of Susan.

'Have you got any recent photographs of Kara?'

'They're still in the camera.' She has taken several snapshots during the course of David's holiday. Kara sitting in her rock pool. Kara splashing in the sea. Kara on David's lap, listening to a story. The memories are too vivid to be endured. That lively little girl seen through the viewfinder cannot possibly be dead.

Susan's tears have the effect of drawing out the love and sympathy which David has come all this way to express. He does his best to console her before becoming businesslike again.

'Let me have the film, then. I'll get it developed in Antalya. Reuters have given me the address of their local stringer. He can get it into the Turkish press as well as sending it through to London.'

'What did the Foreign Office say?'

'They recommended no publicity. Leave negotiations to them. I don't go along with that. How are they going to find out who to negotiate with? And anyway, if she's been taken by any kind of terrorists, then publicity is what they'll want.'

'It could be a kidnap just for money.'

'In that case, surely the kidnappers would have made contact by now. The most likely thing, it seems to me, is that she's going to be offered to some couple who want a child. The mere fact that the abductors came to such an out-of-the-way spot as this suggests that there may have been a very specific requirement: abduction to order, so to speak. But I can't believe that any woman will accept a child stolen from a happy home, if she knows that to be the case. So what we need to do is make sure that anyone who is offered a child for adoption in the near future is made aware that to take this particular one will be a criminal offence as well as a cause of great distress.'

'A reward!' exclaims Susan. 'We ought to offer a reward.' Why hasn't she thought of this before? Because in her heart she has believed that Kara is already dead; that's why. That may still prove to be the case, of course. No doubt at this moment Captain Zeybel is studying currents and tide tables to see where a small body might be washed up. But the unproductive search of the area is allowing her to hope again. From that point of view, Yilmaz's departure is a good sign.

It may be illogical, but the thought of a reward begins to cheer Susan up. This is something positive that she can do, instead of waiting passively for something to happen. The mere suggestion of the offer helps her to believe that someone, somewhere, will have cause to claim it.

'One of the press agencies asked about that.' The tone of David's voice suggests approval of the suggestion, but he does not endorse it immediately. 'What I thought, though, was that we should let the story appear first of all in terms of what's happened. Then we can get it back on to the front pages in a couple of days' time with the offer of a reward. Two bites at the cherry of publicity. What do you think?'

'Yes. Yes, I expect you're right.' Susan's mind is on money. David has only his salary, so any cash sum will have to come from her private fortune and she will offer every penny of it if it will produce the result she longs for. But too great a sum may produce hoax claims and false leads. It's not a question of putting a value on a life, but of calculating the most efficient way to achieve a particular result. Well, the timetable David has proposed will give her the chance to think about that. She goes off to fetch her camera.

After David has left for Antalya she wanders round the house with nothing to do. The boys are in the schoolroom. It is sensible of Peter to insist that lessons should continue as usual, but when she pauses on the verandah to look in she can tell that he is finding his teaching hard work this morning. As a rule, the tutor has proved to be imaginative in devising ways to engage all the boys at the same time, before setting them tasks suited to their individual abilities. But this hour is apparently devoted to maths and he is giving a quiet explanation to Murdo and Calum while the other three work at exercises. They are not trying very hard; there is an air of distraction in the room. But it is unfair to spy on Peter in such unusual circumstances. Quietly she moves on.

She is still feeling weak and listless after her miscarriage, and is glad when the afternoon siesta time arrives. No one will think it odd if she rests for an hour or two, for by this point in the summer the midday sun is relentlessly hot and bright. The boys, it seems, have no more energy than their mother. Usually they celebrate their release from lessons in boisterous fashion, but today Calum and Roy and Tam are all content to read in the shade of the verandah and Donnie, like his mother, has retreated to bed. Murdo has gone to what he calls his practice tower, but instead of playing the trumpet has taken his mouth organ with him. As she lies on her bed, Susan can hear the sound faintly. He is not playing recognisable tunes, but seems merely to be breathing chords in and out. The effect is to induce drowsiness. She allows herself to drift into sleep.

Her awakening is an abrupt one. Murdo,

it seems, must after all have carried the trumpet to his tower as well as the mouth organ, and now he emits a sudden blast, almost a call to arms. Startled, Susan sits up in bed, groping for her watch. Four o'clock. Perhaps Murdo, less sleepy than his brothers, is indicating that he wants to go down to the sea.

If so, he doesn't get his way. Although the other four boys do now emerge from the house, it is to the rocky castle that they make their way. Once inside it, they cannot be seen. All that Susan can deduce from their quietness is that for once their private domain is not Troy or Jericho or Valetta or any other historic city to be besieged and defended.

Peter too has been disturbed, and ten minutes later knocks on her door with news that she has a visitor. 'The first of the journalists,' he tells her.

It is foolish to be taken by surprise. For some reason Susan has assumed that The Lookout is too far off the beaten track, that no one will be able to find it or will even want to try. She is reluctant to face an interview, but David is right; publicity is needed.

There is no shame in looking tired and haggard. That is what is expected, and what she wants the reporter to report. She takes a moment, though, to put on a neatly tailored dress with sleeves and a V-neck. The shorts and sundresses in which she spends most of her days here will give too great an impression of holiday light-heartedness.

Asking the cook to provide tea for two is within her capability. Then she joins her visitor on one of the verandahs.

He is a grey-haired Irishman in his fifties, with the crimson scar of a recent wound slashed under his left eye. Susan finds it hard not to stare at it.

'Afghanistan,' he tells her after he has introduced himself as Patrick Milligan. 'Everyone thinks that the war there ended when the Russians left, but they're still blowing each other to bits. I go back from time to time, don't you know, just to see what's going on. I don't expect anyone was shooting at me deliberately: they just like letting off guns. Now then, Mrs Rolph, may I say to start with how sorry I am about what has happened.'

His voice is soft and sympathetic. Back in England, Susan has read with indignation about cases of press harassment, but she feels under no pressure now. They are on her side, his voice seems to be telling her as he takes out his notebook.

What he wants is facts: a description of Kara, the precise time when she was last seen, and then a list of names: all the other members of the family, with their ages. That includes Susan. She winces at the thought of seeing herself in print as Susan Rolph, 34, but provides the necessary information.

Later in the interview, however, she begins to hedge. There is no reason why Hugh should be brought into this. When she is asked in that polite, uncritical voice to explain why she has taken her children out of school for such a long period, she speaks vaguely of a family connection with the place and hurries on to emphasise that their education is not being neglected. This has the useful consequence of diverting the reporter into an inquiry about Peter's name and age.

He asks about her husband, naturally, and she is glad that David's movements—the need first of all to get back to work after a holiday, and then the haste to return and support her—will read so well. It seems to be almost the only piece of sensible behaviour in the whole sorry story.

'May I speak to him?' asks Mr Milligan.

'He isn't here at the moment.'

'Ah. Well, now, a photograph. Have you a photograph of the little girl?'

'That's what my husband's gone down to get. You may meet him on the track when you leave. You could ask him.'

He nods and stands up. 'Could I be having a word with little Kara's brothers?'

'No. They're very upset, naturally. I don't want to make it worse.'

Once again he nods, although this time he appears to disagree with her reasoning. 'I suppose they may be frightened for themselves. Of the bogeyman returning. Although there's not much danger of that. It's mainly girls. And children of seven and over can speak up for themselves. Too risky.'

'What do you mean, mainly girls?'

The reporter is reluctant to answer, but Susan presses him.

'As I understand it, we're talking about an abduction here, rather than an accident or a murder. Is that right?'

'Yes.' The word sticks in Susan's throat, but she forces it out. Yes, it must be an abduction.'

'Well, I've no doubt you've been asking yourself over and over in the past day or two why anyone should want to steal a child.'

'Have you come across this sort of thing before in your work?' It is a question that Yilmaz has shrugged away; probably because the reputation of his country as a tourist area might be at risk of damage.

'Oh, yes. Two German girls from Turkey this summer, and three British kiddies from the Greek islands in the past four years. There's not much doubt that there are gangs operating. Not just round here. There are more of them out east, where the girls look younger for longer. They tend to finish up in Holland. Given drugs to smuggle if they're lucky. Travelling as innocent little daughters of families. If they're not so lucky, then starring in films.'

'What sort of films?' Susan's throat is dry with horror. But she knows the answer, and he doesn't bother to give it. Instead he stands up, ready to leave.

'Are you and your husband offering any reward?' he asks casually. Too casually for Susan's liking. She is suddenly suspicious and frightened.

'Which paper did you say you worked for?' she asks.

'I didn't. I don't. I'm a freelance. I only get paid for the stories I provide. Your husband contacted a couple of agencies. I get tipped off about anything in my territory so that I can put some flesh on the story.'

'May I look at your identification again, please?'

'Surely.' He pulls a card from his wallet and this time hands it to her instead of merely waving it in front of her eyes. It bears his photograph, although without the

227

scar, and a date stamp which bears the word 'Accredited'. Accredited by whom? She doesn't know the right questions to ask. She doesn't know who can be trusted.

'You're right to check. But I am what I say I am. I'll be expecting, then, to meet Mr Rolph on my way. And I certainly hope that your little girl will be back with you before long.'

His voice is as sympathetic now as it was when he first arrived. Susan doesn't really suspect him of being in league with kidnappers, not when she stops to think about it. If she is angry with him—and she is—it's because he has put into her mind a thought which she hasn't the courage to bear.

Chapter Eighteen

The arrival of the reporter has distracted Peter from his work. He isn't finding it easy in any case to concentrate on his dissertation. What possible use to the world is the understanding of a language that has not been written or spoken for almost three thousand years? Even if his study of the Lycian tomb inscriptions does eventually lead to more knowledge of the history of this small area, what does it matter? This is scholarship for scholarship's sake—or, more accurately, for the sake of earning the right to call himself Dr Quigley. It is a low rung on the ladder of a career, nothing more.

He has never felt like this before. Indeed, there is a sense in which the very lack of any practical usefulness has made him in the past enjoy his work all the more. But the events of the past two days have reminded him that living people are more important than pieces of stone.

Equally unsettling is the memory of the hour Esin spent in his bed. He still doesn't know whether she was deliberately keeping him out of the way while a crime was committed or merely strengthening her case for an invitation to England: neither possibility does anything for his self-esteem. What makes him especially angry with himself is the fact that he didn't really find her attractive. He was missing Mandy—but not missing her quite enough to feel that no other woman would do. It was a sordid incident, and he is ashamed of himself.

He tries to make amends by doing everything he can to help and protect Susan. For this reason he remains within earshot, although concealed from view, while the man who calls himself a journalist is on the premises. Probably a journalist is just what he is; but it is not beyond the bounds of possibility that a kidnapper might turn up in some apparently legitimate guise instead of sending a ransom note.

To some extent his fears are realised. When Susan appears outside the house to watch the reporter leave, her appearance is that of a woman who is cracking up. Her eyes are too bright and too wide open. She holds on to the doorframe as though she would otherwise fall to the floor. Peter hurries across.

'He's upset you. What's happened? What did he say?'

'Nothing that I hadn't thought of for myself already. It's just that when somebody else says it, it seems more, well, likely. Peter, I'm going to lie down again for a little while. Will you keep an eye on the boys until David comes back? He shouldn't be long now. I don't mean that you need to *do* anything with them but just be around.'

'Yes, of course. You're right; you ought to rest.'

'And Peter, thank you for not saying anything to David about what happened yesterday.'

'It's none of my business.' He watches, disturbed by her weakness, as she turns wearily away and makes for her bedroom.

The boys are still in the castle. Perhaps they would like to be taken down to the beach. Peter collects his own towel and swimming trunks and walks across the football field towards the circle of rocks. To begin with he makes no attempt to conceal his approach but, as he draws nearer, he remembers Yilmaz's request that he should eavesdrop on the boys' conversation. He finds himself treading more lightly and swerving so that he can approach the castle in a less conspicuous manner. One of the tall fingers of rock offers a solid screen of concealment. Cautiously he moves his head to one side so that he can see through a gap in the rubble infill what is going on.

Three of the boys—it is hard to be certain which three—are sprawled on the ground with their backs to him. Tam, sitting on the 'throne', is facing them—and facing Peter, who pulls his head back into the shelter of the rock. He has had time to tell, though, that Tam appears to be under verbal attack from his brothers. His face is flushed with indignation.

'Yes, I know we agreed that,' he says, his voice at a higher pitch than usual. 'But things change. When Mum was so upset, I had to decide—'

'Hi, Peter!'

Peter spins round, startled by what is

not so much a greeting as a challenge. Murdo, who has appeared silently behind him, is soft-spoken as a rule, making use of his trumpet when he feels the urge to be noisy. But on this occasion he shouts out the words in a manner which makes it clear that he is warning his brothers of their tutor's presence—and, indeed, that he has been appointed to act as a sentry. The discussion inside the castle comes abruptly to a halt. Peter feels about nine years old as he steps out of cover.

'I've come to find out if you'd like a swim,' he says in as casual a voice as he can manage.

The boys look at each other and then at Tam, who answers for them all.

'Yes, thanks, if there's time before supper.'

'Just about. Go and get your things, then. Roy, will you bring Tam's for him, please?'

Tam looks even more worried and flustered than before as the others leave him alone with Peter. He doesn't know, of course, how much of the recent discussion may have been overheard. Unfortunately for Peter, though, it was not enough even to act as support for a guess.

'You were all looking very earnest when

I arrived,' he says lightly. 'What were you arranging?'

'Well, we were disarranging it really.' A flicker of relief is visible in Tam's eyes as his face takes on its usual earnest expression. 'We'd been planning to have a sports day, like at school, and of course Roy would have won most events but we thought that Donnie and Kara ought both to be given a chance, so we'd worked out a few special races, with handicaps. But now that Kara isn't here, I thought it would upset Mum. We decided—at least, *I* decided—to leave it for a bit. Roy was rather fed up.'

The glibness of the lie—which Peter doesn't believe for a moment—takes his breath away. Because Tam is such a law-abiding boy, he has always assumed him to be truthful as well. It's a mistake that Yilmaz has never made. Peter promises himself that he will be more on his guard in future.

In the meantime, however, a new thought has occurred to him, prompted by the earlier glimpse of Tam on the stone slab which the boys call their throne.

'When Captain Zeybel and his men were searching for Kara, did they look into your dungeon?'

'I don't know. I expect so. They came

into the castle a lot. The one with the night telescope and camera had his things set up exactly there.'

'But they wouldn't necessarily know that the stone could be moved, unless you told them.'

'They'd find it if they were looking properly. Anyway, Kara couldn't possibly have fallen in, because we never left it open and she wouldn't be able to move the top by herself.'

'Help me open it up now,' says Peter abruptly. He has a sudden mental picture of a little girl pestering to join her brothers, of a game that went wrong. Tam gives a shrug of the shoulders and swivels the flat slab of stone round on his own to reveal the opening of the hole.

As one of the boys asserted when the dungeon was discussed on that first tour of exploration, the underground chamber, although clearly man-made, is not particularly deep. It is obvious enough now that it is empty but, to make sure that there are no secret tunnels leading from it, Peter lowers himself into the space and feels round the walls. There is no indication that Kara, either dead or alive, has ever been there.

Tam watches without offering to help as his tutor hauls himself out. Together they slide the stone back into place.

'Let's start moving towards the headland,' Peter suggests. 'The others will catch us up.'

Tam, who seems uneasy at the prospect of a one-to-one conversation, hurries ahead, but Peter calls him back.

'Steady on. We don't want to be too far ahead. Tell me, are you looking forward to starting at Winchester in September?'

'Yes. Though I've got to learn the school song before I go, and all the special words they use for things there.' Tam's voice is less strained now. School is a safe subject.

'In a way,' suggests Peter, 'I suppose it will come as a bit of a shock. I mean, you've always been the eldest at home, and for this past year you've been at the top of your school as well. And suddenly you're going to find yourself one of the youngest in a large community.'

'Yes.'

'You may actually find it a relief, of course. Your mother does expect you to take rather a lot of responsibility for your brothers. In a big school, everything will be organised. The masters and the big boys—young men, really—will be in charge.'

'I shall still be responsible for myself,' Tam points out. 'I mean, I have to do

235

my own work. No one's going to do it for me.'

'No. But you know what I mean.' Peter grabs at Tam's hand to hold him back. 'Tam, what has happened to Kara?'

Tam doesn't turn round, but tugs his hand away. 'I don't know. How should I know?'

He is lying again. Peter didn't originally believe Yilmaz when he claimed that the boys were almost certainly involved, even if only indirectly, but he believes it now. 'For your mother's sake,' he begins. But Tam interrupts.

'There's Grandfather! Where's he—? Grandfather, Grandfather!'

He breaks away and runs at top speed towards the headland. Dr Sutherland is walking with long strides down the steep path towards the sea. As an experienced mountaineer he doesn't bother with the elaborate arrangements which he has made to keep his grandsons safe, but Tam, on reaching the top of the path, stops uncertainly. He is still a boy who obeys rules. 'Grandfather!' he calls again.

Dr Sutherland comes to a standstill. As he turns and looks up, his face expresses a momentary irritation, but it is quickly replaced by a smile.

'Hello, Tam. Going swimming? I thought I might have a dip myself after a few days away from the sea.'

He nods politely in Peter's direction and begins to climb back towards the two of them. But as he nears the top of the path, a third person arrives to welcome him. Yilmaz, whom everyone thought to have left The Lookout, has suddenly reappeared.

'Bad timing, Tam,' mutters Yilmaz. 'He was on his way to inspect the tomb, wasn't he? I would have liked him to go a little further. Still, it can't be helped.' He raised his voice. 'Dr Sutherland, will you please come back to The Eyrie with me and answer a few questions?'

It is an order, not a request. Dr Sutherland stops in his tracks and looks round, as though estimating whether there is anything to be gained by running away. But common sense prevails. He takes the last few steps towards the level land more slowly and asks Yilmaz who the hell he is. His face is pale beneath its wind-weathered tan.

Peter and Tam watch the two men walk away. They both know about the stolen antiques; they are both well aware that Yilmaz suspects Dr Sutherland of being involved. Tam is a favourite grandson. As his grandfather disappears from sight, he sits heavily down on the ground. His face is white with shock.

Chapter Nineteen

The news that Dr Sutherland has been arrested reaches Susan later that day, when his cook, in tears, comes running down to The Lookout's kitchen to be comforted by her friend. There is a brief period in which Susan is disturbed to realise that the younger boys are almost excited by what has happened; it is as if a story in a book or television programme is coming true, and they are part of it. But Peter explains to them how very seriously the Turkish government regards any illegal export of its antiquities. The punishment, if their grandfather is found guilty, could be a long prison sentence—and Turkish jails are not renowned for their comfort.

Tam already knows this, because he was told by Yilmaz when the stolen antiquities were first discovered; and of all the boys he is the closest to his grandfather. From the moment when Yilmaz walked up the hill with Dr Sutherland, he has been withdrawn and anxious; and after hearing Peter's warning, the other boys become anxious as well. They talk in whispers and at mealtimes keep their heads down, concentrating on the food.

Susan tells herself that she ought not to be surprised by what has happened, because Yilmaz made it clear from the first moment where he expected his investigations to lead. She suspects him of being lazy; a man who looks for the easy answer, the obvious suspect. Why, he even believes that Kara's disappearance may be a domestic matter, and that's ridiculous! If he is wrong on that score, he may be wrong in the matter of the smuggling as well.

But although she tries to persuade herself that it must all be a mistake, Susan is disquieted. She was speaking the truth in telling Yilmaz earlier in the investigation that she did not suspect her one-time father-in-law of harming Kara: the idea would be unthinkable. But the suggestion that he might choose to increase his income by trading in antiques is not so easily dismissed. Turkey is littered with the abandoned sites of once prosperous cities. They have not all been excavated and they cannot all be guarded. A man who for many years has enjoyed climbing alone to remote mountain spots will have had the opportunity to find and abstract objects that have perhaps never been officially catalogued.

The presence among them of something stolen from a museum is less easily explained, though, and the only explanation that does come to Susan's mind is not an easy one to accept. Assuming that Dr Sutherland is in fact involved, and that this consignment, stumbled upon by accident, was not the first, he has presumably needed help to transport and sell articles that would never be allowed out of Turkey through any legitimate channels. It would be easy for these accomplices to put pressure on him to use his land as a staging post for regular smuggling operation.

All this is mere speculation. Susan reminds herself that she must think of him as innocent until he is proved guilty, but she is not at all sure that Yilmaz has the same attitude. She writes a note to Hugh, who needs to be told at once what has happened so that he can find a lawyer for his father. Because she is still feeling weak, she asks Peter to take the note up to The Eyrie and instruct Dr Sutherland's manservant to drive down with it to Professor Sutherland's lodgings in Antalya. It all seems very complicated.

David has by now returned from Antalya. He has sent most of the photographs off from there, but has brought back one complete set. He is reluctant to show them to Susan because he knows how much they will upset her; and they do. Here is Kara, only a week ago, glowing with health and happiness as she smiles and splashes. Whatever has happened to her during the past two days, she will not be smiling now. Susan groans aloud and runs to her bedroom. She is ashamed of herself for cracking up, but she can't take much more of this.

She is still losing a little blood and uses this as her excuse to keep her distance from David when, later, he comes to bed. He is not in a good mood. In the years since their marriage he has always tried to be pleasant and friendly towards his stepsons, but Susan has taken pains to ensure that he should only find himself responsible for looking after them when it is by his own choice. Presiding over supper tonight, with the only child of his own missing from the table, has left him testy, and now he is frustrated by his wife's refusal to let him make love to her.

Susan knows that she is behaving badly—because David is as much in need of comfort as she is herself. There are plenty of ways in which she could relieve his frustration. Even a cuddle would be better than nothing. But she can hardly bring herself even to kiss him goodnight. Something very important is happening in her mind, and until it has been resolved she doesn't wish to be made conscious of her body. Not to touch; not to be touched.

David is asleep by the time she reaches a decision. There will be no more babies. No more children for other people to steal and hurt. Always before she has thought of child-bearing as something intrinsically good. She is bestowing the gift of life. It is an act of creation with no dark side—or so she has believed until now. Tonight she realises that what she has also created is the possibility of pain and fear, and the inevitability of death. What right has she to inflict this on children who never asked to be born?

Keeping very still in the bed, so that David will not be disturbed, she thinks about her five sons. She has been lucky so far. They are all healthy and happy. But sooner or later some kind of tragedy is bound to strike their lives, and it will be all her fault that they have to bear it. Guilt overwhelms her. No, there must be no more babies. As soon as she gets back to England, she will arrange to be sterilised.

David won't mind. But perhaps that's not quite true. As long as David has Kara, his own child, he wouldn't mind. But he hasn't got Kara, has he? Why should he want to spend his life bringing up another man's children? If Kara never returns, will he choose to stay with a wife who denies him the further chance of a family of his own?

It is a worrying question, but the thought that pushes it out of her mind is more devastating still. Would she really care if David were to leave her? He is a good-looking man, an honest and well-organised man; but he is not—now that the first illicit excitement of their affair is over—in any way stimulating. He works hard in his office and comes home, when they are both in England, simply to relax. Susan can offer him food and comfort and domestic security; but what, outside the bedroom, does he have to offer her? Thanks to her father's trust, she is financially independent. If David were to leave, she would still have her home, her sons, her income, her hobbies. Without Kara, what has she in common with him?

Another disturbing thought follows from this. Hugh's reason for wanting to limit his family to his five much-loved sons is not the same reason that is prompting her own present decision, but the effect will be the same. They need never have divorced. But no, that's not right either. She wanted Kara; and desperately now she wants Kara still. It is just that Kara's absence is making it insistently clear to her that she still loves Hugh more than she has ever loved David.

This is disloyal and unfair, but she is

unable to dismiss it from her mind as she tosses restlessly through the small hours of the night. But tomorrow, in the sunshine, everything will seem different. So at least she tries to persuade herself.

But tomorrow, when it comes, brings with it no cheer. Susan herself, although now recovered from her miscarriage, is tired after an almost sleepless night. Peter and the boys settle down in the schoolroom as usual after breakfast, but she can tell from the quietness that they are all low in spirits and are slogging on through school textbooks with none of the liveliness that Peter originally brought to the lessons. As for David, he is unusually silent; he is working himself up to something.

In the middle of the morning Hugh comes to call. Even he has lost all his usual ebullience and looks tired and strained.

'I've been up at The Eyrie, keeping an eye on that Yilmaz chap while he goes through the house and the account books. He's finished now, so I'll be getting back to work. But I'm proposing to come back this evening to dig around for myself and see if I can sort out what's been going on. I thought I'd better warn you in case you saw the lights and wondered.'

'Did they find anything?' asks Susan.

Hugh sighs. 'There was a folder of bank statements. Obviously they're going to ask

Dad to account for all the sums paid in. I really don't know if he'll be able to. There did seem to be more in his account than I might have expected.'

Susan can think of no useful comment. 'Will you stay and have a cup of coffee?' she asks instead.

'No, thanks. I don't like to leave my team unsupervised for too long. 'Bye for now.'

David, who has been present for this conversation, although not included in it, uses it after Hugh's departure as a cue for what he has been wanting to say.

'Susan, like Hugh I need to get back to work. As you know, we're not supposed to be away for more than three weeks at a time. Naturally, in the circumstances, I was given compassionate leave. But I feel now that there's nothing more to be gained by staying out here. We've got the publicity moving. The next step is to put pressure on the Foreign Office, and that's most easily done in England. As long as the police here know how to make contact, there's no point in hanging around.'

'Yes, I expect you're right. You go. I'll be OK.'

'I'm not talking about leaving you and going back on my own, for heaven's sake! Of course you must come too. The whole family.'

'That's not possible. Hugh has the right—'

'If Hugh wants to stick to the letter of the law on access rights, then he can look after his sons himself, instead of using you as a sort of unpaid housekeeper. But this whole system is ridiculous—going off for so long at a time, taking the boys out of school. We'll have to make a more sensible arrangement in future. For the moment, Hugh must surely understand how disturbing it is for the boys to stay here, wondering whether there's someone prowling around, wondering who may be the next one to be snatched. Well, that's up to him. But your place is with me, at home.'

'I can't leave here.' Susan's voice is faint with astonishment that such a suggestion should ever be made. 'I must be here when they find Kara.'

'Susan, darling, look at this sensibly.' David grips her hands in an effort to persuade her. 'You can't really believe that Kara is still in Turkey. If she'd been kidnapped for ransom, we'd have heard by now. There must have been some other reason for taking her, and the first thing they'd do would be to get her out of the country. We need to be back in England so that we can make direct contact with Interpol. Stuck out here, we're too helpless. Just waiting for something to happen isn't good enough. We must take active steps ourselves.'

'She can't have left the country,' Susan argues. 'I've got her passport.'

There is a silence: the kind of silence that makes Susan realise that she is being stupid again. Not for the first time since his return, David is controlling any exasperation he may feel when she speaks without thinking, but his restraint is almost more humiliating than a gentle correction would be. She has to work out for herself what kind of mistake she has made this time.

It doesn't take long. What difference would a passport make to a kidnapper? No one would walk up to a frontier post holding the hand of an unwilling child. She would have to be sedated and hidden. In the boot of a car, probably. A small parcel, tucked under a blanket. The picture is too vivid to be endured—and so are the implications of it.

'No!' It has been bad enough envisaging Kara among strangers somewhere in Turkey, but the thought that she could be anywhere in the world by now overwhelms Susan with terror. She tries to get a grip on herself. 'I'm sorry, David. I expect what you say is sensible, but I don't feel sensible. I have to stay. I have to be here for her. You go back. That's all right. But

I'm not coming with you.'

David does not give up easily, and the insistence with which he tells her that she is acting foolishly leads to a quarrel. The rage they should both be directing only against Kara's abductor is preposterously turned against each other. Although David does not in so many words claim that by her lack of care she is responsible for their daughter's disappearance, Susan's own feeling of guilt makes her read the accusation into even the faintest criticism and she defends herself more vigorously than is justifiable. By the time David sulkily packs his own bag and asks Peter to drive him to Antalya airport, they are both angry. Just when they should be closest to each other, united in grief! Susan can't comprehend how this can have happened.

That evening, tired after her sleepless night, she goes very early to bed without even bothering to have supper. She has no appetite, and Peter can look after the boys. But each time that her eyes start to close she has a mental picture of a small child, sedated, in the boot of a car. Going where? She jerks herself awake again. She needs to sleep, but is afraid of what sleep may bring. For perhaps an hour she fights her tiredness, but in the end the struggle is lost and she tumbles into the darkness of a nightmare.

Chapter Twenty

Kara is four years old. Wearing nothing but her white cotton knickers, she has been rolled up in a blanket and tied tightly with her arms down her sides so that she is unable to move her hands. She is lying in the boot of a car which is being driven fast over a rough road. In spite of the blanket, every bump bruises her and the darkness terrifies her. Where is Mummy? Where is Daddy? Why are they allowing this to happen to her? She tries to express her fear in a scream, but a wide piece of sticky tape is sealing her lips.

A radio is turned on. It is playing loud music, with drums thumping at her ears. The car comes to a halt. She can hear voices outside. She tries to call out, but only a sort of grunt emerges. She wriggles around in an attempt to bang against the metal of the boot, but she is wearing no shoes and her soft, small feet do not make any noise. The car drives on. The road has become smoother, but that is no consolation. How will Mummy and Daddy ever be able to find her again?

Kara is crying now, but not in any of her

usual ways. In the past she has often fallen down and hurt herself and Mummy has heard her sobs and come to kiss her better. Or she has cried with rage and frustration because the boys won't let her play; and one of them has tried to explain patiently, if not always successfully, that their games would not be safe for her; she will be able to join in when she is older. Now, though, she is crying in fear, and there is no one to comfort her. Her shoulders shake and tears run down her cheeks, but she is still unable to make any sound. Her nose begins to run and becomes stuffy. She can't breathe through her mouth. She can't breathe properly through her nose. She can't breathe. She can't breathe. She is overwhelmed by terror.

Kara is still four years old, but she has been taken from the car. Her knickers are wet and dirty. A woman whom she has never seen before takes them off and gives her a bath. She doesn't speak, and Kara herself feels unable to open her mouth even although the tape has been painfully stripped away. She allows herself to be cleaned and dried. She doesn't know where she is.

Now she is lying on a bed, with no clothes on and no sheet to cover her. A bright light shines down into her eyes.

She can tell that there are people standing around the bed, but the light is so bright that she can't see their faces. A finger touches her face. It doesn't hurt her, but she doesn't like it. It touches each eye in turn and then strokes down her nose, over her chin, down the middle of her body. It pauses for a moment on her belly button and then continues down, parting the little lips between her legs, lingering on the parts of her which no one is supposed to touch except Mummy or Rosie or Esin when they bathe her, or a doctor if she is ill.

She is not ill now, but merely frozen with unhappiness and bewilderment. The man to whom the finger belongs moves a little to one side, and for a second or two she can see his face. He is nodding his head.

It is Kara's fifth birthday, although even Kara herself is not aware of this. On all her other birthdays she has had a party at The Lookout. Her brothers are always specially nice to her on her birthday. She is the Birthday Girl, and for once can choose what games to play; no one will tell her that she is too small. They all give her presents. Murdo makes up a special tune to play as she cuts her birthday cake. There is a small parcel from Mummy and Daddy as well, but her real present will be waiting at home in England. To celebrate her fifth birthday they have bought a proper bicycle, with two little side wheels to stop her from losing her balance. But nobody in this strange country knows that it is her birthday. She will never have a chance to ride the bicycle.

She has become completely silent. All around her people are speaking in a language she doesn't understand. They try to show her what they mean by moving their hands and arms a lot, pointing and acting, but she refuses to watch. Something of what they are trying to teach her does in fact become clear, but she doesn't admit it.

A stranger is pretending to be her mummy. Kara is supposed to call her Mama, but she won't. The Mama woman doesn't call her Kara, but Sophia. Kara refuses to answer to that name. Every time she refuses, she is slapped. The slaps are becoming harder. Soon she will have to start coming when she is called. But she will only do it sulkily. She sulks all the time, refusing to speak or to smile. She is angry, because her real mummy and daddy don't want her any more. They only want to have boys. She was a nuisance to them and so they have let someone take her away.

No, Kara. Never believe that. Never. A different dream, please.

Kara is six, but she is not Kara any more. Her name is Arianna and she lives in a big house with a swimming pool. She is looked after by someone called Maria. Maria is kind, and so are the two people who are her parents now. They speak a little English at first: just enough to tell her that she has become their daughter. But Maria is teaching her new words every day and soon there is no more English spoken in the house.

Arianna is told every Sunday how pretty she is. A dressmaker makes new clothes for her at Easter and Christmas and whenever she grows too big for the old ones. Maria ties ribbons in her hair and admires the bracelets which jangle on her wrists. She can eat sweets whenever she wants. A day has been chosen to count as her birthday, and she is given a puppy of her own. There are no other children in the house. She is the only one, the special one, the chosen one.

She can still just remember that once upon a time she had brothers, but they have all in an odd way merged into one. She has a vague picture of a boyish face, but is not sure whose face it is. She is unable to remember her first father at all. Of her first mother she retains an impression of warm hugs and sweet smells and loving smiles, but the memory is fading fast. She has been told that her first mother is dead, and that must be true, because otherwise she would surely never have let Arianna go.

Kara is seven years old and her name is Ingrid. Her parents are both dead and she lives with her uncle. He used to live by himself before he started looking after her, but now he has someone called Greta to do the housework and prepare the tea while he is out at work. His house is very cold and has hardly any toys for Ingrid to play with. Greta is not very friendly, so Ingrid is lonely in the house; but she is happy at school. By now she has learned to understand the language her schoolmates speak and because she is clever she is doing well in class. She is especially good at English lessons, and often is able to think of words that she can't remember having been taught.

Uncle Bernhardt has told her stories about her mother and father, and her life with them before the fire which killed them, but she doesn't seem to remember any of the incidents he describes. She wishes there were some photographs; but everything was destroyed in the fire.

From Monday to Friday Uncle Bernhardt is at work and Ingrid hardly sees him. But at weekends, when Greta isn't there, he becomes friendly. He takes her for walks in the country or holds her on his knee in fairground rides. Wherever they go, he takes her photograph. Sometimes she has to keep still and sometimes he films her doing cartwheels or turning somersaults. He calls her his little film star.

Playing at film stars is his special Sunday game. There is a room at the top of his house which has been made to look like a tent—except that not many tents have mirrors in such surprising places. Instead of an ordinary bed, there is a mattress on the floor, covered with rugs and cloths. Uncle Bernhardt gets Ingrid to sit on the mattress wearing just her knickers.

Their game is that he says just a word, like 'bored' or 'excited' or a sentence like 'your cat has been run over' or 'the person you love most in the world has just come into the room', and she has to act whatever he says. Sometimes he makes her a present of a new pair of knickers, made of lace, and goes on filming while she takes off the school pair and puts the new ones on instead. He doesn't very often touch her, except to make her lie in a particular position or stretch her arms up in a special way. But once or twice he has suggested that she should wear stockings and a suspender belt, and then he helps her to do up the suspenders. She had better not talk about being a film star when she is at school, he tells her: the others will be jealous.

Kara is eight years old and her name seems to be different every few weeks. She keeps being told to make journeys in aeroplanes, although she doesn't know why; and almost as soon as she arrives somewhere she is told to go back again. When she flies out of England she is an Unaccompanied Young Passenger. She wears a name pinned to her coat, which helps her to remember who she is this time, and both in the airport and on the plane there are friendly hostesses to look after her. They give her books to read and games to play and orange juice to drink, and they make sure that she never gets lost. When she arrives in Lagos she is sometimes frightened because there are so many people shouting and milling around and everything smells of sweat; but a man called Billy is there to meet her and she is told that she has been a good girl.

When she flies the other way, from Lagos to London, there is always someone with her, although not the same person each time. Sometimes she has a small suitcase to carry and sometimes she wears a satchel on her back. The suitcase is filled with books, but she is never allowed to read them, and the satchel is filled with soft toys, but she is never allowed to play with them.

If anyone at Heathrow or Gatwick asks her, she has been told to say that she is being taken back to boarding school. Her father is too busy to make the journey himself, so he has asked his personal assistant to look after her instead. Kara knows that this is all a lie, because she hasn't got a father and she isn't going to school at all. But if she doesn't do what she is told she will be whipped.

Billy's whip is a stick with something like an animal's tail fixed on to it. He has only whipped her once; to show her what it would be like, he said. He promised not to hit her very hard, but it was hard enough to make her cry out with pain and the red line across her shoulders went on hurting for a long time. It wasn't fair, because she hadn't done anything naughty to deserve it. She doesn't want to be whipped again and so she continues to fly between Lagos and London, ready to tell lies if anyone ever asks her.

Kara is nine years old and she has no name. When people want her, they simply point. She has no home either. She lives for a few weeks at a time in a tent made of animal skins, and then one day the tent is rolled up and strapped on to camels and she has to start walking to a new place. Sometimes she walks through deserts, which are very hot, and sometimes she climbs high into mountain ranges, which are very cold.

The women who ride on the camels or horses, while she walks beside them, are dressed like princesses. They wear gold necklaces and dozens of gold bracelets and three or four skirts at the same time, made of bright colours and sometimes embroidered in gold or silver thread. But they don't smell like princesses. They are dirty, and Kara is dirty as well. She is given all the most unpleasant jobs to do and there is never enough clean water to wash more than her hands. Her face has become quite brown, and she doesn't think it will ever wash clean again.

She is unhappy on these long walks, which seem to go on for ever. But one day the tribe arrives at a town and pitches its tents just outside the walls. There is plenty of water here and she is told to wash herself all over. Then she is given a new dress and her old rags are thrown away.

She has not had much to do with the men of the tribe while they are on the move, but now one of them takes her into the town, where there is a busy market place. He holds on to her wrist and begins to shout. People gather round in a circle, staring at her. A woman comes up to pinch the muscles of her arms, and takes out a purse. Kara realises that she is being sold. Although she has never been happy with the wandering tribe, she is frightened at the thought of leaving them and wonders whether the woman will be kind.

The man holding her wrist is still shouting, and now the woman who wanted to buy her is elbowed aside. A man is taking out his purse instead. He is a very tall man, wearing a grey cotton gown which comes down to his ankles. He looks her up and down in a way that she doesn't like. Then he smiles; but it is not a friendly smile. He is not smiling at Kara, but about her. He is smiling because he has bought her and can do whatever he wants with her. Kara is sure that there is something evil about him. Terrified, she opens her mouth to scream, but no sound comes out.

No! No, not that. Something else quickly.

Kara is ten years old and she is Arianna again. Maria is still looking after her and her father is richer than ever. Her dresses are even more beautifully made than before; she goes to dancing classes and has learned to play the piano. When she is eleven she will be sent to school in Switzerland. One day, her father tells her, she will be the most beautiful woman in the world and will marry a rich man who will buy her presents and give her everything she wants. But until then she is fortunate to have a mother and father who have always wanted a daughter just like her. She is a lucky little girl. Cling on to that. She is a lucky girl.

Kara is eleven years old. Her name is Yasmin and she lives in a very hot country. The household seems to consist mainly of women and children and servants. Sometimes she hears men talking in one of the courtyards, but she never sees them. She has been taught to read and write, but she doesn't go to school: in fact, she hardly ever leaves the house. She doesn't have the same complexion as the other children, and none of the women seems to be specially fond of her, so perhaps she had a different mother once upon a time; but she can't remember anything about that.

Now that she is eleven, it's time for her to earn her living. One of the women leads her across a courtyard and hands her over to a man she has never seen before. He orders her to follow him and leads the way through narrow, dusty, crowded streets. Yasmin could run away if she chose, but she has nowhere to go and no money—and perhaps she will enjoy the work that has been found for her. So she follows as she has been told.

She is taken to a very large house. A woman is waiting to greet her in a hall which has sofas and divans all round the walls. The woman has dyed her hair red, which doesn't suit her, but apart from that she looks quite ordinary. She says that the girl must be examined by a doctor, to make sure that she is fit for work. This seems reasonable, although it is the first time that Yasmin has ever had to take her clothes off in front of a man. She shivers with cold and thinness and nervousness as she lies down and allows him to press and poke.

By the time she has dressed again, the man who brought her to the house has gone. The red-haired woman takes her to a bedroom. The light bulb is pink, which seems odd, and the room is very small, but it looks comfortable. Yasmin sits down on the bed and waits to be told what sort of work she will be expected to do.

There seem to be a lot of people living in the house. Footsteps come and go along the corridor outside. Yasmin waits patiently, wondering when she will be given something to eat. At last the door opens and a man comes into the room.

He is a large man, very tall and very fat. He has a dark moustache and an oddly shaped beard curving round his chin in a way which makes his mouth look cruel. He smiles, but she doesn't like his smile. Standing up, she tries to back away from him, but there is nowhere to go. He steps forward, standing so close that his stomach is pressed against her. She tries to push him away, but lacks the strength. He is still smiling as he bends down to take off her clothes.

'No! No, not that! No! No!'

This time the sounds break out of Susan's nightmare. She screams, over and over again. Her body is drenched with sweat as she jerks herself upright in the bed. She has lost control of herself. There is nothing she can do to save Kara. She continues to scream.

Chapter Twenty-One

Hugh has found a notebook in his father's bedroom and doesn't like the look of it. It was concealed inside what appears at first sight to be a coat hanger but is in fact designed as a mini-safe. Yilmaz has failed to discover this hiding place. Hugh, when he has at last located the tiny key which opens it, wishes that he had failed as well.

He sits cross-legged on the floor, staring at a list of dates. They cover a period of almost eight years, and the last of them is the day on which his father left for his most recent climbing trip: the day on which Kara Rolph disappeared: the day before the police, searching for a child, discovered instead a hoard of antiques waiting to be collected. Against every date except the last one is written a sum of money.

While he tries to decide what to do, anger and disappointment mingle with fear of what will happen to his father.

As an archaeologist and teacher he has always preached the importance of recording the exact site and position in which any antique work of art is discovered. When a work is stolen and sold, it not only lacks a true provenance but is frequently given a false one in order to avoid awkward questions. It is of no further use to scholars and instead may lead them on a false trail.

As a son, he is being forced to see in a new light the father he has always admired. It was his father who first introduced him to the mysteries of old stones, who held him by the hand while pointing to the carved inscriptions and decorations on the Lycian tombs and describing the little that was known about the craftsmen who made them. Is this the same man who is prepared to make money out of theft and desecration? And is it Hugh's duty to betray him or to betray his own principles of scholarship?

His dilemma is interrupted by a harsh buzzing which he recognises as coming from the intercom linking The Eyrie with The Lookout. Perhaps he is going to be invited to dinner. But no, that isn't very likely. David's expression, on seeing him for the second time in two days, was not that of a welcoming host. He lifts the receiver.

'Hello.'

'It's me, Peter. Hugh, Susan's having hysterics. She was trapped in a nightmare, I think. I can't stop her and the boys are getting in a bit of a panic. Perhaps she ought to have a doctor. But if you could come down...?'

'Yes, of course. Straight away.' Hugh shouts to tell the servants where he is going and covers the rough ground at a run. He is almost at the house when he realises that he has left the notebook on view in his father's bedroom. But it doesn't matter. He'll be back there before any police are likely to return.

The three elder boys are looking out for him anxiously and show their relief at his arrival.

'She won't stop screaming,' says Murdo. 'Peter tried to wake her up because he thought it was a bad dream, but she won't open her eyes. And she won't answer when we talk to her.'

'OK, leave it to me. Look, it's nearly ten o'clock. Time you were in bed.'

'Donnie and Calum are already.'

'Well, off you three go as well. And try not to worry too much. It's natural for a mother to be terribly upset when something like this has happened. And much better to make a noise, scream it out, than try to pretend nothing's wrong. We'll talk about it later.'

Peter is standing outside Susan's bedroom.

'I tried to hold her and bring her out of it, but she won't...' His voice fades helplessly away. He is still a young man, and out of his depth in this family tragedy.

'Where's David?' Hugh asks him.

'He's gone back to England. He tried to get Susan and the boys to go with him, but she wouldn't. They had a bit of a row. We couldn't help hearing. That may have something to do with her being so upset again.'

Hugh nods and goes into the bedroom, closing the door behind him. The screams, which he could hear even before he stepped inside the house, have abated slightly because she has turned her face into the pillow in an effort to muffle the sound. But her breath is coming in painful gasps and she is expelling it again in a mixture of small shrieks and moans.

Hugh grasps her shoulders firmly.

'Susie, love, it's Hugh. You must calm down, sweetheart. You're frightening the boys. Steady now. Steady.'

Her body shudders with effort as she does her best to obey, but noisy sobs and groans still break through.

'Tell me about it,' he says gently. 'Was it a bad dream?'

'It's what's going to happen. I can see it all.'

'Not really, you can't. You're imagining things that are never going to come true. Talk me through them. Just hold on a moment, though, while I turn off the light.'

Before moving to do that, he stands up and looks down for a moment at the convulsive movements of her shoulders. Taking a quick decision, he unfastens his shirt and trousers and pulls them off. As soon as the room is dark he slides into the bed beside her, wearing only his boxer shorts. He presses his body close against her back—as comfort, not in passion. His hand strokes her arm gently, repetitively. When at last she ceases to groan, he turns her so that she is lying on her back.

'Open your eyes,' he commands. 'Are they open? Sure? Now tell me what you've been dreaming.'

'I have this picture. Every time I close my eyes. Of Kara sitting in an Amsterdam window, for sale, and men coming in and out and, and...'

She is starting to cry again. Hugh continues to stroke her skin, but can tell that she is not aware of his touch.

'And then when I fall asleep I imagine all the ways she might have got there. All the things that must have happened on the way. All the pain and fear. And the worst of it, even more than the men buying her and hurting her, is that she'll think I let it happen. She'll believe that she must have had a mother who didn't love her.'

'Tell me about all those things you think happened on the way. Keep your eyes open while you talk.'

He listens without interrupting as she paints one vivid picture after another. Only when she has come to an end does he try to argue her fears away.

'You're on the wrong track here, Susie

267

love. Those girls in the Amsterdam windows are there because they want to be, because they're making a good living. There are plenty of girls all over the world who actually choose to be prostitutes, and thousands more who go into the life more or less willingly because they can't find any better way of supporting their families. No one has any need to steal a child for that purpose, especially a small child who'd have to be fed and looked after for years before she was any use. If Kara's been stolen, it's because there are people in Europe who want a child of their own to love. Hang on to that.'

'Even if that were true, just think how frightened she must be now. Such a small person in such a huge, strange world. But I don't believe it *is* true. I think...'

She is about to start crying again. Hugh turns her on to her side, so that they are lying face to face, and presses her head against his chest. How often in the past they have lain like this, talking in the darkness about the boys, their plans for the future, their love for each other! He gives a deep sigh, wishing that nothing had changed.

Until this moment Susan has been lying passively in his arms, allowing him to move her and stroke her but without making any response. Now, though, she grips him tightly as she prepares to make a confession.

'It would be better if she were dead. While I was having those dreams, I kept trying to wake myself up, but the only way out of the nightmare was to think that she might be dead. I don't mean that I *want* her to be, of course I don't. But if she is, it would help me to know. I told Tam—was it yesterday or the day before?—that I didn't want to be told that she was dead, because I had to be able to go on hoping. But it's not hoping; it's fearing. I do need to know, after all. But how can I ever find out? I may have to spend the rest of my life not knowing.'

There is nothing that Hugh can say. Susan has not in the past been good at facing up to unpleasant facts, but she is facing this one and it will bring her no comfort in the long run to talk about possible happy endings. He tightens his embrace.

Everything about Susan is familiar to him: the shape of her, the smell of her, the sound of her breathing, the way their bodies fit with each other. He can tell that her need for him is as desperate as his for her, and he feels no guilt, but only an urgent desire. They have sworn to love each other until death shall part them. It is David who is the interloper—and Susan, most certainly, is not thinking about David now. This is a form of comfort which she is able to accept.

In the years since their divorce High has not led a celibate life, but there has been no one important. There is a sense in which he has kept himself for Susan and now that the moment has come it is not enough to love her once, or even twice. Exhausted at last, he turns on to his back. Kara and David are both forgotten. Surely he and Susan can somehow start again? And while he daydreams, Susan sleeps peacefully beside him. For a few hours at least he has drawn her out of the nightmare.

Chapter Twenty-Two

Hugh is wakened by the sound of his sons' early-morning bustle. Susan continues to sleep as he lies without moving, listening for the moment when they are all assembled round the breakfast table. Then he will slip unobtrusively into the room that has been abandoned by the Turkish girl. Not that he cares about being found in bed with the woman whom he once again thinks of as his wife, but for her sake he ought to observe the conventions of adultery.

This plan is foiled by Donnie, who enters the room without knocking. While Roy holds open the door for him, he carefully carries in a tray which he has prepared.

'Breakfast in bed,' he announces, shaking his mother's shoulder to wake her. He shows no surprise at seeing his father in bed beside her: it is the natural place for him to be. But Hugh has not been catered for. Donnie looks at him inquiringly.

'Would you like some as well, Dad?'

'No thanks, Donnie. I'll get up and join you. Shut the door after you, will you?'

Susan, blinking sleep away, pulls herself up in the bed. She tries and fails to control a smile.

'Did we—?'

'Of course we did. Several times. And very nice it was, too.'

Stretching her arms above her head, she is happy for a moment. She has not yet remembered about Kara.

'I shall have to ask the boys to be discreet,' is all she says.

'Do you think they will?'

'Oh yes. They'd be on your side, not David's, in any case. And they're good at keeping secrets. Tam makes them swear oaths. I shudder to think what he threatens them with if they sneak.'

'I miss all that,' Hugh tells her fiercely.
'Not just you.' He kisses her to make it
clear how much he misses her. 'It's not
right, not seeing how the boys are growing
up. Every year I notice these huge leaps in
how they've changed. But I ought to be
there all the time, sharing it.'

'Yes,' agrees Susan. 'I'm sorry.'

Briefly he wonders whether to press the
point into a serious discussion. But this
doesn't seem the right time. He makes
for the shower room before dressing again
in the clothes he wore on the previous
evening.

Before joining the others for breakfast,
he steps outside to enjoy the dawn air. To
his surprise, the man from the Department
of Antiquities is sitting on the edge of one
of the verandahs, obviously waiting for him
to appear.

'Dr Sutherland's servants told me I
might find you here,' says Yilmaz. 'I
have to thank you for your discovery of
your father's notebook.'

Oh, God! Hugh swallows a lump in his
throat which threatens to choke him. He
had forgotten all about the notebook.

Yilmaz has no difficulty in understanding
his horror.

'As a scholar, you must have found it a
difficult point of ethics. A hard decision,
whether to destroy the notes or hand

272

them to me. If you would prefer it to be thought that I made the discovery without your help, that would of course be to my professional advantage, as well as avoiding any personal recriminations within your family.'

There is a question mark in his voice, but Hugh is unable to speak. He is frozen with the enormity of what he has done and of what is inevitably going to happen to his father. Perhaps it would have happened anyway. There are those unexplained sums of money in bank accounts. But that doesn't excuse Hugh's own contribution to what will become the prosecution case.

'You ought to be looking for the child,' he croaks at last, anxious not to make any remark which might further strengthen the indictment against his father.

'You can help me in that search too, Professor Sutherland.' Yilmaz leans back against one of the posts which support the verandah's roof. His thickset body is relaxed and there is an easy smile on his fleshy face.

'How?'

'Well, to begin with, the girl Esin has been traced. She claims that she knows nothing of Kara's whereabouts. She ran away because she felt guilty at her neglect of her charge, and ashamed when she realised that it would be necessary to confess the reason for it.'

'Which was?'

'That she was in bed with your tutor. Did you not know? Anyway, I accept her story as true.'

'Then what—?'

'I don't believe that your father was involved in any way. It was not at all to his advantage that his property should be so thoroughly searched at just this time. Nor do I believe any of the possibilities that so much distress your wife—your ex-wife. Terrorists, kidnappers, nomads.' Yilmaz shakes his head dismissively. 'I have felt sure from the start, and I feel sure still, that your sons, or one of them, could provide the vital piece of information. They may not understand the value of what they know. But if there is any clue waiting to be found, it is inside their heads.'

'Have you asked them?'

'I have asked each boy individually, with none of the others listening. But it may be that they have pledged together to keep a secret. They tell me nothing. I have asked their tutor to discover what he can, and he has failed. I have asked their mother also, but she will not even consider the possibility that they can be in any way concerned. So now I am asking you. It is not good for anyone that the mystery should be left unsolved.'

Hugh's immediate instinct is to refuse. Already, by accident, he has betrayed his father. He can surely not be expected now to betray one of his sons, should he discover some unhappy secret. But two things make him pause. Less than half an hour ago Susan has talked of secrets and of Tam's authority over his brothers. If there is anything to be discovered, it will be just as well for their father, rather than a Turkish investigator, to discover it, for then Hugh can consider what best to do.

The second argument is more compelling still. Susan needs to know the truth.

'I'll see what I can find out,' he says huskily. 'But about my father...'

Yilmaz shrugs his shoulders. 'He knew the risks. Next time I come here I'll give you the name of a good lawyer in Istanbul. But if the law has been broken, justice must be done. I think, Professor Sutherland, that you should persuade Mrs Rolph to take your sons back to England.'

Hugh has no problem in understanding that Yilmaz is giving him a warning rather than making a threat. It would be the last straw for Susan if any of her sons were to be caught up in the long processes of Turkish justice.

'I quite agree,' he says quietly. 'She

275

wouldn't listen to her husband when he said the same thing. But she only comes here for my sake. If I tell her to leave, she will.'

He considers what he will say as he watches Yilmaz rise to his feet and walk back towards The Eyrie. Although he joins the boys for breakfast, he eats almost in silence. By the time he has finished, his mind is made up.

'Tam, come outside with me, will you? There's something I want to talk about.'

It is the kind of summons to make any twelve-year-old search his conscience uneasily and Tam is no exception. Only with reluctance does he follow his father out to the football area, but he manages to postpone any unwanted interrogation with a quick question of his own.

'Dad, are you and Mum going to get together again?'

'Would you like that?'

'Of course we would.'

'It would be a bit hard on David, of course,' Hugh suggests. 'To lose Kara and then to lose his wife as well.'

Tam shrugs his shoulders, making it clear that he doesn't care about David. It is tempting for Hugh to ask his eldest son for an opinion on the state of that marriage, but he manages to resist.

'I'm going to ask your mother to take

you all back home,' he says instead. 'She needs to get away from here. I shall miss you, of course, but I'll try to fix myself a couple of weeks in England before I go back to Texas, and maybe we can all have a holiday together.'

Tam nods, recognising that this is not the central point of the conversation.

'But of course, she's not likely to budge until she's discovered what happened to Kara, and so that's something we've got to clear up. I think Kara is dead. I think you know that she is dead. None of the others is likely to tell me the truth unless you give them permission, and that's why I'm asking you.'

'I don't know—'

'Hold it, Tam.' Hugh, who has been pacing up and down the scythed area of scrubland, stops and turns to face his son. 'I don't want you to lie to me. I'm a historian. Truth is very important to me. People who tell lies muddle up history and make it impossible for anyone to trust them. I've already had to face the possibility that my father may have done just that. I don't want to be deceived by my son as well. If Kara is dead, it's very important that your mother should know.'

'No, it isn't.' Tam's unbroken voice is high with indignation. 'She said herself, she didn't want to know. She said it the first time when she was screaming. I don't mean the time yesterday, before you came. It was when she saw one of the statues and thought it was Kara's body. She said she couldn't bear the thought of Kara being dead. She specially said that if that was what had happened, she wouldn't want to know. She wants to go on hoping. She's never liked to think of anything being dead. She won't swat mosquitoes. And when Prince was run over last Christmas, she wouldn't even come and look at him. We had to bury him all by ourselves.'

'Ah. I think I see. Tam, you've got to believe me when I tell you that she's changed her mind on this. You heard her screaming last night, after she had that nightmare, didn't you?'

Tam nods.

'Was it worse than the time before?'

He nods again. There is a troubled expression on his face.

'It's because she's recognised that in a sense hoping and fearing go together. She's started to realise how unhappy Kara will be if she's still alive, and to imagine what terrible things might happen to her in the future; and she can't bear it. What she is feeling now—and you can check it with her if you don't believe me—is that naturally she hopes that Kara isn't dead. But if that is the case, then it's very important indeed that she should know.'

It is asking a lot of a twelve-year-old to keep pace with the shifts of an adult's emotions, and Hugh is careful not to press Tam faster than he can easily go.

'No need to say anything just now,' he tells his son. 'I realise that if there are any secrets, they may not be yours. I'll give you time to discuss all this with the rest of the gang. But there is one other thing you ought to consider. A feeling of guilt is a terrible thing to live with.'

'That's what teachers always say.'

'Then teachers are right. Even something like cheating in an exam will change you, although you may not be aware of it at the time. And when someone has reason to feel guilty about a bigger thing, which can never be put right, it can ruin his whole life. Honestly, Tam. There's only one way to escape from that kind of guilt, and that's to own up to it before you're found out. Whatever the punishment you may get from someone else, it won't be as bad as the punishment you'll inflict on yourself. I'm not necessarily talking about you personally, but whoever it might apply to. If it's one of the younger ones, he can't be expected to understand the damage that can be done. You can understand it, though, and you must persuade your brothers.'

Tam, who is probably not convinced by this part of the argument, doesn't answer.

'Is that all?' he asks.

'Yes.' Hugh pauses and then speaks more briskly. 'I'm going to spend the day here, Tam, to look after your mother. And so I shall ask Peter whether he'd be willing to drive over to Termessus and keep an eye on the site for me. I'd like you all to go with him. It will give you a chance to have a private talk. You've got a lot to think about.'

Tam is glad to escape. Hugh has a word with Peter and then telephones to inquire about booking airline seats. The plane that flies from Antalya to Istanbul is not a large one, and travel agencies make their block bookings well ahead. But a cancellation has left six seats free tomorrow. That will do. Peter can travel separately. Hugh makes a provisional reservation and then goes out to wave the boys goodbye as Peter drives off. Squashed up together, the four younger boys look pleased about the interruption to their lessons. What will their mood be when they return?

Chapter Twenty-Three

Susan is still in bed when Peter and the boys leave, but her reluctance to get up has nothing to do with her health. She has had a good night's sleep and has put the miscarriage behind her, both mentally and physically. The pregnancy was not, after all, very far advanced. Her reaction to the loss of the baby was a matter more of shock and disappointment than of pain. If she is feeling lazy now, it is because she is in no hurry to wash away the smell of Hugh's body; the smell of love.

She had forgotten how exciting Hugh was as a lover, and how enthusiastically he played his part as husband and father. At the time of their divorce, resentment of his decision to have no more children caused her to put out of her mind his bubbly personality, the wholeheartedness with which he would devote time to his sons, the praise which he would heap on her paintings, or even on the way in which she ran their home. Now, lying in bed, she remembers all that.

David is quite different—but that doesn't mean that she has any cause for complaint.

He adores Kara, is loving towards his wife and behaves in a friendly manner towards his stepsons. If he takes it too much for granted that his household will run smoothly without much effort on his own part—well, so do most men. If her marriage has become somehow flat and predictable, lacking in the spark of excitement which she once enjoyed—well, so do most marriages, no doubt, after the honeymoon is over. It is unfair to compare her two husbands.

Nevertheless, swinging her legs out of bed at last, she sighs at her own stupidity in provoking Hugh to divorce her. She still feels that she was justified in being angry about the vasectomy—although at this moment she has good reason to be glad about the operation, which means that there is no danger of David finding himself with a child who happens to have the Sutherland sandy hair and blue eyes. But that anger did not excuse her own subsequent behaviour. And now she is cheating on David just as earlier she cheated on Hugh.

'I ought to feel guilty,' she exclaims aloud as she opens the shutters to let the sunlight flood in. 'But I don't!' She doesn't feel like an adulteress. She just feels happy.

If only she could have decided earlier, as she decided a day or two ago, that she would have no more children. Hugh was right all the time. Five are enough.

But she has six. That is the moment when, for the first time since waking that morning, she remembers Kara. Outside her bedroom the sun continues to beat down on mountains and sea, but through her clouded eyes the day has become dark and she shivers with a chill which comes from the heart.

Hugh is waiting for her on the verandah. He tells her of the plane reservations he has made and she nods in acceptance. Guilt has replaced happiness. She can't stay here. If David has lost his only daughter, he mustn't be robbed of his wife as well. Packing up will not take long, but she starts to collect things together while Hugh confirms the reservations and makes the necessary onward booking from Istanbul to London.

She is still in a listless mood when Peter brings the boys back for a late lunch. Hugh has apparently told him to do this, since there would not be enough food available on the site. Susan does now try to make an effort. She is not exactly ashamed of herself for breaking down in front of her sons but it is time to show more self-control and to demonstrate that she loves them just as much as their missing sister.

Hugh is watching the boys with a particular interest. Susan, who knows him

283

so well, can always tell when he is in his observing mode; his concentration narrows even while his words and gestures are as expansive as usual. The boys too are in an unusual mood. They keep looking at Roy. He is just about to say something when Susan sends them off to wash their hands; and when they return they wait for Roy again.

'Mum, I did the dice thing while we were at Termessus,' he begins when they are seated at the table.

'What do you mean, the dice thing?'

'Didn't Dad tell you about what he'd found carved on the walls?'

'Even if I did, you need to be more precise in your words,' Hugh tells him. ' "Thing" is not allowed.'

The boys grin at the familiar criticism, but then return to their food with a quietness which makes it clear that Roy is for some reason chatting on behalf of all of them. But now there is a second interruption. Captain Zeybel has arrived with a copy of Esin's statement. Yilmaz is with him, on this occasion returning to his role as interpreter. The two men indicate their willingness to wait until the meal is over.'

'Go on then, Roy,' Susan urges him; but her second son seems reluctant to continue.

'Out with it!' Hugh commands him. 'Start by telling your mother about the dice.'

'Well, Romans who couldn't afford to go to the oracles used to come to walls like the one Dad's found. To ask advice.' Roy is gabbling and his expression reveals uncertainty. He glances towards the two Turks as though wondering whether they can hear. 'While we were there, Tam said it would be fun to play it. We made some dice with four sides, like they used to have, and we each had a turn. Most of the answers didn't make much sense, but when it was my turn I asked, "Where is Kara?", and the throw was three fours and a six and a one.'

'And what was the answer?' Hugh is staring intently at Roy as though what he is saying is important. Yet it can't be, not really: Susan doesn't believe in fortune-telling. Nevertheless, she is waiting for the answer—and so, she can tell, is Yilmaz, whose hearing is obviously keen.

Roy swallows a lump in his throat. 'It said, "Three fours, six and one; this is the god's advice. Search in the house of the dead" '

There is a long silence before Susan pushes her plate aside. 'This is ridiculous. It isn't something to play games about.'

'No, wait a minute.' Hugh's voice is

gentle. 'That's your translation, I take it, Roy. What did the Latin say?'

Roy pulls a piece of paper out of his pocket and reads from it carefully. 'The numbers were written as numbers. Then it said, *"Hic est dei consilium. Mortui domum inspice."* '

'So what do you conclude from that?'

'That we ought to make another search. In any graveyards or—or tombs.'

'Surely all the tombs round here have been searched already?' Hugh looks interrogatively towards Yilmaz, who indicates with a nod of the head that he is following the conversation.

'Yes, I know, but perhaps one was missed out or perhaps there are hidden bits of something. Anyway, I just think we ought to do what the dice said.'

'Right!' Hugh speaks with a brisk decisiveness. Susan listens in bewilderment as the plan is translated to Captain Zeybel and two search parties formed. Hugh himself volunteers to explore the tombs that have been cut out of the cliff face. Although he is not as experienced a mountaineer as his father, he has been taught from boyhood how to climb.

'Hugh!' Susan clutches his arm to hold him back. 'You can't believe in this sort of thing. It's just superstition.'

He looks at her with an unusually serious

286

expression on his face.

'If the words Roy read out were actually incised on any piece of stone that we'd discovered, no, I wouldn't believe them for a moment. But they're not. There's no need for you to tell your friend Yilmaz that, though.'

'I don't understand.'

There is a grave sympathy in his eyes as he bends over to kiss her forehead. 'I think we're going to find Kara very soon, Susie, my love. You must prepare yourself. Be strong.'

There are a few moments of bustle while torches and ropes are collected and the police driver is called down to join in the search. Peter also volunteers to help, but the boys are told to keep away from the headland. They disappear in the direction of their castle before Susan has time to question them about the inscription which apparently does not exist.

She is being stupid again. Why are other people so quick to understand the significance of things that mean nothing to her? She reminds herself that she mustn't use the word 'things': it is on Hugh's blacklist. But as she sits alone at the untidy table, one statement at least remains clear. Kara is about to be discovered. And she cannot possibly be alive.

So it is that when for a second time

she sees a man—it is Yilmaz on this occasion—walking towards her with a small white bundle in his arms, she doesn't scream or faint. She is not even conscious of the fact that tears have begun to trickle down her cheeks. Although her chest is churning with emotion, she is able to give an impression of calmness as Yilmaz comes to a halt in front of her.

'I'm very, very sorry, Mrs Rolph.'

She nods her head in acceptance of his sympathy. 'May I look?'

'I think it will distress you if you do. In a hot country... It's better for your last memory of her to be as she was in life.'

Susan is silent, remembering. 'There is nothing in the world more beautiful than the body of a four-year-old girl,' she says talking to herself. 'Nothing.' Then she looks Yilmaz straight in the eye. 'I expect you're right, but I must see.'

Shrugging his shoulders, he stands unmoving while she takes the necessary two steps towards him, clenching her fists to give herself courage. For the whole of her life she has managed to evade the sight of death and even the thought of death. But this is something she must learn to face. Not merely that she herself will one day lie stiff and shrouded, but that death must come also to the five boys to whom she has given life. This lesson will strengthen her resolve to have no more children. She reaches forward, pulling away the white sheet in which Kara's body has been wrapped and lifting off the bloodstained T-shirt which covers her face.

Yilmaz was right to give her a warning. Half of Kara's head is covered with dried blood, in the middle of which is a hole where her left eye once was. The hole is filled with squirming maggots.

Susan gives a gasp of horror. The taste of bile fills her throat and mouth. She is going to be sick. No, she is not. She is going to faint. No, she will not. But her head is swimming. She covers up the hideous head and stretches her arms out towards Yilmaz.

Yilmaz is still holding Kara's body and is unable to support her. Susan grips his upper arms in order to prevent herself from falling. For a moment, as she breathes deeply, bringing herself under control, they are so close together that she can feel his breath on her lips. His eyes are full of sympathy. He is a kind man.

The faintness passes and she is able to stand unsupported again.

'Are you all right, Mrs Rolph?' he asks.

'Yes, thank you. I suppose I knew, really. I must have known all the time. In a way I've done my mourning already.

Perhaps the greatest pain is over now, for both of us.'

She turns to go into the house. Hugh is approaching Yilmaz and will deal with any formalities which have to be observed. But Yilmaz's next comment stops her in her tracks.

'The suspense is over for you, yes. But for me, there are still questions to be asked.'

'What do you mean?'

'Kara's body was found in the tomb in which the stolen artefacts were earlier discovered, and in which we hid our own substitutes: the tomb that was left empty after the arrests were made. I think we shall find that she died on the day you first realised that she had disappeared. But her body must have been carried to that tomb after the completion of our operation against the smugglers. It is necessary for me to know what has been happening.'

Chapter Twenty-Four

Captain Zeybel had taken Kara's body away. It will presumably have to be examined in case there should prove to be a bullet wound or stab wound or other sign of foul play. Hugh doesn't expect anything like that to be discovered. It has become clear to him in the past hour that Yilmaz was right to suspect that at least one of his sons is implicated in the little girl's death. He sends Roy off to summon them all to a meeting in the schoolroom, but Calum cannot be found in any of the quiet places to which he usually disappears with his book. The other boys wait uncomfortably while Hugh himself searches the house and eventually discovers the eight-year-old learning new Turkish words from the cook in the kitchen.

As Calum is unwillingly interrupted and sent to join his brothers, Susan emerges from her bedroom. She has been crying and her face is pale, but for the first time since Kara's disappearance the normal calmness of her expression has returned.

'All right, love?'

She nods. 'I suppose so. At least I know that Kara's at peace now.'

'Have you told David?'

'Not yet. It's not the sort of thing he'd want to hear at his office desk. I'll wait until he's home this evening. And tell him at the same time when we shall be arriving at Heathrow. I shan't ever want to come back here, Hugh.'

'No, of course not. We'll work something else out.'

'Where are you going now?'

'I've got to have a talk with the boys. It's time to find out what really happened.'

'Yilmaz said the same thing. But I don't see... I'll come with you.'

'I don't think that's a very good idea, Susie love. They won't want to talk in front of you. I may have to promise not to tell you anything I find out, at least to start with. Later on I should be able to persuade them how important it is for you to know.'

'Are you suggesting that one of them...?' Her face, already pale, whitens with the shock of the suggestion. She has not yet managed to interpret the clues that have led Hugh—and undoubtedly Yilmaz as well—towards the truth.

'I'm suggesting nothing because I don't know anything. But I intend to find out.'

He kisses her in what he hopes is a reassuring manner and then hurries to the schoolroom before the boys become tired of waiting and start to disperse.

'Thank you, Peter.' He dismisses the tutor, who has been lingering, unsure whether his presence is required. Then he closes the door and studies each young face in turn. They look nervous, but that is natural enough; it is not often that they are summoned to so formal a meeting. Hugh takes a moment to adjust his own expression. Somehow, while keeping his voice neutral, he must manage to convey a mixture of sternness and sympathy, and, above all, determination to get at the truth. His moment of silence increases the discomfort of the boys.

'This is a confidential conversation,' he says at last. 'Nothing that anyone says in this room will be repeated outside it, except with permission of the one who says it. I'm under no obligation to tell the police the answers to any questions I may ask. But sooner or later they'll come back and make their own inquiries. I hope that I'll be able to get you all back to England before that. I can't protect you, though, unless I know the truth.'

He pauses to give them time to absorb this.

'What I've realised already is that between you all you've been keeping your sister's body out of sight. I'm prepared to be persuaded that you've acted from what you thought were good motives. But I need to start at the beginning and find out what actually happened. No more secrets.'

He is looking at Tam as he speaks, and the younger boys all look in Tam's direction as well. As their father has guessed already, his eldest son has at some point sworn all the others to secrecy.

There is a long pause. Almost imperceptibly Tam nods his head. Taking advantage of this permission, two boys speak at once.

'It was an accident,' says Roy—and, at the same moment, Calum says, 'It was a sort of accident.'

'Tam?'

'It was an accident.'

'We don't know. We just found her.'

'Who found her? Look, I don't want to have to drag this out of you one sentence at a time. Give me a narrative version. What happened?'

'We were playing in the castle.' Tam has accepted his usual role as spokesman. 'We were playing Jericho. Making a lot of noise. I suppose Kara woke up from her rest and heard us and wanted to join in. I suppose she tried to climb into the castle. She must have climbed a bit of the way up and then she couldn't manage the rest and fell off and hit her head on a pointy bit of rock. Somebody yelled at me to come, but by the time I got there she was dead already.'

'I told you I wanted the truth,' says Hugh. 'I'm not getting it, am I? When you unexpectedly find a little girl lying on the ground with a bloody head, you send someone running to fetch her mother, to get a message to a doctor. You don't hide her away in different places and pretend you don't know what's happened. Did you see her coming out to join you, Tam? Did you see her fall?'

'No. I was inside the castle, defending it. I didn't know anything about it until I heard someone shouting. A different kind of shout from what was in the game.'

This statement, unlike the earlier one, has the ring of truth about it. Hugh turns his attention to one of the younger boys—a boy who even at the age of only eight is surprisingly precise in his choices of words.

'Calum, what did you mean by saying it was a sort of accident?'

'The same as Tam.'

'It's not quite the same, is it? Sort of. You didn't think it was a real accident, did you? You thought it was someone's fault. That's why she had to be hidden, because someone was going to be blamed. Was it you?'

Calum doesn't answer and Hugh finds himself becoming irritated.

'Oh, come on, boys.' He waits again. 'All right then, I'll tell you what I think happened. If you don't correct me, I shall know I'm right. Yes, Kara wanted to join your game. She saw some of you outside the castle and trying to get in. You told her to go away because she wasn't big enough to play with you. It's too dangerous, you said. It's a boys' game, you said. Go back to whoever's supposed to be looking after you. But she wouldn't go and so you got cross. Yes, she did try to climb in herself. And you wouldn't help. Perhaps one of you even pushed her down. And then, of course, when you saw she was hurt, that one of you who had done the pushing was very frightened, because if she was dead it was all your fault. Is that it?'

There is a pause before Tam gives a reluctant agreement.

'Something like that. But not a real push. She was holding on to someone's foot, trying to climb up after him, and he just gave a sort of waggle, nothing very much, he said, and his sandal came off while she was holding it and so she fell off. Not very far, really. It was bad luck that there was such a spiky bit of rock just where she landed. And we've all promised each other, Dad, that we're not going to say who it was, so there's no good asking us. Because it could have been any one of us and no one really meant it.'

'But why didn't you get someone to help? Or at the very least, to come and see what had happened?'

'No one could have done anything to help. She was dead already, straight away, before I got there. I know how to tell. I

296

used the mirror that we have for sending signals. She wasn't breathing. There was no pulse in her neck, either. And her head... We covered it with Roy's T-shirt, but the blood came through.' There is a moment in which Tam looks as though he is going to be sick at the memory, but he pulls himself together. 'If there'd been anything a doctor could do, or Mum, then of course we'd have run for help straight away. But there wasn't.'

'Even so...' Hugh finds it hard to understand how all five boys could have conspired to keep such a happening secret.

'We knew how upset Mum would be. We wanted to think about the best way for her to find out.'

'How could you make her less upset by keeping quiet about it, when she was bound to learn what had happened in the end? What you're saying is that you didn't want her to know that it had anything to do with any of you?'

Silence provides the answer. At last, reluctantly, Tam attempts to put his train of thought into words.

'Well, she was dead anyway. Nothing we did would make any difference to that. So we thought it might be better if she seemed to have died in a different sort of accident.'

'Such as?'

'Well, suppose she'd tried to go down to the sea by herself. She hasn't got a harness, because someone always carries her. So she might start running, because it's steep, and then when she got to the place where the path turns back at the tip of the headland, she might be going too fast to stop or make the turn and so she'd fall off and straight down on to the rocks below or into the water.'

'So you were going to carry her to that corner and throw her down?'

Tam nods unhappily. Perhaps only now is he realising the enormity of his proposal.

'But you didn't.'

'We'd only just decided all that when Calum said that he could see Esin coming. So I told him to go outside and try to keep her away, and two of us pulled down a bit of the rubble wall of the castle and lifted Kara over. We put her in the dungeon and pulled the stone back on top, in case Esin looked into the castle.'

'We were all in a bit of a panic at the time,' Calum tells his father. 'We didn't really know what to do.'

Calum's interjection with its precise choice of word, reminds Hugh that he must not judge his sons as though they are adults. They are children, horrified by the situation in which they have found themselves. Yes, of course, they were in a panic. Perhaps he ought not to be too harsh about the wrongness of their decisions.

One of them—he doesn't know which, but one of them—must have been sitting on the ground, guilty and frightened and in shock, while Tam was holding the mirror in front of Kara's lips and then shaking his head. It would be typical of his eldest son that he should try to protect an unhappy brother once it was clear that his half-sister was beyond help. Hugh is doing his best to understand the reasoning that has entangled the boys in so many lies. He moves on.

'But you left her in the dungeon, in spite of what you'd decided.'

'There wasn't time to do anything,' Tam explains. 'Almost as soon as Esin went off again, we saw Peter coming out to take us swimming. And then Mum and Peter were dashing around looking for her and after that there were police all over the place. I meant to do it by myself when everyone was asleep, but first of all there was a guard having his supper there and then Mum locked all the doors and windows up. Then the smuggling business made it even worse. There was someone in the castle all night. I didn't suppose it mattered how long I had to wait, though. I thought that once Kara was in the water, no one would ever see her again.'

'You must have realised, surely, that your mother would need to find out what had become of Kara? It was terrible for her, not having any idea what had occurred.'

Tam shakes his head vigorously. 'No. Like I told you before—by that time, the next morning, Mum was screaming about how she didn't want Kara to be dead. Even if she was, she didn't want to know. She wanted to go on looking for her and hoping.'

'But in spite of that, you still didn't carry out your plan.'

'There was something that changed my mind. When I was talking to Yilmaz, he said bodies that went into the sea were always found again sooner or later. And then Mum wouldn't have been able to hope any longer. So I had to think of something different. After the police told me that all the pretend antiques had been taken out of the tomb, I thought that was a good place to hide Kara, because no one would think of looking there any more. The others didn't know what I was going to do. They pitched into me because I changed the plan. But I reckoned it was a perfect hiding place—well, until I saw Grandfather on his way to find out whether the stolen pieces had been collected. He never got there, though, because Yilmaz stopped him.'

'So you would have left her body there for ever, would you, and left your mother wondering for ever what had happened?'

'Well, that was what she *wanted!*' The pitch of Tam's voice rises as he tries to justify himself. 'Anyway, that was what she *said* she wanted. But then you told us that she'd changed her mind and wanted the opposite. Wanted to know that Kara wasn't alive and having terrible things done to her.'

'So you cooked up this crazy business about the dice oracle.'

'Well, if we just said, go and look in the tomb again, everyone would realise it was us. When it all started, we didn't mean to tell so many lies. Just the one: that we hadn't seen Kara that afternoon. But then it all got so complicated. The tomb business: we thought—oh, I don't know. It was all such a mess and we're ever so sorry.'

Boys of twelve and a half don't cry, but Tam is very near to breaking down. Hugh moves quickly to put his arms round the shoulders of his eldest son and hug him.

'Of course you are, and of course you didn't mean Kara to die. Thank you for telling me the truth at last. You must look at it this way, all of you. Any children who have any spunk in them at all are liable to have accidents from time to time. Adults know that. Every parent has to decide whether to keep the children sitting safely and stuffily in front of a television set or to let them get out and use their imaginations and exercise their bodies. There are always risks and some risks have to be taken. This seems to have been a particularly unlucky accident. Kara might well have escaped with a twisted ankle or a bruised forehead.'

Moving away from Tam, he looks around the little group, wondering which of them he is addressing.

'It's right that all of you should be sorry about what happened that day. And it's right that one of you should wish that you'd been a little kinder, a little less impatient. But what that one has to feel bad about is what was in your mind when you waggled your foot and not what happened as a result of it. You didn't intend to kill Kara. It really was an accident.'

'Mummy won't ever believe that,' says Murdo miserably.

'Yes, she will. As Tam said, you made it into a mess by trying to cover up what happened, and she's been very upset as a result of that. If she'd been told the truth

302

straight away, it would actually have been much better. And she needs to know it now. I want you to stay here while I fetch her, and then to describe everything just as it took place.'

Five unhappy faces look towards him before each boy in turn drops his eyes and swallows the lump in his throat.

'You can think of it as part of your punishment if you want to,' their father tells them briskly. 'But in fact it's the only way for you to get out of the mess. Until you talk it out with her, you'll never be easy. It's got to be done—and you need to do it before she works it out for herself. Shall I fetch her?'

'Yes.' Tam's hoarse whisper gives the go-ahead; but Hugh does not in fact move immediately.

'One more thing,' he tells them. 'This business of protecting the owner of that waggling foot isn't going to work, you know. It's like the situation that arises in school when no will own up to some misdemeanour and so the master keeps the whole form in. Some of the innocent boys may get a bit resentful because they think they're under suspicion, and the one who has been passing notes or whatever feels worse and worse because other people are getting the blame and punishment for what he did. You've got five minutes on your own together to think about that.'

There is no immediate reaction. He goes in search of Susan.

Chapter Twenty-Five

In the absence of its usual defenders Susan has stormed the castle. Now she sits on a flat slab of stone, looking down into the empty hole in the ground in which her daughter's body lay hidden while she searched in panic. It is hard to forgive her sons for inflicting that torture on her. But they are only children. Because as a general rule they are children who behave sensibly, she has perhaps in the past been unfair in treating them as though they were adults, capable of reasoning in an adult way.

For the larger matter of Kara's death she has forgiven them already as she listened to their tearful story. Yes, it was an accident—and it was her own fault for not looking after her four-year-old properly. She has hugged and kissed each of the boys, telling them how much she loves them all, how much she will always love them. It has been a harrowing half-hour.

'So there you are!' Hugh's head appears

above the breach in the rubble. He climbs over one of the encircling rocks and comes to sit beside her. 'Have they confessed?'

'Not who did it. Only what was done. I ought to have guessed. Why didn't I guess? That Turkish chap, a complete stranger, he's known all the time, hasn't he. What a rotten mother I am, not to understand my own children at all! I've never been any good at anything else, but I did think that at least I was a good mother.'

'And so you are.' His arm encircles her shoulder. 'You bring up your children to be healthy and happy and independent.'

'Not Kara.'

'The logic of encouraging independence is that it may not always be used wisely. Look at Africa.'

As so often in the past, Susan fails to follow her ex-husband's allusion. 'What's Africa got to do with it?'

'Nothing. Sorry. Look, I expect you're feeling a bit stirred up. Later on, it might be a good idea for you to have a chat with each of the boys separately. Somehow or other we must find out which of them was responsible—and from the boy himself, not by getting the others to sneak. Until he's confessed, he'll never be sure that we wouldn't turn him out if we knew.'

Susan nods. She is emotionally drained, unable to take in anything more. Hugh is quick to realise this.

'Come down and have a swim with me. It's what we both need. Clear, clean, refreshing water.'

'The boys—'

'I've asked Peter to take charge. Come on.' He helps her to climb over the castle ramparts, holding out his hand to catch her as she jumps down the last few feet.

'I feel guilty about Peter,' she says. 'Asking him to act as a sort of nanny. He hasn't had much of the free time he was promised lately.'

'I've had a word with him. I could only get six seats on the plane, not seven. If you feel that you need him at home, he could follow you back the next day, but if not, he could stay on at The Lookout. I might as well move in myself with a couple of my students instead of renting rooms in Antalya. I can probably give him a bit of help with his thesis as well. Where are you going?'

'To fetch my swimming things.'

'You don't need those. Come on.'

Susan tells herself that she ought not to be surprised by the suggestion. The beach can be seen only from a boat or by the inhabitants of The Lookout—and then only if they approach the edge of the cliff. She and Hugh, in the days when they were married, regularly took an evening swim in the nude. They are not married now, of course, but at the moment she lacks the emotional stamina to argue the point. She follows him carefully down the steep and narrow path.

Hugh's fair skin, like his sons', burns easily and so he always wears a shirt on his dig. As he slips it off, his chest looks absurdly white against the dark brown of his neck and forearms. Susan herself is lightly tanned all over except for the pale triangle usually protected by a bikini bottom. Hugh makes no attempt to disguise his admiration.

'You're the most beautiful woman I've ever seen. You're the most beautiful woman in the world. I love you, you know. I've never stopped loving you. Will you marry me, Susie?'

Susan is shocked not so much by the question as by the strength of her wish to say yes. She stands without moving, unembarrassed by her nakedness and his. They are Adam and Eve—but this idyllic spot is no Garden of Eden. Crimes have been committed here. She manages to speak at last.

'I'm married already,' she reminds him.

'For how long, do you think? In an hour or so's time you're going to be phoning David. He must have guessed years ago that you were only interested in him as the father of yet another baby.'

'That's not—' Susan attempts to protest, but Hugh speaks through the interruption. 'Now you have to tell him that his daughter is dead. Are you also going to confess that her death was caused by one of his stepsons? I'm not trying to knock David. From what the boys tell me, he's tried to act as a decent stepfather, even though they don't think he has any particular interest in what they do. But if you tell him the truth, he'll start to feel suspicions, anger, even hatred of the boys. You'll try to defend them, no doubt. I don't give your marriage a hope in hell.'

Susan has no answer. He is almost certainly correct, and she is too stunned by the events of the past days to argue the point. She turns away and runs into the sea. Hugh catches her up and holds her back when the water is still only up to her waist.

'There's been no one else,' he tells her. 'No one who matters, I mean. I've always reckoned that sooner or later we'd get together again. It's the sort of fantasy that kids always have about their parents. Our boys certainly do, and I've gone along with it. Haven't you as well, in your heart?'

Without answering she flings herself forwards into the calm water of the bay. It seems to be at the same time both warm and cool and as her arms move in the strong, regular rhythm of a crawl she does indeed feel refreshed, as Hugh has promised. Little by little some of her unhappiness and self-reproach falls away, to be replaced by a kind of acceptance. What's done is done.

Nevertheless, she can't resist asking a question when, half an hour later, the two of them emerge from the water. They have brought no towels down with them but, although the sun is by now low in the sky, the rocks at the foot of the headland are still hot from their midday baking. Susan and Hugh lie face downwards, close together but not touching, their arms folded under their chins.

'Which of them do you think it was?' Susan asks. 'Who pushed Kara?'

'That's the sort of question that worries me. I mean, I'm worried about whether you're going to spend the rest of your life wondering about it.' But in spite of himself, Hugh cannot resist making a partial attempt at an answer. 'I'm pretty sure it wasn't Tam, though. He's told a lot of lies, but I don't believe he'd do that to save himself. Only to shield someone else.'

'I don't think it was Murdo, either.' This is Susan's own contribution. 'He was always very fond of Kara. And he seemed genuinely distressed when she disappeared, even though it can't have been quite the kind of distress that I assumed at the time. I don't think he can have known what had happened—not to start with, at least. Once the walls of Jericho had fallen down in their game, he may have decided that his part in it was over. He often goes off on his own with his trumpet, to that special place he's got. No, probably not Murdo.'

'As for Calum.' Hugh pauses to consider. 'There was something Calum said that made me feel he wanted the truth to come out. But whether that meant he wanted to confess himself or hoped that someone else would, I'm not sure.'

'If we see Tam as the protector, he's always been very protective of Roy. The two of them have been a pair ever since Roy was born.'

'But as well as that, Tam sees it as his duty to look after the youngest of his brothers. I don't think we ought to go any further with this, Susie.'

'I ought to know! I'm their mother. There ought to be some instinct to tell me.' For a moment she is silent, and when she speaks again it is with an unusual firmness. 'I'm never going to have any more babies, Hugh. What right have I got to go on pumping new life into the world as though it were nobody's business but my own? I didn't ever think of it from their point of view at all: the babies, and the lives they'd have to live, the deaths they'd have to die. Just because I wanted them myself, to love me and give me something to do that seemed worthwhile. I simply didn't realise how selfish I was being. You did, didn't you?'

To her surprise, Hugh shakes his head. 'If everyone felt like that, the human race would soon come to an end. The acceptance of death—other people's, as well as our own—is something we all have to face. Having babies is a natural function. Nothing to be ashamed of there. If I tried to set a limit, it was because of my own inadequacies. I simply didn't feel that I could cope with any more children—not in the way that I wanted to cope, I mean. It doesn't really matter if we've chosen different ways to come to the same conclusion. The important thing is that there's nothing to come between us any longer.'

Except David, of course. But in the long silence which follows, Susan realises that she has unwittingly answered Hugh's question. There was never more than a single disagreement to divide them. She used it to justify her adultery, and now

311

she is ashamed of that. Is it shame that makes her feel that she can hardly bear to see David again? She had no right to love him: no right to hurt her husband and unsettle her sons by destroying their family life. Now that she and Hugh have each owned up to their different kinds of selfishness, she can admit to herself that he is the man whom she truly loves. It isn't easy to see a way through what is bound to be a messy and even cruel procedure but, yes, in her heart she does indeed want to be back with Hugh again.

She has turned her head to look at him. He doesn't move to touch her, but instead gives a slight, abrupt nod of his head: the mannerism Tam has inherited from him.

There is no more warmth in the sun. Hugh offers her his shirt to rub dry any wet patches on her body. It is the shirt he has worn for two hot days. She rubs the smell of his sweat under her arms and between her legs and is overcome with love for him. Nevertheless, when he suggests that he should stay the night again, she shakes her head.

'Tonight is for Kara,' she tells him. 'I want to remember her and say goodbye.' That is the truth—but there is more to it than that. She doesn't want to do anything else of which she will feel ashamed. She is still David's wife, and it is time to make the call to her husband.

Without speaking again, she leads the way up the steep and narrow path.

Chapter Twenty-Six

There are no sounds to be heard when Susan leaves her room at five o'clock the next morning. No boys are stirring, no birds are singing; even the sea, pale turquoise in the dawn light, is calm and silent. The air, which all too soon will become heavy with heat, is cool enough to make her shiver when she first emerges from the house.

Not wishing to go near the castle, nor even within sight of it, she turns away from the water and makes her way up the steep track towards The Eyrie. Skirting the side of the house, she continues to climb upwards, although here there is no path and she has to scramble over rocks. Her sandals are unsuitable for this and after a little while she stops and sits down, clasping her knees as she stares across to Antalya, to the boats in the little harbour and the terraces of the big hotel.

She feels wide awake and clear-headed,

even though she has hardly slept at all. As she told Hugh, it was a night to be shared with Kara. Lying awake in the darkness she has relived the pain of her daughter's birth, the delight of learning that she had a little girl, the joy of holding the baby for the first time. As vividly as though it were actually happening, she has felt the tug of Kara's mouth on her breast and has smiled happily at the vigorous splashing of bathtime. She has remembered bedtime cuddles and the kissing away of tears. She has swung Kara round and round in the air and has accepted her demands for proper lessons like her brothers by teaching letters and dealing out words written on cards to be recognised.

Kara's short life was a happy one. There is no pain in these memories. The only pain that persists must be caused by self-pity. Kara will never grow up into womanhood, but she will never know what she has lost: only her mother knows. Susan's earlier nightmares have taught her an important lesson: it could have been worse.

This is only half a comfort. The death of a child before her parent goes against nature. The ache is Susan's heart will never be completely healed and there will always be a gap in her life. She will never be able to hear her daughter's name spoken without tears coming to her eyes, because where once there was Kara there is now only silence: a silence which will last for ever.

But from now on her mourning must be a private affair. She is still a mother. Her sons must never be allowed to believe that she values them less than their dead sister. To conceal her heartbreak will take self-discipline and courage: she draws on that courage now as she stands up.

Someone else stands up at the same moment: someone who has been hidden by a rock a little nearer to The Eyrie. Susan is momentarily alarmed by the movement, but it is only Yilmaz.

'How long have you been there?' she demands as he waits for her to scramble down towards him.

'All night. I was just about to leave when you came past, but then I didn't want to disturb you.'

'All night? Why?'

'To watch Dr Sutherland's house. We hold the men who came by boat to collect the stolen artefacts and we hold the man who put them ready to be collected. But there must be one more link in the chain. Dr Sutherland may have stolen from unguarded mountain sites, but I don't believe that he would have stolen from a museum. There has been no publicity about the arrests. I'm hoping that we can catch someone trying to make contact. May I help you down?'

He holds out a hand. Susan is quite capable of jumping down without help, but it seems churlish to refuse. He uses his other hand to steady her and stands for a moment without letting go.

'I was in any case intending to call on you, although not so early in the morning,' he tells her. 'Your daughter's body has been examined. Death was caused by a blow to the head by a sharp piece of rock. Fragments have been found in the wound. With the new information available about the area in which the death occurred, we have been able to search for traces of blood, and we have found them. There are no indications of any bruising or restraint prior to death and no weapon of any kind were used. Kara fell on to the rock that killed her. Death was accidental.'

'Yes. Yes, I'm sure.' Susan looks down at her captive hands but is reluctant to make the positive gesture of pulling them away.

'So from our point of view, there is no longer a criminal case to be solved. First of all I have to ask you formally whether you wish to bring charges against anyone, and whether you wish our investigations to continue?'

'No, I don't. And I would be very happy to sign a statement, if you like, to say how considerate you have been while trying to find her.'

'That would certainly be appreciated. You know by now what happened, I suppose?'

'Yes. Although not who did it. And you—did you know all the time?'

Yilmaz shrugged his shoulders. 'Not for sure. One can never be sure at the beginning. But in a list of probabilities, this was always the most likely. I have one more question. The body of little Kara—will you wish it to be buried here or in England?'

'In England. I have insurance to cover the arrangements, I think.'

'So you don't propose to return to my country?'

'No.' Susan's answer is definite, although not without a trace of regret. She has had happy times in Turkey, starting with an idyllic honeymoon; but they are over. She does now gently release her hands from Yilmaz's grip.

'You will return to live with Professor Sutherland, I suppose?' he says sadly.

'I think that's my private business.' But something in the tone of his voice catches her attention. Startled, she looks more closely into his eyes.

'Oh, yes,' he agrees. 'How could I not fall in love with such a beautiful woman? But don't be afraid. I know that you will never associate me with anything but sadness. You will come down to Antalya to sign the release forms and then I shall never see you again. Well.' This time the shrug of his shoulders has a different significance: the acceptance of a situation.

The awkward conversation is interrupted by the sound of a boy shouting. 'Mummy! Mummy, where are you?'

'Here!' Susan shouts back. 'Coming!' She has recognised a note of panic in the voice. Slithering and sliding, she hurries down towards The Lookout.

It is Murdo who is calling, panting as he hurries up the track towards her.

'What's the matter, Murdo? What's happened?'

'It's Donnie. He was crying last night. Into his pillow so that me and Calum wouldn't hear, but I did hear. And now he's got up early and he's gone too near the cliff. He gets dizzy when he stands near the edges of things.'

Susan can feel her whole body going white with fear, as though every drop of blood in her veins has frozen.

'Murdo, tell me quickly. Was it Donnie who pushed Kara? It was, wasn't it? Tell me.'

318

Murdo clearly wants to answer, but is unable to force out the word. Susan goes down on one knee and takes his hands.

'I'm your mother and I must know. Whatever Tam may have ordered, I've got to know the truth, and fast. Was it Donnie?'

He nods miserably. Susan begins to run.

As she reaches the more level area between The Lookout and the cliff, she pauses for a moment. Yes, there is Donnie; a pale, slight figure wearing only pyjama trousers. Although he is tall for his age, his age is only seven; he looks small and vulnerable. He is standing close to the edge of the cliff with his back to her, looking down. Susan is about to dash forwards again when she feels herself being grabbed, almost roughly, by Yilmaz, who has followed her down.

'Be steady,' he warns her. 'If you run too close he'll step forwards, even though he may not really mean to. Go slowly and no nearer than three or four metres. Talk to him all the time. Make him turn round to look at you.'

He speaks with such authority that Susan automatically obeys. Her pace slows and she takes two or three deep breathes in order to steady her voice.

'Donnie! Donnie, darling, it's Mummy.

Can you hear me?' She is continuing to move quietly forwards as she speaks. 'Can you hear me, or am I too far away? Turn round if you can hear me, so that I can talk to you properly. I love you, darling. I know what happened and I know it was an accident. You didn't mean to hurt Kara, of course you didn't.'

Very slowly Donnie turns round. His face is swollen with tears.

'Yes, I did,' he says.

'Not to hurt her in the way that happened. I expect you wanted to stop her spoiling your game, but you didn't mean her to be dead, did you? I know you didn't. It was an accident. Come here and tell me you're sorry, because I'm sure you are, and we'll have a cuddle and forget all about it.'

She has stopped moving now that he is looking at her, but her alarm returns when he shakes his head.

'You thought it was all of us, but it was only me.'

'Well, now you've told me, and that's very brave of you. So it's nothing to do with the others. Just the two of us need to talk about it. I'm not angry, Donnie. I just want to tell you how much I love you. Come a bit closer, please. I'm frightened of going so near the edge of the cliff. It makes me dizzy. Come here so that I'll feel safe.'

He shakes his head and turns away, taking another step towards the edge which is too close already.

'Donnie!' Susan can't control her voice, which shrieks out in panic. 'Donnie, I can't lose you. I love you so much. I can't do without you. You're frightening me. You don't mean to do that, do you?'

He isn't listening. She feels sure that he isn't listening. He has cut himself off from her and is trying to screw up his courage to do something that terrifies him as much as it terrifies her. Susan looks wildly round to see who can help.

The four elder boys are standing in a little group, staring at their brother in alarm and not daring to move in case they frighten him. They are too far away to intercept him if he moves to throw himself down. But at this moment they are joined by Yilmaz, who only a few seconds ago was at her side. For such a big man he has moved with extraordinary speed and quietness. Now he takes Tam's arm and whispers something in his ear. He is giving an instruction which the eldest boy accepts immediately.

'Donnie!' There is nothing cajoling about Tam's voice. He is issuing a reprimand and an order. 'Donnie, you've gone past the white posts. You know that's against the rules. Get this side of them straight away.

321

Otherwise none of us will ever be allowed to play out here again. Come on! Get a move on!'

The last exhortation is unnecessary. At the first sound of Tam's voice Donnie has turned to face his brothers, has glanced guiltily at the line of posts and has automatically stepped forwards out of forbidden territory. Now he is hesitating, perhaps on the point of turning back—but now it doesn't matter any more, because Yilmaz has moved to stand behind him. It is safe for Susan to rush forwards and pick up her youngest son as though he were still a baby. At first he holds himself stiffly away from her, refusing to be forgiven, but within a few moments they are both crying together. The crisis is over.

Chapter Twenty-Seven

The crisis may be over, but the situation remains unchanged. Donnie eventually ceases to sob and slips off his mother's lap before drawing a little way away. Lacking a handkerchief, he sniffs and tries to dab his nose and eyes dry with his bare forearm. Then he waits to learn what is going to happen next.

Susan for her part continues to shudder with shock and fear and indecision. She is not a psychiatrist. At this juncture in her son's life there must be a right and a wrong thing to say, but she lacks the confidence to know which is which. Her instincts have betrayed her so often during the past few days that now she doesn't trust herself to speak.

Hugh, who has spent the night at The Eyrie and heard Murdo's shouts, arrives on the scene at a run and settles the matter for her. He has no greater knowledge of psychology than she has, but he makes a decision and puts it into practice. As Susan takes her youngest son's hand and leads him to join the rest of the family, she can tell from the tone of his father's voice, even before the words are clear, what conclusion he has reached. Hugh has decided, it seems, that guilt can best be assuaged by rebuke and punishment. His anger, as he faces the four elder boys, is controlled but not concealed.

He interrupts his lecture as Susan and Donnie approach.

'Come here, Donnie, with the others. This applies to you as much as to them. I've been telling them how disappointed I am that sons of mine should be liars. I've always thought I could trust you all to be honest. No one expects you to be perfect, but I do expect you to own up when something goes wrong.'

'We thought—' Tam, who has organised the lies, recognises that he must be the one to defend them.

'Telling the truth isn't something to think about. It's something to do. Automatically.'

'Sneaking isn't something to do, though.'

'Agreed, Donnie ought to have owned up straight away and then some of this unhappiness might have been avoided. Instead of that—'

'We were trying to make it better for Mum.'

'No. Be honest, now. You were trying to make it better for Donnie.'

'Well, that as well, but we could have done that in a different way. We really did try to let Mum think whatever she wanted to think.'

'You were taking too much on yourself.' Almost imperceptibly Hugh's voice softens, although probably Susan is the only one to notice this. Tam is his father's pride and to attack the boy like this must be going against the grain. 'You have to take responsibility for your own actions. I've always taught you that. But you aren't expected to make yourself responsible for adults; not until you're grown-up yourselves.'

'I was trying to be responsible for the

younger ones. You taught me that, as well.' Tam is upset as he tries to defend himself.

'Then you got it wrong, didn't you? Being responsible for them means helping them to become responsible themselves. By telling the truth.'

'Oh, Hugh!' Susan can't hold back a protest. This is too complicated for children.

'Yes. Well, I can see that you all recognise that you've made mistakes. But however good your intentions may have been, the consequence of telling so many lies has been a great deal of extra unhappiness. I intend to punish you for it. I hope you recognise that that's fair.'

The younger boys await sentence in apprehensive silence, but Tam is their defender to the last.

'Murdo didn't know anything about it, not till afterwards. After the walls fell down, pretending I mean, he went on playing his trumpet in his special tower. And when he did find out, he wanted to tell Mum straight away.'

'I liked Kara,' says Murdo sadly. 'But I did do what the others told me.' He wants to make it clear that he is to be included in the punishment and not cut off from his brothers. That this is just as well becomes clear immediately, because Hugh's choice

325

of penalty is an all-or-none affair.

'There's no punishment for Kara's death,' he announces. 'That was very, very sad, but small children do have accidents and they can happen anywhere. We nearly lost Tam when he rode his bike out of the school gate in front of a car; do you remember?'

There is a murmur of remembrance from Roy: the others were too young to have been aware of what was happening at the time.

'If Tam had died then, it wouldn't have been the fault of the driver. He would have felt sorry, as I'm sure Donnie feels sorry, and that's enough. What I'm going to punish you for is for the lies and silences, and for breaking the rules. We've been bringing you here for your summers—to a place which we all know has dangerous areas—so that you could have marvellous adventures. We could only go on doing it as long as you could be trusted to keep the rules which we laid down to keep you safe. Well, we can't trust you any longer, and so you're never going to come back here again. Not till you're grown-up, at least. You are exiled from The Lookout.'

Distressed, the boys look toward their mother, hoping that she will protest on their behalf, but Susan makes no comment. Hugh is making good use of her own refusal ever to return. It is Calum who puts his brothers' anxiety into words.

'But then we shan't ever see you again, Dad.'

'You needn't worry about that. This is only intended to teach *you* a lesson, not to punish you. Your mother and I will have to make a new arrangement.'

Donnie looks from one to the other. Over the past few days he has reverted to being the baby of the family again instead of striving desperately to keep up as one of the gang. 'Are you and Mummy...?'

'That's our business. Your business is to go inside and collect everything to be packed. Everything. Even the games that are usually left here.'

Too subdued to run, the five boys make their way towards The Lookout. No doubt they are upset by their banishment, but they have accepted it. By paying for their misjudgements they can avoid a lasting millstone of guilt. Hugh has got it exactly right.

Susan turns to face him. 'So what is *my* punishment?' she asks.

'You? You're not guilty of anything.'

'I'm guilty of bringing Kara into the world. None of this would have happened except for me.'

'There's no life without death, certainly. No death without life. But that doesn't

327

mean that there's any need to feel guilty about giving life, giving birth. You're not to reproach yourself. Kara's death is a tragedy for you and for David, but in no sense at all was it your fault.'

'I'm guilty of other things as well. Destroying our marriage. Robbing the boys of their father.'

This time he doesn't contradict her. How can he, when she is speaking the truth and he was the first to be hurt by it? But his eyes are loving.

'Yes, well, perhaps there should be a penalty for that,' he agrees, taking hold of her hands to give her strength. 'It may turn out that your sentence is the toughest. Somehow or other you have to disentangle yourself from David. I don't imagine you'll find it a very pleasant task.'

Susan makes no immediate comment on this. This is something that may be happening already, although not as a result of any decision of her own. Her conscience tells her that it would be unforgivable to desert her second husband now, at a time when he is mourning his daughter. But she has reason to wonder whether he may be ready to desert her.

In a call to David on the previous evening she broke the news of Kara's death. It ought to have been a sad conversation but instead erupted in bitterness. She told him the truth—or, at least, as much of it as she knew at that time—and his reaction was to say that she can surely not expect him to go on living with the boys who never showed any affection for his daughter and now have killed her. They must make a new home with their father.

David cannot possibly have expected her to agree to this ultimatum. Probably it was shock that caused him to put such a thought into words—but the thought will still be there even if he later denies it and pretends a willingness to continue as they were before. Susan finds it hard to understand why tragedy should be separating them instead of drawing them closer together, but it would be foolish to pretend that the relationship is any longer a satisfactory one.

If they had been truly happy as a couple at the moment when the sad truth became known, perhaps they could have clung together. But Susan has felt for some time that her second marriage was a mistake. A sense of duty would have prevented her from running away from it; but if David himself is unhappy with the situation, then she will make the choice he apparently wants to force upon her. Naturally she will choose her sons. And Donnington Manor belongs to her. It is David, not the boys, who will have to leave. She must

329

give him a chance to withdraw his outburst and apologise for it, but probably what he said is what he genuinely feels. It may well be that the marriage is over already.

Hugh wrongly interprets her silence as indicating that she finds the mechanics of regaining her freedom too daunting.

'Look at it this way, Susie,' he said beseechingly. 'We've all, every one of us, been damaged. Think of the sherds I pick up on my digs. Once upon a time they formed a piece of pottery, useful, elegantly shaped, beautifully patterned: a single item. Now the pot is just a handful of broken pieces. With a little skill it can be pieced together again. And part of the skill lies in recognising the odd piece that doesn't belong and discarding it. Chucking it away may seem ruthless at the time, but until it's done all the broken pieces will remain just that: rubble. Putting the pot together again will be right for everyone—even for David in the long run. How happy can you expect him to be with the present situation?'

He pauses, perhaps expecting Susan to argue on David's behalf; but with the memory of last night's conversation still fresh in her mind, there is nothing she can say in disagreement, and so after a moment Hugh continues to plead his own case.

'I've banished the boys from one

kingdom; now you must give them the chance to return to another, in which they have a father as well as a mother. Getting us all back to where we were before is your job. Just take it one day at a time and it will all work out.'

'Yes.' Susan is ashamed of herself, and knows that she has good cause to be. But if she allows herself to be overwhelmed by guilt for the rest of her life, other people will suffer as much as she does. Although the process of mourning her dead daughter cannot be hurried, Hugh is quite right. She must force herself to pick up the pieces of her shatterd life and restore the security which her sons deserve. And perhaps, one day at a time, the pain of losing Kara will fade at the same pace as her self-reproach. 'Yes,' she says again.

Hugh kisses her, lightly at first, before enfolding her in his arms. But they are both too emotionally drained to be passionate.

'I'll be up with an extra jeep to help get you all to the airport,' he promises. 'After that, I'll wait to hear when I can come home. Goodbye for now.'

As he strides away, Susan moves towards the edge of the cliff and breathes in the silence of the dawn. Although so much has happened since she left her bed, it is still only half past six. But there is some movement now in the sea below her. Thousands of tiny ripples sparkle in the pale-pink light of the rising sun. In the hotel across the bay, as well, there are signs of activity. Mattresses are being laid on the terrace loungers and colourful umbrellas are unfurled. The world is waking up.

So now a new life stretches before her: a life which must embrace the acceptance of death. Take it a day at a time, Hugh has told her; and the first day has already begun.

The publishers hope that this book has given you enjoyable reading. Large Print Books are especially designed to be as easy to see and hold as possible. If you wish a complete list of our books, please ask at your local library or write directly to: Magna Large Print Books, Long Preston, North Yorkshire, BD23 4ND, England.

This Large Print Book for the Partially sighted, who cannot read normal print, is published under the auspices of

THE ULVERSCROFT FOUNDATION

THE ULVERSCROFT FOUNDATION

. . . we hope that you have enjoyed this Large Print Book. Please think for a moment about those people who have worse eyesight problems than you . . . and are unable to even read or enjoy Large Print, without great difficulty.

You can help them by sending a donation, large or small to:

**The Ulverscroft Foundation,
1, The Green, Bradgate Road,
Anstey, Leicestershire, LE7 7FU,
England.**
or request a copy of our brochure for more details.

The Foundation will use all your help to assist those people who are handicapped by various sight problems and need special attention.

Thank you very much for your help.